D0983799

MURDER IN MANHATTAN

WRITTEN BY
THOMAS CHASTAIN
MARY HIGGINS CLARK
DOROTHY SALISBURY DAVIS
LUCY FREEMAN
JOYCE HARRINGTON
WARREN MURPHY
BERNARD ST. JAMES
WHITLEY STRIEBER

CONCEPT BY BILL ADLER

MURDER IN MANHATTAN

WILLIAM MORROW AND COMPANY, INC./NEW YORK

A portion of this book originally appeared in *Playboy.*

Printed in the United States of America

INTRODUCTORY NOTE
BILL ADLER

About a year ago a group of nine writers in the mystery-suspense field began meeting for dinner once a month at a Manhattan Upper East Side restaurant to discuss their craft. Most of the writers were already known to one another, and were brought together by Thomas Chastain and Mary Higgins Clark. They call themselves Adam's Round Table, Adam being the name of one of the restaurant owners who made available to them a round table in the back room.

The objective of the group has been summed up by one of its members, Bernard St. James, as "a unique opportunity for each of us to examine the minds of other writers to find out how they work, why they work, how they do what they do, how they got where they are."

When I heard about the group, I suggested that each of the members write a short story to make a collection that would be entitled *Murder in Manhattan.* It was my suggestion that each story be set in a different section of the city to reflect the various facets of Manhattan. The idea was appealing to the group since all of them live in or around Manhattan and most of them have used the city as a setting in their work at one time or another.

This book is the result.

The reason there are eight stories here instead of nine is that one member of the group, Frederick Knott, author of *Dial M for Murder* and *Wait Until Dark,* is a playwright.

In one way or another the members of Adam's Round Table have expressed their feelings about the place where they live and work as: "Manhattan is a city of possibilities waiting to be realized."

CONTENTS

MURDER IN MANHATTAN

DIRECTED VERDICT

THOMAS CHASTAIN

The homicide report was logged in by the dispatcher at Manhattan's Sixteenth Precinct at 11:41 P.M.

Two Sixteenth Precinct patrolmen, after responding in their squad car to a police emergency 911 phone call, radioed in that they'd found a young woman strangled to death in her apartment. The apartment was in a luxury high-rise building on the east side of the city in the Kips Bay area.

The dispatcher immediately notified Detective Sergeant John Cluett, the ranking homicide officer on the four-to-midnight shift of the precinct.

"Got it," Cluett told the dispatcher. "Roust Detectives Melchior and Pappas. Tell them to meet me down front, ready to roll. I'm on my way."

At age thirty-four, after thirteen years with the NYPD, John Cluett had realized a lifelong dream when he had been promoted to homicide detective sergeant six months earlier. Now, although he had no way of knowing it, he was about to embark upon the most fascinating, and often most frustrating, murder case of his career.

When he got down to the street, the two detectives were waiting for him in an unmarked Plymouth, the motor idling. They were in the front seat, Melchior at the wheel. Cluett slid into the rear.

Melchior and Pappas were veteran cops. They had worked together as a team for longer than Cluett had been on the force. Big men, similar in build and bulk, they could have been mistaken, by a stranger seeing the three men together, for Cluett's bodyguards. In fact, Cluett sometimes suspected the two got a secret kick out of deliberately giving that impression.

Although Cluett himself was younger than most of the men he commanded in his unit, he did not— except when he was with Detectives Melchior and Pappas—particularly look it. From appearance alone it would be difficult to fix his age any more exactly than that he was in his thirties or forties, somewhere; there was gray in his dark hair, which was worn combed flat against his head; there was bulge around his beltline; there were set-in lines and creases in his face, which gave him a look of maturity beyond his years.

The station house was on the west side of the city, and on the drive across town Melchior and Pappas talked between themselves, the car's police radio a static sound in the background. Cluett tuned them all out.

The late-July night was hot and humid, the sky overcast. There had been a drenching cloudburst within the hour, but the rain had done little to cool the almost ninety-degree temperature of the evening. This was the eighth straight day and night of the kind of heat wave in the city that frayed nerves, triggered tempers, and set the crime record soaring. Cluett had seen the statistics.

For the moment, though, he was thinking that as much as he'd wanted his promotion to detective sergeant, he had had to pay an unexpected personal price to meet its demands.

Two weeks ago the live-in girl friend he'd hoped, and expected, to marry had moved out on him. She told him that since his promotion she spent more time with her hairdresser once a week than she did with him. And, she'd added, even then he wasn't home long enough to notice when she'd had her hair done.

Now, stuck with a case that could keep him on duty until God only knew when, he supposed he ought to feel a sense of relief that she wasn't at home waiting up for him. But he didn't.

He put all such thoughts out of his mind as Melchior parked the Plymouth in front of the East Side building where they'd been told the young woman had been strangled. The apartment house was twenty-two stories high, of brick, and looked well kept up.

There were three prowl cars lined up along the block, and a few curious onlookers were standing on the sidewalk observing the scene. Two patrolmen stood at the entrance to the lobby and, just inside the glass doors, was a uniformed doorman.

Cluett pinned his shield to his coat lapel and stepped out of the car. Melchior and Pappas followed as Cluett crossed the sidewalk and entered the building. The lobby was spacious and air-conditioned. An assortment of potted ferns and other plants were set along one wall, and there were a couple of attractive sofas and a long coffee table arranged in front of the ferns and plants.

Another police officer was standing with a second uniformed doorman near the bank of four elevators.

The police officer said to Cluett, "Sergeant, this is the fellow who found the body. His name's Harold Schmidt."

Cluett nodded. "Bring him along. Let's go up."

Schmidt was tall, of medium build, in his mid-thirties, and had sandy hair and an angular face with high cheekbones, the skin fair with a reddish splotch of what looked like razor burn under his jaw.

He appeared nervous and ill at ease in the self-service elevator with Cluett and the other policemen. Cluett knew the fact that he seemed intimidated had no particular significance. Most civilians reacted in a like manner when involved in a police matter.

As they rode the elevator up to the eleventh floor, Schmidt repeated the story he had already told to the first patrolmen to arrive at the building.

He had taken a coffee break in the locker room in the basement. The doorman now on duty—Marty Olin—had come in early. Schmidt had returned to the lobby in about fifteen minutes. By then it was raining heavily. There were people waiting in the lobby while Marty Olin, outside, was trying to get them taxicabs. The lobby intercom phone was buzzing insistently.

Schmidt took three intercom calls in a row, two from apartments on the eleventh floor, one from an apartment on the tenth floor. All reported loud noises, some kind of disturbance, a scream, coming from Apartment 11-E. Schmidt told the callers he'd check it out.

He knew that Apartment 11-E was occupied by Jacqueline Holby, a young fashion model who lived alone. He also remembered that a boyfriend of hers, a regular visitor, had gone up to the apartment about an hour earlier.

Schmidt said he tried to call Apartment 11-E on the intercom, but there was no answer. Normal procedure at that point, he added, would have been to inform the building superintendent, who lived on the premises, but he knew the super and his wife were out for the evening.

Schmidt then got a key from the super's office in the basement and went up to the eleventh floor. He tried knocking on the door and pressing the buzzer, but there was no answer.

Before he opened the door with the key, Schmidt explained, he asked one of the tenants who had called down on the intercom, Mr. Hendricks, in 11-F, to join him.

Schmidt unlocked the door, and the two men went inside. "Right away we could see there'd been trouble—chairs overturned, a drawer pulled out and lying on the floor, all the lights on, and the whole place too quiet. Then we saw her. Stretched out on the living-room floor. Something—a necktie, I think—wound around her throat. We could see she wasn't breathing. I hollered out, 'Anybody here?' Then we got out. I locked the door again, Mr. Hendricks called 911 from his place, and we both waited in the hall until the police came."

Cluett was making notes on a pad he'd taken from his pocket. "You said her boyfriend had visited her tonight. You see him leave?"

Harold Schmidt shook his head. "And when we got back down to the lobby, I asked Marty Olin had he seen the boyfriend leave. He said no, too."

"This boyfriend, you know his name?"

"Phillip something," Schmidt said. "I can't remember his last name. He was here so regular, we'd stopped announcing him when he showed up."

Cluett was the first one off the elevator when it reached the eleventh floor. Doors to most of the apartments all along the hallway were open. Some of the tenants were looking out from the open doorways, others were partway outside in the hall. A uniformed officer was at the closed door of 11-E, which was directly across from the bank of elevators.

Cluett, after motioning to the officers to keep Schmidt in the hall, opened the door to 11-E and went inside with Melchior and Pappas close behind him.

Later, the medical examiner and the men from the Forensic Unit would be arriving, but for the moment the detectives had the place to themselves.

The scene looked much as Harold Schmidt had described it. Two chairs were overturned in the foyer and a drawer, pulled out from a small desk, lay dumped on the foyer rug. All the furnishings in the apartment were modern, the carpeting wall to wall, all of it expensive looking. The dining area and the living room were on one side of the foyer and, as Cluett could see through an open doorway, the bedroom on the other side.

Cluett led the way into the living room. Jacqueline Holby lay on her back on the deep-pile carpeting. She wore a fluffy white robe partially open down the front to reveal that she had nothing on underneath. A man's necktie was knotted tightly around her throat, deeply impressed into the flesh. She was so lovely, even in death, that Cluett could well imagine that she had been a successful fashion model.

Cluett used his pen to flip the necktie over so that he could see the label: RICHARDSON'S, FIFTH AVENUE, which was an exclusive men's clothing shop. All three detectives made a note of the name.

Cluett waved a hand in the air. "Spread out, see what you can find before the place gets overrun."

Melchior and Pappas went to check out the rest of the apartment.

Cluett, alone, bent down to look more closely at a broken glass that lay near the body, its red contents spilled across the carpeting. Forensic would later determine that the red liquid was tomato juice.

At that moment the telephone rang.

Cluett hurried out to the foyer, where the phone sat on the small desk, and answered it.

The voice on the other end of the line was female, and the caller was confused when she heard Cluett's voice.

Cluett quickly identified himself, told her there'd been an accident, and asked her name.

"I'm Trudy Quinn. Jackie and I are good friends. What happened?"

Cluett asked if she'd come to the apartment if he sent a police car for her. He'd explain everything then. She said she would and gave him her address and phone number.

He had just finished the call when Melchior and Pappas returned, both men excited.

"Paydirt!" Pappas announced.

Each man held up a hand to show Cluett what had been found.

"Her diary!" Pappas said.

"Her address book," Melchior said. "The boyfriend's name, address, and phone number are all there. Phillip Rimmer. Lives on East Sixty-third Street."

"Get him," Cluett said.

* * *

Months later Cluett would admit that he'd disliked Phillip Rimmer at first sight.

But before the detectives brought Rimmer back to Jacqueline Holby's apartment for questioning, Cluett had already done some of the tedious detail work that was necessary as part of the homicide record.

The three tenants in the building who had reported the disturbance in Apartment 11-E had given statements.

Mr. and Mrs. Albert Hendricks, in Apartment 11-F, next door, to the east, of the Holby apartment, were a gray-haired couple—he was a retired stockbroker—who had lived in the building for nine years. They appeared somewhat embarrassed to find themselves caught up in an unpleasant situation. They reported they'd heard a loud, crashing sound and a scream from just beyond their foyer wall, which adjoined the foyer of 11-E.

Mrs. Hendricks added, hesitantly, that while her husband had tried to call down to the lobby, she had gone to the peephole in the door to her apartment and looked out into the hall. After some time had passed, she said she had seen the figure of a man hurry down the hall and disappear through the exit door to the inside stairwell. She could not say whether or not the man had come out of 11-E, and he was too far away for her to be able to describe him.

Terence Evans lived in Apartment 11-D, next door, to the west, of the Holby apartment. He was in his early thirties, thin for his almost-six-foot height, and had dark hair prematurely balding. He was a commercial artist with a Manhattan advertising agency. He had lived in the building for seven years. He stated that he'd heard indistinct noises from 11-E, followed soon after by the more distinct sounds of glass shattering and a scream from just beyond his living-room wall which adjoined the living room of 11-E. He had then immediately gone to the intercom to try to call the lobby.

The third tenant, Mrs. Sophie Fischer, lived in 10-E, directly below the Holby apartment. She was a gray-haired widow in her late fifties, a tenant in the building for five years, who, despite the fact that she wore a hearing aid, could report that the sound of crashing from above was quite loud. She had heard it clearly from above the ceiling of her foyer, which was identical to the foyer of the apartment one flight up.

The value of these statements, to Cluett, was that they matched the physical disarray he'd observed in Jacqueline Holby's apartment and helped him visualize the sequence of what might have transpired in 11-E; that is, that the struggle began in the foyer, near the door, continued across the foyer, and ended in the living room.

All four tenants stated, when questioned by Cluett, that they had not known the victim personally. Mr. and Mrs. Hendricks and Terence Evans said they knew her by sight but not by name as a next-door neighbor when encountering her in the building. Mrs. Fischer said she did not know that much about her. All of which showed, Cluett supposed, the anonymity of most New Yorkers even when they were living in close proximity to one another.

In addition to the statements from the four tenants, Cluett also had a chance to talk to Trudy Quinn, who arrived at the apartment before Phillip Rimmer did.

She was twenty-three years old, a cute, rather than pretty, brunette, a trifle overweight, who was a graduate student working for a master's degree in literature. She was clearly shocked and frightened by the news of her friend's death. "I kept trying to phone her all evening," Trudy Quinn said in a shaky voice, "and wondering why she didn't answer. And all the time she was dead." She shook her head.

When she had recovered sufficiently to talk coherently, she was able to provide Cluett with information about Jacqueline Holby—and Phillip Rimmer.

"Jackie and I were best friends," she said. "We met at a party a couple of years ago when she first came to New York and didn't know many other people. In fact, I was the one who introduced her to Phillip."

Jacqueline Holby, according to Trudy Quinn, was twenty-two years old and had come to New York from Winter Park, Florida where she had grown up and where her parents and a sister still lived. She had wanted to become an actress and, as a first step, had found work as a model as soon as she had moved to the city. Her picture had appeared on the covers of several magazines and in various magazine ads.

"She was always working," Trudy Quinn said.

"And Phillip Rimmer," Cluett prompted softly. "Tell me about him."

Trudy Quinn, speaking slowly, said she had known him about a year longer than she had known Jacqueline Holby. He was from Fairfield County, Connecticut, had a degree in law—"We met in college," she explained—and was working now as a clerk in a law firm in the city while studying for his New York State bar exams.

Cluett nodded encouragingly. "And he and Jackie had been going together for a while?"

Trudy Quinn frowned. "They *were* a couple. But I thought it was all over with them about a month ago."

She paused. Cluett waited.

Finally, she spoke again, hesitantly. Jackie had told her that she'd broken off with Phillip Rimmer. The reason Jackie gave was that he had become too possessive, jealous, always questioning her about where she went, what she did, suspecting her of seeing other men, smothering her, until she had had to tell him they were quits.

Trudy Quinn brushed back a strand of her hair with her hand and said, "That's why I was so surprised when Phillip phoned me earlier tonight and said he had just been here with Jackie and they'd made up."

Cluett frowned. "He phoned you tonight? After he'd seen Jackie? Why?"

"He said when he got home after seeing her, he'd tried to phone her and there was no answer. He wanted to know if I had talked to her. He said he was worried."

"Worried?" Cluett repeated. "Did he tell you why he was worried?"

Phillip had told her, Trudy Quinn said, that Jackie had told him she was frightened, that someone had been following her, that she had been getting strange phone calls at all hours of the night and she'd answer and all she would hear was heavy breathing at the other end of the line. "Phillip wanted to know if Jackie had said anything about all this to me," Trudy Quinn added. "I told him she hadn't. Then I tried calling here myself, and there was no answer until you picked up the phone."

She sat, looking at Cluett, until he said, "You've been very helpful."

A few minutes later, after he had sent Trudy Quinn home in a squad car, Melchior and Pappas appeared with Phillip Rimmer in tow.

The medical examiner and the forensic-science team were on the scene by then, busy in the living room where Jacqueline Holby's body still lay.

Cluett had already decided he was going to confront Rimmer with the corpse before interrogating him, so he motioned to the two detectives to lead Rimmer directly into the living room as soon as they came into the apartment. Cluett himself stepped to one side to size up the boyfriend and observe his reaction to the murder.

Phillip Rimmer was in his mid-twenties, about five nine or ten in height, his body lean and appearing to be in good physical shape. His hair was brown and thick and clearly carefully barbered. He had the kind of dark, brooding face and implacable expression that Cluett imagined many women would consider handsome. He was dressed in designer jeans, an open-collar sport shirt with an embossed symbol over the shirt's breast pocket, a neatly pressed linen jacket, socks, and loafers. The overall impression the sergeant had was of a man, a look, too precisely—"Not a hair out of place, not a loose thread," Cluett would recall later—calculated.

And Cluett, looking at Phillip Rimmer as Rimmer looked down at Jacqueline Holby's body, noted that while some of the color drained from Rimmer's face, the expression on it remained impassive.

Cluett delayed entering the living room until Rimmer had turned away from the body and began looking around the room. Then he went in.

Again, Cluett had already decided how he was going to question Rimmer: right there in the living room, with the body there, the M.E. examining it, the police photographer shooting pictures of it, the forensic team checking the entire apartment for any possible clues that might be analyzed as evidence later in the police lab.

Cluett approached Rimmer, introduced himself, and motioned to the sofa, taking out a notebook and pen. They sat side by side while Melchior stood near Rimmer, Pappas near Cluett, the two men towering over the sofa. Pappas leaned down and whispered in Cluett's ear, "While we were in his place, I managed to get a look at his tie rack. He's got several ties from the same place as the one around her neck."

Cluett nodded. He looked hard at Rimmer. "Let's talk about tonight."

"Obviously," Rimmer said coolly, "you know I was here. And I suspect you just heard that that's probably my tie that killed her. I wondered what your friend there was snooping around for in my place. As soon as I saw the tie around her neck, I knew."

"Is it your tie?"

"Sure. I took it off when I first got here. It's a hot night. I forgot all about it. It was over the arm of a chair in the foyer when I left."

Rimmer paused, shook his head, and then he said softly, "I should have known something like this might happen."

"Like what?"

"Like her getting killed."

"Why's that?" Cluett asked.

Rimmer settled back on the sofa and told them that in the late afternoon he had received a phone call from Jackie asking him to come to her apartment that evening. When he got there, he found her to be upset. She told him somebody had been following her for days now and that she had been getting phone calls at odd hours of the night, with a lot of heavy breathing on the other end of the line. She was, Rimmer said, scared out of her wits. She was convinced some weirdo was after her. "I should have taken it more seriously," Rimmer said. "I thought it was just her imagination. I tried to quiet her down. And then I left."

"Uh-huh," Cluett said and then said abruptly, "Tell me about you and Jackie."

Rimmer spread his hands in the air. "What's to tell? We'd been going together for about a year now. So what?"

Cluett frowned. "Trudy Quinn told me Jackie broke off with you about a month ago."

For the first and only time, Rimmer seemed caught by surprise. "You've already talked to Trudy tonight?"

Cluett nodded.

"Then you already know that Jackie was being followed, about the phone calls she got," Rimmer said. "Didn't Trudy tell you about that?"

"She told us," Cluett said, "that you told her about them. Jackie never mentioned them to her, Trudy said. But let's get back to the other point. Did or didn't Jackie break up with you about a month ago?"

"It was just a dumb argument, a misunderstanding," Rimmer said. "We made up tonight. Anything else?"

Rimmer had remained calm and composed throughout the interview despite the body in the room and the presence of the Forensic Squad prowling everywhere in search of evidence. Cluett even got the feeling that Rimmer was playing games with him and enjoying the experience.

"Yeah, there is something else," Cluett said, standing. "I want you to come with us now to the station house so we can take a formal statement from you."

Rimmer shrugged. "Glad to accommodate you."

"And I think I should warn you. You have a right to a lawyer—"

"I don't need a lawyer," Rimmer said, cutting Cluett's words short. "And you don't have to waste time telling me about my rights. I have a degree in law. I know what my rights are. And what yours are, too, for that matter."

Cluett simply nodded.

As they were leaving the apartment and passed by the drawer dumped on the floor from the desk in the foyer, there occurred an incident that puzzled Cluett.

Rimmer, pointing to the drawer, asked, "Did you find her revolver in there?"

Cluett knew that no such revolver had been found and he said so.

"She had one," Rimmer insisted. "A thirty-two silver-plated revolver. She brought it with her from Florida. There's a receipt for it somewhere around here. She showed it to me once."

Cluett instructed Pappas to stay behind to look for the receipt, and then Cluett and Melchior left with Rimmer.

Two hours later, at the Sixteenth Precinct, Cluett tape-recorded his interrogation of Phillip Rimmer.

Cluett asked the same questions he'd asked at Jacqueline Holby's apartment. Rimmer gave the same answers.

Now it was a documented part of the record of the case.

Before he had begun his interrogation, Cluett had notified the district attorney's office of his intention.

The assistant D.A. they sent to observe the proceedings was a stranger to Cluett, a young woman pretty enough herself to be a fashion model.

Assistant District Attorney Suzanne Barents was wheat-blond, brown-eyed, in her late twenties, and stylishly attired in a pale-lemon jacket and skirt that fit her too perfectly to have come off any department-store rack.

After Cluett finished the tape recording, he and Suzanne Barents left Rimmer with Melchior in the interrogation room and went out to the corridor to discuss the case.

Cluett was convinced Rimmer was guilty. They could place him at the scene of the crime, he had admitted that "the murder weapon"—the tie—was his, and Trudy Quinn had supplied them with the motive, that Rimmer had been too possessive, jealous, of Jackie and she had broken off with him. He had gone to see her, hoping to make up, and she had rejected him. Something snapped in him and he strangled her. Then he had slipped out of the building unseen so that the time couldn't be pinpointed. Shortly thereafter he had phoned Trudy Quinn to plant the idea that Jackie had been followed and frightened by some "stranger" and had received some weird phone calls. Thus, he had introduced the possibility into the case that she had been killed by some person, unknown, who had been stalking her and who had visited the apartment after he left. "Which will probably be his defense argument if he goes to trial," Cluett concluded.

"You make him sound awfully clever," Suzanne Barents said.

"He is. He's a cunning improviser. The ones who get away with murder always are."

"And he's arrogant and he knows the law," she said softly.

Cluett nodded. "That, too."

"It's all circumstantial. It'll be hard to convict him," she said thoughtfully, staring down at the floor.

Cluett waited.

She raised her head and looked at him. "But let's try."

He grinned.

Later that day Phillip Rimmer was formally charged with the murder of Jacqueline Holby, arraigned, and freed on bail.

Cluett was satisfied with the way events had progressed so far in the case, but there were two aspects of it that puzzled him. One was that Detective Pappas, in searching Jacqueline Holby's apartment, had found a sales receipt for a .32 revolver sold to her in Florida. The receipt contained a serial number for the weapon. However, no trace of the gun was to be found in the apartment.

The other puzzle concerned a discovery police had made at the apartment. On one section of wall in the living room there was a picture hook surrounded by a square patch lighter in shade than the paint on the other walls of the room; an object, a picture perhaps, had obviously hung there. No such object could be located anywhere in the apartment.

Ever since his girl friend had moved out, Cluett followed the same routine after he finished his four-to-midnight shift. He'd stop in one restaurant or another and eat a late meal, then drive home to his apartment in Jackson Heights across the East River from Manhattan.

Once there, he'd put a tape of a movie on his video cassette recorder—bought after she'd left him—and make himself some drinks or open a six-pack of beer while he watched. Sometimes he'd fall asleep before the movie ended.

He was aware, during this period, that he was drinking too much, sleeping too much, and putting on weight.

All this began to change, slowly, in the weeks that passed between the arrest of Phillip Rimmer and his trial. Cluett was dedicated to proving Rimmer had murdered Jacqueline Holby and relentlessly drove himself and his men to assemble every possible piece of evidence to prove Rimmer's guilt.

He even spent most of his hours off-duty working on the case. Now, instead of heading home at midnight from the precinct, frequently he, Melchior, Pappas, and some of the other men would meet in a restaurant or bar or, on occasion, at Cluett's apartment to argue about or agree upon the strength of the evidence they were compiling against Rimmer.

The district attorney had assigned Suzanne Barents to prosecute the case, and sometimes she met with the detectives or she and Cluett would get together during the day. This would be her first big case to try, and she was eager for all the help she could get. Especially since they all had learned, in the meantime, that Phillip Rimmer had hired as his attorney one of the country's leading criminal lawyers, Stephen Krebs.

By then the detectives knew that Phillip Rimmer came from an affluent family and had attended the best schools as a top student before receiving his degree in law. But also, digging into his background, they had unearthed a previous girl friend, Jan Phelps, who told them she had broken off with Rimmer because of his temper and jealousy. Once in a rage he had slapped her around, she said, and broken two of her teeth. She agreed to testify for the prosecution.

The trial of Phillip Rimmer for the murder of Jacqueline Holby began on a Monday in the second week of September in the Criminal Courts Building in lower Manhattan.

In her opening statement to the jury of seven men and five women, Assistant D.A. Suzanne Barents outlined the prosecution's case:

On that fateful night in late July, Phillip Rimmer went to Jacqueline Holby's apartment unannounced. Although she had not expected him and had ended their relationship some weeks . . . a month before, they had been going together for a time earlier, and so she let him in. He had hoped they could make up. But she rejected him. She tried to get rid of him, he wouldn't go, and they struggled in the foyer of the apartment. He forced her back into the living room. And there, in a fit of violent anger, he yanked off his necktie and strangled her. Then he made his way out of the apartment and the building unobserved. Those are the facts we will prove to you.

Stephen Krebs, Phillip Rimmer's lawyer, was a large forceful-looking man with a florid face and a mane of white hair that fell almost to his shoulders. He loomed large over the jury box, leaning in as he made his opening remarks.

The defense, Krebs said, did not dispute that Phillip Rimmer had, indeed, been at Jacqueline Holby's apartment on the night in question. *She* had phoned Phillip and asked him to come by. When he got there, he found her to be in an agitated state. Krebs explained:

As Phillip Rimmer told the police who questioned him, Jackie related to him that she was being followed by some stranger and had been receiving phone calls, anonymous phone calls, at all hours of the night. She was terrified. Phillip, believing she was just overwrought, managed to quiet her down. They patched up their differences, and he left her. Left her alive. He did not try to slip away from the apartment and the building unnoticed, as the prosecution would have you believe. He went down on the elevator, the lobby was filled with people, the doorman was busy outside getting taxicabs and did not notice him when he left. Later, when he got home, he tried to phone Jackie. There was no answer, and he then called Jackie's friend, Trudy Quinn, because he had begun to be alarmed. Someone else, most likely the person who had been following and phoning Jackie, went to Jackie's apartment after Phillip had gone. She let him in, probably thinking it was Phillip who had returned when he discovered he had forgotten his necktie. This is the person who killed Jacqueline Holby.

Cluett saw, as he had suspected, that the defense was going to construct a "reasonable doubt" argument to try to get Rimmer off, claiming that it was some unknown stranger who had murdered Jackie.

The trial lasted ten days, and Cluett was present at every session.

One by one, Suzanne Barents presented her witnesses to tell their story to the jury.

The tenants—Mr. and Mrs. Hendricks, Terence Evans, and Mrs. Sophie Fischer—gave an account of the sounds of the disturbance coming from Apartment 11-E before Jackie's body was found. The defense attorney did not bother to cross-examine, conceding there had been violence in the apartment.

Harold Schmidt testified that Rimmer had gone up to the apartment that evening and that he had not seen Rimmer leave. Under cross-examination, Schmidt had to agree that it was possible Rimmer had left in a normal fashion, taking the elevator and exiting through the lobby and the front entrance, and still not been observed.

The medical examiner gave the results of the autopsy on Jackie's body. She had been strangled, and there were no other marks of assault on the body, sexual or otherwise.

Defense Attorney Krebs asked only one question of the M.E.: "Simply because there were no such marks found on the body does not preclude the possibility that the murder could have been an act of passion?"

"No," the M.E. answered.

Trudy Quinn related an account of her friendships with Jackie and with Rimmer. She stated that Jackie had told her that she had broken off with Rimmer, and why.

Then, under questioning by the defense attorney, Trudy admitted that she and Rimmer had been going together before Jackie came along. Trudy also grudgingly revealed that she and Jackie were not as close friends once Jackie and Rimmer began dating.

The other young woman, Jan Phelps, who had dated Rimmer some years earlier and who testified that he had struck her in an angry fit of jealousy, became rattled when Stephen Krebs cross-examined. She could not recall the year it had been when she claimed Rimmer had struck her, she could think of no one else who had known of the incident, and she left the witness chair weeping and shaking when the attorney dismissed her.

Cluett himself took the stand. He described the scene of disarray inside Jackie's apartment when the police arrived, the finding of her body, and related his tape-recorded interrogation of Rimmer. The tape recording was allowed into evidence.

Throughout the trial Cluett had noted the many whispered comments Rimmer, at the defense table, was making to Stephen Krebs and was convinced that Rimmer, not Krebs, was directing the defense. In the past months the excess weight had disappeared from Cluett's waistline, and he felt fit and eager to handle what he expected to be a grueling cross-examination by the defense.

Instead, the defense attorney, with a wave of the hand, said he had no questions to ask of the sergeant at this time but reserved the right to call him to the stand at a later time.

At that point, a week into the trial, the prosecution rested its case.

In the following days, the defense called a number of witnesses to the stand, one of Rimmer's law professors, several of the lawyers from the firm where Rimmer was employed, two of his friends, and a minister from the church the Rimmer family attended.

As the trial approached its final days, Cluett was recalled to the stand by the defense attorney.

The first question asked by Krebs set the tone for the ones that followed: "Did you or any other police officer ever make the smallest attempt to locate the stranger who had been following and phoning Jacqueline Holby?"

Cluett had a bad head cold that day. He had to blow his nose and clear his throat before he answered: "No."

"Because you had already made up your minds to convict Phillip Rimmer, isn't that the fact?"

"Based upon the only evidence—"

"Just answer the question, yes or no!" Krebs thundered.

"Yes," Cluett said. "*Because* there was no proof there was any stranger—"

"How could you *know* that?" Krebs demanded. "If you didn't pursue the matter?"

When Cluett tried to explain that the police couldn't pursue a phantom, Krebs cut him off again. Suzanne Barents objected, protesting that the defense was badgering the witness. The judge sustained the objection.

The defense attorney kept Cluett on the stand for another forty minutes, hammering away at the possibility that there *could* have been someone else who had murdered Jackie. Cluett continued to answer, one way or another, until his voice was a hoarse whisper, but without conceding the existence of some unknown killer of Jacqueline Holby.

The next day the defense and the prosecution summed up their cases.

Stephen Krebs recounted all the issues of doubt remaining in the case, especially the fact that the real killer remained at large.

"Phillip Rimmer has explained every piece of evidence the prosecutor has assembled against him. Yes, he was there—she had phoned him asking him there. Yes, his tie was used—he had taken it off because of the heat of the night and left it there. And, no, no, no, he did not have a motive, because he and Jackie patched up their differences! Did the police, did anyone, make the slightest effort to look for the real killer of Jacqueline Holby? Again, no, no, no, I say to you! The law requires you to find the defendant guilty beyond a reasonable doubt. The real killer of Jacqueline Holby exists, and I say to you, so does reasonable doubt as to Phillip Rimmer's guilt."

Suzanne Barents recounted all the evidence pointing to the guilt of Phillip Rimmer and the equal lack of *any* evidence that someone else might have committed the murder.

"*He* was there, *his* tie was used to strangle her, *his* motive was that he was angry enough to commit murder because she had rejected him."

All through the trial Cluett had expected the defense to bring up the matter of the disappearance of Jackie's .32 revolver. But it was never mentioned. The revolver and whatever it was that had been hanging on the apartment wall continued to puzzle Cluett.

The case went to the jury late in the day and, when after several hours had passed and they had reached no verdict, the jury was locked up for the night.

Cluett and Suzanne Barents stopped and had a cup of coffee together before he went on duty at the Sixteenth Precinct. She was depressed, certain that Rimmer was going to go free. Cluett tried to cheer her up, although he felt miserable himself, from his cold and his own doubts about the outcome of the trial, despite his own conviction that Rimmer was guilty.

Cluett overslept and was late getting to the courthouse the next morning.

He had had to work overtime the night before because an emergency situation had developed in the city about an hour after sunset.

A police helicopter flying over Manhattan had crashed into a construction crane atop the sixtieth floor of one of the many buildings seemingly always being thrown up eastside, westside, uptown and down. This one was on Third Avenue in midtown. The crane should have had a lighted warning beacon on it, but somebody had goofed and forgotten to turn it on. The helicopter pilot and passenger had been killed, and debris from the helicopter and the wrecked crane had scattered over several blocks of the streets below. Fortunately, no other persons had been injured or killed. But the traffic gridlock that resulted from the accident had taken hours to untangle and had forced most of the police on duty, including those in homicide, into overtime.

When Cluett finally reached the courtroom, the jury foreman was announcing the verdict: *not guilty.*

Cluett was sickened by the sight of Phillip Rimmer, a great smirk on his face, raise his arms in a gesture of victory as his lawyer and friends surrounded him, shouting congratulations. Congratulations for what? Cluett wondered. For getting away with murder?

Suzanne Barents had hurried out of the courtroom, and Cluett caught a brief glimpse of Jackie Holby's mother, father, and sister as they slowly exited, anguish plainly etched on their faces. Cluett left.

It was too early for him to report for duty at the precinct, but as he headed up the FDR Drive toward midtown, he decided to stop by the station house. Today was payday, and since he still had a bad cold, he decided he'd pick up his check, then take sick leave for the night.

He never had a chance to do either of those things, however. As soon as he reached the precinct, the desk sergeant called him over, saying, "Detective Jorgenson phoned in a message for you. Says he's on a case that looks like it's connected to one you've been working on, the murder of that model, Jackie what's-her-name." The desk sergeant handed a slip of paper to Cluett. "Here's the address where he's at. He said if we heard from you, you might want to look in on this one."

Detective Jorgenson was in Homicide on the day shift. The address written on the slip of paper was a number on Second Avenue.

Curious, Cluett took the slip of paper and drove across town to the address, which turned out to be a small store-front building a block away from Jacqueline Holby's apartment. Once again, there were police cars pulled up in front of the building, along with the morgue wagon and the Forensic Unit's station wagon.

The windowpanes on either side of the door had been painted over black and had lettering on them that read, PRINTING PHOTO COPYING.

Cluett made his way inside, past the uniformed patrolman at the door.

The interior was filled with detectives, members of the forensic team, and the medical examiner. A young woman in her late twenties was weeping in a chair on one side of the office. Detective Jorgenson, who was at the back of the room, came forward when he spotted Cluett. A man's body lay on the floor.

"Got a funny one here, Sergeant," Jorgenson said. "Looks like the guy shot himself. Name's Willard Pope." Jorgenson indicated the weeping woman. "That's the wife, she called us. She says he didn't come home last night. She came here today and found the body. The peculiar thing's here."

He led Cluett over to a typewriter on a desk. There was a sheet of paper in the roller. On it was typed:

> TO WHOM IT MAY CONCERN:
> I STRANGLED JACQUELINE HOLBY. THE POLICE HAVE CHARGED THE WRONG MAN. I CANNOT LIVE WITH THIS ON MY CONSCIENCE.

The note was unsigned.

"Where's the gun?" Cluett asked quickly.

Jorgenson pointed to where the weapon lay, on a sheet of plastic. It was a .32 silver-plated revolver.

Cluett would have bet Jackie Holby's gun had finally surfaced.

He gave Jorgenson instructions to check with Detective Pappas at the precinct later and see if there was a match-up between the serial numbers on the revolver and the serial numbers on the sales receipt Pappas had taken from Jackie's apartment. He also told Jorgenson he wanted an extra-thorough dusting of the premises for prints and other evidence that someone other than Pope himself might have fired the fatal shot.

Cluett still felt feverish and ill and wanted to get home to bed. He stayed long enough, however, to find a phone in the back room of the shop and call Suzanne Barents.

He told her of the latest development in the case, and when she asked, voice incredulous, "You mean Rimmer was telling the truth all along about someone else strangling Jackie?" Cluett answered, "Not if I have it figured right. Rimmer set this whole thing up himself. Rimmer lifted the revolver from Jackie's place the night he killed her so that he could use it just exactly the way he did here. He'd already planned it. He picked out this guy, Willard Pope, because he was in the neighborhood. Rimmer came here sometime last night, killed this guy, and typed up a phony suicide note."

"But the jury cleared Rimmer," Suzanne said.

"Sure," Cluett answered. "But Rimmer couldn't be certain of that last night. So he took out a little extra insurance just in case he was convicted. Rimmer's always directing events."

"You really think that was the way it was?"

"I do," Cluett said. "And if Rimmer slipped up anywhere along the line this time, we're going to nail him."

Cluett headed home from the printshop, bought himself a bottle of liquor, and when he was home, fixed several stiff drinks and went to bed to nurse his cold.

He was more asleep than awake when, around 11:00 P.M., his phone rang. It was the desk sergeant at the precinct calling to say that a Mr. Albert Hendricks was trying to reach Cluett, said it was urgent, and left a phone number.

Cluett called Hendricks, Jackie Holby's neighbor. Hendricks said he had to see Cluett immediately, that it might be a matter of life and death, and he didn't want to discuss it on the phone.

Cluett sighed, said he'd be right there, dressed, and went to Hendricks's apartment in Kips Bay.

Hendricks and his wife met Cluett at the door to their apartment and led him into the living room, where a young woman, in her early twenties, quite pretty, sat huddled on the sofa. She had on a nightgown, robe, and slippers.

Mrs. Hendricks introduced Cluett, explaining to him that the young woman was Millie Singleton and that she had moved into the apartment next door that had been occupied by Jacqueline Holby. Millie Singleton worked as an executive secretary to the president of an investment firm. The Hendrickses had become friendly with Millie Singleton, so she had come to them with her problem. "She's terrified," Mrs. Hendricks said.

Mrs. Hendricks smiled encouragingly at the young woman and said, "Tell Sergeant Cluett here the story."

Millie Singleton told Cluett that soon after she had moved into the apartment, she had begun getting anonymous phone calls. Sometimes there was just heavy breathing; sometimes a male voice made obscene suggestions. The calls came at different times, usually when she was getting into bed, and then later throughout the night. Millie Singleton had not known about Jacqueline Holby's murder until that evening when she told the story of the calls to the Hendrickses after receiving such a call an hour or so before. The strange part, she said, was that she had an unlisted phone number.

"We thought you should be informed," Mrs. Hendricks said to Cluett. "We don't want—want anything else happening. Do you think Millie's in any danger?"

The truth was that Cluett did think she might be in danger. He didn't want to alarm any of them, however, so he said only that probably the calls were coming from some nut and were unconnected with the earlier case. Merely as a precaution, he added, he'd like to put a recording device on her phone and assign one of his detectives to man the phone at night, if she'd give her permission.

Millie Singleton agreed eagerly.

Cluett thanked the Hendrickses for phoning him and went with Millie Singleton back to 11-E, where he phoned the Sixteenth Precinct and asked for one of the detectives to come over with a tape recorder to hook up to the telephone.

The sergeant stayed on in the apartment until the detective, Frank Masters, arrived and hooked up the tape recorder.

Cluett noted that Millie Singleton had furnished the apartment in a different decor from Jacqueline Holby's, with Scandinavian furniture, throw rugs on the floor, framed modern prints on the walls. The interior had been repainted, so he could no longer see where the bare spot had been on the wall when Jackie Holby lived there.

Before Cluett left, he told Millie Singleton there would be a man assigned to her place to monitor her calls until they caught the creep who was bothering her.

Then Cluett went home again and to bed, but not to sleep. Normally, of course, he would not have taken the report of a series of obscene phone calls so seriously. They occurred frequently in a city where the population of single women living alone was high. But it was too much to expect that there was nothing but coincidence between Jackie Holby's death and the phone calls Millie Singleton was receiving. He didn't want another murder on his hands.

That night, for the first time, Cluett had to consider the possibility that Phillip Rimmer had told the truth about someone else stalking and phoning Jackie before her murder. And if there *was* a connection, Cluett realized, the likely link was the apartment itself, someone who had been there, a delivery person, repairman, movers, or someone who worked in the building itself and had had access, at one time or another, to 11-E.

When Cluett presented this new development to Detectives Melchior and Pappas and other members of the Sixteenth's Homicide Squad the next day, Harold Schmidt, the doorman, became the chief suspect.

Cluett assigned a three-man team to keep an around-the-clock surveillance on Schmidt and to check on his background. This, in addition to a man to be posted in 11-E throughout the night to monitor any phone calls Millie might receive.

Cluett picked another team of men to check on any persons who might have visited apartment 11-E during the time Jackie lived there and then again while Millie lived there.

Meanwhile, it had been established through the serial number that the .32 revolver in the printing shop was the one purchased by Jackie Holby in Florida.

Later that same day there came yet another intriguing twist to the case. All three of the New York City newspapers carried a story on Phillip Rimmer's acquittal, and the *Daily News* and the *Post* also ran a photograph of Rimmer. And, in the late afternoon, Elizabeth Pope —wife of Willard Pope, the man found dead with the suicide note and the .32 revolver—contacted the precinct. She said she had seen Rimmer's photograph in the newspapers and swore that he had been outside her husband's printing shop early in the evening on the day before Pope's body was found. She had been leaving the shop. It was the last time she saw her husband alive. She said she would be willing to come to the precinct and make a sworn statement to that effect.

Cluett immediately got in touch with Suzanne Barents, and the assistant D.A. was present at the station house when Elizabeth Pope arrived. As soon as Cluett had her sworn affidavit in hand, he sent a couple of men to pick up Phillip Rimmer and bring him in for questioning.

"Damnedest case I ever worked on," Cluett remarked, shaking his head.

This time when Rimmer was escorted into the interrogation room and confronted with Elizabeth Pope and her accusations, he refused to talk unless his lawyer was present.

There was another wait while Rimmer called the lawyer and until he arrived. Then Rimmer and Krebs had to confer privately, after which it was the lawyer who spoke first.

"My client did a very foolish thing," Krebs said. He went on to explain that on the day in question Rimmer, after he got home from court, found an unsigned letter in the mail. The writer of the letter confessed to the murder of Jacqueline Holby, said he was writing to Rimmer to let him know this in case Rimmer was wrongly convicted, and that he was going to commit suicide. The letter had a typed name—Willard Pope—and address on it.

"Naturally, but foolishly, my client rushed to that address immediately." The lawyer went on to say that once Rimmer reached the printing shop, he had hesitated to enter. Rimmer admitted he saw Elizabeth Pope leave, at the time she saw him. But still he had not gone inside because it occurred to him that the whole thing might be a trap or that he had been lured there to be killed himself. He had lingered on the street until he heard a shot from inside. It was then that he went into the shop, found Pope dead, the suicide note in the typewriter, and the gun—which Rimmer immediately thought might be Jackie's.

"At that awful moment," the lawyer said, "Phillip realized finally that if he was discovered there, under those circumstances, it might very well be concluded that he had killed the man. Just as you now possibly suspect him of doing," Krebs added.

Rimmer produced the typewritten letter and the envelope it had been mailed in. The envelope had Rimmer's name and address on it and had been postmarked three days earlier. The lawyer handed the letter and envelope to Cluett to keep.

Krebs stated further that he believed Rimmer had given a satisfactory explanation of what had occurred and that Rimmer would not, on advice of counsel, answer any more questions.

Cluett had to accept the fact that he either had to arrest Rimmer again—which he was not prepared to do—or release him. Cluett nodded to the lawyer, and once more Rimmer, accompanied by Krebs, walked away from the police.

"He's going to try to stonewall us again, the sly, conniving sneak," Cluett raged.

Assistant D.A. Suzanne Barents agreed with the sergeant that they didn't have sufficient evidence to arrest Rimmer.

Cluett ordered Pappas and a couple of other men back to the printing shop where Pope's body had been found. "I want you to fine-comb the premises," Cluett said. "If there's anything there to tie Rimmer into Pope's death, I want it."

A cold early fall rain had been coming down hard all day, and at about 8:00 P.M., as Cluett was about to leave and check in on Frank Masters, who was with Millie Singleton in Apartment 11-E, Pappas returned to the precinct.

Pappas had brought a sheaf of papers with him from the printing shop. He spread them out on the desk in front of Cluett.

"These are job orders Pope kept for the past year," Pappas said. "Orders for photostats of advertisements he made for one particular customer." Pappas pointed to the customer name on the more than a dozen pages lying on the desk. "That name look familiar?"

Cluett read the name and sat back in his chair. "I'll be damned," he said. "The neighbor in Eleven-D, Terence Evans."

"It could explain a lot," Pappas said. "He could have done it and then set up Rimmer to take the fall, could be setting up Rimmer a second time—"

"There's no time to work it all out now," Cluett said. "If Evans is our man, let's get over there."

The four detectives in Apartment 11-E—Cluett, Pappas, Melchior, and Masters—had been there for hours. The time was a few minutes before midnight. Millie Singleton had made them coffee and then left them in the living room and gone to shower and get ready for bed in the rear of the apartment. There was a phone in the living room and an extension in the bedroom. The tape recorder was connected to the phone in the living room.

Cluett had his eyes fixed on the phone in the living room, which so far had remained silent. "Ring, ring!" he said softly.

He got up and wandered over to a window. They had kept the window blinds closed all evening as a precaution, so that they couldn't be seen in the room even though the way the windows in this apartment and in Evans's apartment next door were arranged, Evans could not have looked into the living room.

At the window Cluett peered out through the blinds. The rain was still falling steadily, and now and then a flash of lightning lit up the sky. Change-of-season weather, autumn in New York, Cluett thought.

Millie Singleton called softly that she was finished in the bathroom and was going to bed. They told her goodnight and heard her door close.

The phone rang.

Cluett hurried over.

Frank Masters switched on the tape recorder.

The phone rang again and then again and was cut off in the middle of the third ring when Millie—as they'd prearranged—answered in the bedroom. Masters eased the receiver off the hook of the living-room phone and handed it to Cluett.

"Hello, hello? Who is it, please?" Cluett heard Millie saying. He heard the answering heavy breathing and several low, but not quite indistinct, sounds. The heavy breathing and the sounds went on for a time until Millie hung up the phone, and so did Cluett.

In the rear of the apartment the bedroom door opened, and Millie asked if they'd recorded the call. Told that they had, she closed the bedroom door again.

Frank Masters rewound the tape and played it again so that the detectives could hear it.

"Not much to go on," Pappas said.

Cluett nodded wordlessly. He said to Masters, "Get the machine set. She says if he calls once, he always calls back."

Cluett walked out of the living room and wandered back to the bathroom. He was restless, looking for something but he didn't know what.

The bathroom was still faintly steamy from the shower Millie had taken, and the air was filled with fragrant scents of bath oil and cologne.

Cluett stood for a moment looking around. The bathroom window was closed and the shade pulled down.

Cluett heard the phone ring again and, on impulse, he switched off the bathroom light, shut the door leading out, and went to the window, easing the window and shade up a few inches from the bottom so that he could see out.

From this vantage point Cluett could see the window of Evans's bathroom directly opposite and, at an angle, the window of Evans's bedroom, which was directly opposite the window of Millie's bedroom. The window of the bathroom across the way was dark and the shade down. The blinds in the window of the bedroom at an angle opposite were up, but the room was dark.

Cluett waited and then was about to turn away when suddenly there was a flash of lightning and a peal of thunder.

Brief as the flash was, lighting up the darkness, Cluett had seen all he had been looking for: Terence Evans—in darkness a moment before, briefly illuminated—standing in his bedroom looking out, the telephone at his ear, a pair of binoculars at his eyes. Cluett slowly closed the bathroom window and pulled down the shade.

He would check, but he already knew that Millie Singleton probably never thought of closing her bedroom blinds, and Jackie Holby probably never thought of it either.

Ironic, he thought. New Yorkers passed each other all the time on the streets and never noticed each other when they were in plain sight. And some of them never considered that, living in such close proximity, they could be observed in some of their most intimate moments—as Terence Evans was now watching Millie and had surely watched Jackie Holby, too.

The puzzle of how a caller could know Millie's unlisted phone number was solved, too: With his binoculars, Evans would have had no trouble reading the number right off the instrument on her bedside table.

Cluett returned to the living room. He looked around at Masters, Pappas, and Melchior.

"We haven't got enough to put him away yet," Cluett said. "But we've got enough to get a court order to plant a bug in his apartment."

A detective named Charley Myers, disguised as a building inspector, went into seven apartments in the building looking for a seepage in the electrical lines in the D row of apartments. It was in midafternoon of the following day. The building superintendent accompanied him. Myers planted a bug in the living room and bedroom of 11-D.

Terence Evans was not home at the time. When he did arrive, as he usually did, at 6:30 P.M., a team of detectives was assembled in Millie Singleton's apartment next door. She was there, too, and so was Suzanne Barents, whose presence had been requested by Sergeant Cluett.

There hadn't been anything for them to do for the past hour that they'd been there waiting for Evans to come home, and when they heard a sound on the amplified receiver they'd set up, which was connected to the two listening devices in the apartment next door, it was like the curtain rising on a play in a theater. Even though the sound was only that of Evans opening and closing his apartment door.

They listened as he moved around in the apartment, heard him whistling, heard the sound of a television set, the seven-o'clock news, and then the television set being turned off. There were only faint sounds for a while after that, and they had to assume he was eating. Later they listened as he made three phone calls, two to men, one to a woman, all concerning his advertising work.

"Not very edifying, is it?" Suzanne Barents asked of no one in particular.

Finally, as the evening wore on, Cluett gave a nod to Millie, and she left the living room and went to the bedroom as they'd planned. A few minutes later, she called out to them softly, "I'm starting now." Which meant she was preparing to undress.

A few moments passed.

The phone rang.

Frank Masters lifted the phone in the living room. The tape recorder began to turn. From the receiver connected to the bug in the bedroom next door, they could hear, quite audibly, the same sounds that were coming from the telephone.

"At least we've nailed him on that," Cluett said. "For whatever it's worth."

They listened for several seconds more until Millie hung up the phone, and then the line went dead, and, over the bug's receiver, they heard Evans laugh softly.

"Okay," Cluett said, "let's go confront him with what we have and see if he breaks down."

Cluett had started to leave the living room when there was a sudden new sound from the receiver: The door buzzer in Evans's apartment was being pressed insistently. Cluett turned back to listen, waving to the others to stay in the living room, too.

They heard Evans move to his door and call out, "Who's there?"

They heard the muffled answer from the other side of Evans's door: "Police! Open up!"

"What the hell's going on?" Cluett exclaimed, and everyone else in Millie Singleton's apartment was equally baffled.

They heard Evans open the door, asking, "What do you want?" And then protesting, "You're not the police!"

They heard the sound of a scuffle, the door slamming, and a voice saying, "Move, Evans."

And then they heard Evans, voice incredulous, say, "Rimmer! You're Phillip Rimmer!"

"Smart boy," the other voice—and Cluett recognized it now as Rimmer's—said.

They heard Evans, voice shaky, say, "What do you want?"

Over the receiver came Rimmer's answer: "You're dead! You're going out a back window and straight down eleven floors."

They heard Evans whining, "Why? You're crazy! What did I do?"

They heard Rimmer's answer: "You watched Jackie in her apartment, when she undressed, when we made love. I spotted you a couple of times."

The voices were fainter over the receiver and then louder again as the two men must have been moving from the front room to the door of the bedroom.

"I didn't kill her!" Evans said, his voice desperate as it came over the receiver.

Cluett motioned to the other detectives in 11-E. "Pappas, Melchior, out in the hall. But don't bust in on them till I tell you."

The two detectives moved fast.

Cluett and the others, still listening, heard Rimmer say, "The police are going to connect it up that you did. I arranged it so they will. That you killed Jackie and Pope. They'll find your name in his records. I followed you at times, knew you went there—"

They heard Evans say, *"You killed Jackie and him!"*

They heard Rimmer's boasting answer: "They couldn't prove I killed her. I was too clever. And once they find you're dead, committed suicide, they'll put together the things I arranged and be satisfied you did, you did it and tried to frame me. That's what they'll believe."

There was a pause for a moment, a kind of whimpering sound from Evans, and then Rimmer's voice came again, as if he couldn't resist proving his cleverness: "There's one thing the police haven't even picked up yet. But they will, they will, in time. You told them, you testified, that you heard glass breaking in Jackie's apartment. But the only glass found was a small one on the rug. You'd never have been able to hear it through the walls. That's why I smashed a picture frame—so you'd hear it—then I took the frame and the picture away with me when I left. After I killed her, I remembered how you'd spied on her and I decided to lay down a trail of clues that, sooner or later, would lead back to you . . ."

Cluett was already on the run from 11-E. Out in the hall, he shouted to Pappas and Melchior, "Bust in! Now!"

The two big detectives went through the door of Evans's apartment, crashing it back on its hinges, Cluett right behind them, all three with their guns in their hands.

In the bedroom, Rimmer twirled around at the sound and the sight of the three men coming at him. Melchior slammed into Rimmer with a flying tackle, Pappas had him around the neck, wrenching away the gun Rimmer held in his hand, all three of them piled up on the floor. Evans was cowering in a corner of the room.

Cluett turned away, saying, "Take them both in."

Cluett would later remark, "Funny thing, if Evans hadn't made those anonymous phone calls to Millie Singleton after she moved in, we'd never have been next door when Rimmer arrived, and Evans would be dead. And maybe, sooner or later, everybody would have been convinced he'd killed Jackie and Willard Pope."

Later that year Phillip Rimmer was brought to trial for the murder of Willard Pope. Assistant D.A. Suzanne Barents was again the prosecutor. The judge allowed the tapes from the listening devices planted in Evans's apartment to be entered into evidence.

This time Rimmer's trial lasted only three days. The jury took just one hour to return a verdict of guilty. Phillip Rimmer was sentenced to twenty-five years to life in Attica Prison.

There's one footnote to be added to this account: A few days after Rimmer's trial ended, Cluett phoned Suzanne Barents and invited her to dinner, saying he'd wanted to do this before but he'd always thought their law-enforcement ranks were too unequal.

She accepted his invitation and added she was glad he had changed his mind about the inequality of their ranks.

He admits that he had great satisfaction in answering, "It isn't that I changed my mind; I changed my rank. I've been promoted to lieutenant."

LUCKY DAY

MARY HIGGINS CLARK

It was a chilly Wednesday in November. Nora walked quickly, grateful that the subway was only two blocks away. She and Jack had been lucky to get an apartment in the Claridge House when it opened six years ago. With the way prices had skyrocketed for new tenants, they'd never be able to afford one in that building now. And its location on Eighty-seventh and Third made it accessible to subways and buses. Cabs too. But cabs weren't included in their budget.

She wished she'd worn something heavier than the jacket she'd gotten at the wrap party of the last film she worked on. But with the name of the film blazoned on the breast pocket, it was a visible reminder of the fact that she did have solid acting experience.

She stopped at the corner. The light was green, but the traffic was turning, and it was worth anyone's life to attempt to cross. Next week was Thanksgiving. Between Thanksgiving and Christmas, Manhattan would be one long parking lot. She tried not to think that now Jack wouldn't have the Christmas bonus from Merrill Lynch. Over breakfast he'd just admitted that he'd been part of the cutback at Merrill Lynch but was starting a new job today. *Another* new job.

She darted across the street as the light turned red, barely escaping the gypsy cab that charged across the intersection. The driver shouted after her, "You won't keep your looks if you get splattered, honey." Nora spun around. He was giving her the finger. In a reflex action she returned it and then was ashamed of herself. She rushed down the block ignoring window displays, stepping around the sleeping baglady who was sprawled against a storefront.

She was about to plunge down the subway stairs when she heard her name called. "Hey, Nora, don't you say hello?" Behind the newspaper stand, Bill Regan, his leathered face creased in a smile that revealed overly bright false teeth, reached out a folded copy of the *Times* to her. "You're daydreaming," he accused.

"I guess I am." She and Bill had struck up an acquaintance over their daily morning encounter. A retired delivery man, Bill filled his days by helping out the blind newsdealer in the morning rush time and then, working as a messenger. "Keeps me busy," he'd explained to Nora. "Ever since May died, it's just too lonesome home. Gives me something to do. I meet a lot of nice people and get a chance to gab. May always said I was a great gabber."

The one mistake she had made was that four months ago, on the anniversary of May's death, she impulsively invited Bill up for a drink. Now he had formed a habit every week or two of calling with an excuse for dropping in. Jack was sick of it. Once inside their apartment, Bill remained wedged for at least two hours until she finally got around either to easing him out or to inviting him for dinner.

"I got a feeling, Nora," Bill said. "A feeling it's my lucky day. There's a big one being pulled out this afternoon."

The state lottery was up to thirteen million dollars. There hadn't been a winning ticket in six weeks. "I forgot to buy a ticket," Nora told him. "But I don't feel lucky." She fished change from her pocket. "I'd better run. I've got an audition."

"Break a leg." Bill was obviously proud of his show-business jargon. "I keep telling ye. You're the picture of Rita Hayworth when she was in *Gilda.* You're gonna be a star." For a moment their eyes locked. Nora felt oddly chilled. The usual mournful expression was gone from Bill's pale blue eyes. Wisps of yellow-white hair were rippling across his forehead. His smile seemed frozen in place.

"One way or another, maybe we'll both be lucky," she said. "See you, Bill."

At the theater there were already ninety hopefuls ahead of her. She was given a number and tried to find a place to sit. A familiar face came over. Last year she and Sam had bit parts in a Bogdanovich film.

"How many parts are they casting?" she said.

"Two. One for you. One for me."

"Very funny."

It was one o'clock when she got the chance to read. It was impossible to tell how well she had done. The producer and author sat with impassive faces.

She went on a go-see for a print ad and then auditioned for a J. C. Penney industrial film. Not bad to get that one; it would mean at least three days' work.

There was one more place where she'd meant to drop off a picture, but at four-thirty, she decided to forget it and go home. The relentlessly uneasy feeling that had been with her all day had grown into a black cloud of apprehension. She walked across town to the subway, just reached the platform as her train was pulling out, and settled down, in weary resignation, on a grafitti-covered bench.

It gave her time to do what she'd not wanted to do all day. Think. About Jack. About her and Jack. About the fact that the apartment was going co-op and they couldn't afford to buy it. About Jack changing jobs again. Even in Manhattan there were just so many investment houses. She'd never even heard of whatever the new one was called.

Face it. Jack hated bond sales. He'd gone into it just so they'd have an income while she tried to make it as an actress and he wrote on weekends. They'd arrived in New York with college diplomas still wet, wedding rings still new, so sure they'd blaze across Manhattan. And now, six years later, Jack's frustration was showing in a hundred ways.

A crowded train lumbered into the station. Nora got on, squeezing her way past the door and grabbing a pole. As she steadied herself in the swaying car, she realized the rain must have started. The people she was next to had damp coats, and the heavy, musty odor of wet shoes permeated the subway car.

The apartment was a welcome haven after the day. Their view included the East River, the Triborough Bridge, and Gracie Mansion. Nora couldn't imagine that either one of them hadn't been born in Manhattan. They simply *were* New Yorkers. If only she could get a running part on a soap, she'd be able to carry the finances for a while and give Jack his chance to write. She'd come close a couple of times. It would happen.

She shouldn't have hammered at him this morning. He'd been so embarrassed when he admitted losing the Merrill Lynch job. Had she unconsciously become so critical that he couldn't talk to her anymore or was he losing his self-confidence that badly? I love you, Jack, she thought. She hurried into the kitchen and pulled a wedge of cheddar and a sprig of grapes from the refrigerator. She'd have the carafe of wine waiting, with them when he got home. Fixing the platter, getting out wineglasses, propping sofa pillows, and turning the lights down so that they glowed softly and emphasized the panorama of the skyline eased Nora's sense of worry. It was only when she went into the bedroom to change into a caftan that she noticed that the light on the answering machine was blinking.

There was one message. It was from Bill Regan. His voice an excited, raspy wheeze, he said, "Nora, don't go out. I gotta celebrate with you. I'll be over by seven. Nora, I told ye. I knew it. *It's my lucky day.*"

Oh dear God. Just what Jack needed, to have Bill Regan around tonight. Lucky day. It had to be the lottery. He probably won a few hundred bucks again. Now he would really stay all evening or insist on taking them to a cafeteria for dinner.

When Jack was going to be late, he always called. Tonight he didn't. At six o'clock, Nora nibbled on a slice of cheese, at six-thirty poured a glass of wine. If only Jack had been early tonight. They'd have had at least a little time before Bill barged in.

At seven-thirty, no one had come. It wasn't like Bill to be late. Surely he would have called if he'd changed his mind about coming. Exasperation mingled with worry. Whether he came or not, the evening was out of kilter. And where was Jack?

By eight o'clock Nora wasn't sure what to do. She couldn't remember the name of Jack's new firm. The messenger service in the Fisk Building on West Fifty-seventh Street where Bill worked was closed. Had there been an accident? If only she'd watched the local news. And Bill always walked through Central Park when he came to their place. He said it gave him exercise. Even in the rain he did that. Thirty blocks through the park. On a night like this there wouldn't be joggers. Had anything happened to him?

Jack came in at eight-thirty. His thin, intense face was dead white, his eyes wide-pupiled. When she rushed to him, he put his arms around her and began to rock her slowly. "Nora, Nora."

"Jack, what happened? I've been so worried. You and Bill, both so late . . ."

He pulled back. "Don't tell me you're waiting for Bill Regan?"

"Yes, he phoned. He was supposed to be here by seven. Jack, what's the matter with you? I'm sorry about this morning. I didn't mean to upset you. Jack, I don't care whether you changed jobs. I'm only worried for your sake. . . . Maybe I can give up acting for a while and get a job that pays regularly. I'll give you your chance. Jack, I love you."

She heard a strangled sound, then felt his shoulders begin to heave. Jack was crying. Nora pulled his head down, cradled it against her face. "I'm sorry. I didn't know it's been so bad for you."

He didn't answer, only held her against him. Nora and Jack. They'd met ten years ago, their first day at Brown. She'd been attracted by the quiet intensity she felt in him, his thin, intelligent face, the quick smile that dispelled his usual serious expression. Boy meets girl. Neither one of them had bothered with anyone else after that first meeting.

Now she made him slip off his bargain copy Burberry. "Jack, you're soaked!"

"I guess I am. Oh God, honey, I want to talk to you, but I'll wait. You say Bill is coming." He started to laugh, then tears came to his eyes again.

Like an obedient child he followed her order to get into a hot shower. Something had happened, but they certainly couldn't talk until Bill Regan had come and gone.

What about Bill Regan? He lived in Queens. He'd shown them pictures of the shabby bungalow. Maybe his phone number was listed. It seemed impossible he'd just forget to come, but he was seventy-five years old.

There were a dozen William Regans in the Queens directory. Despairingly Nora racked her brain to see if she could remember an address. She hung up, dug out her Christmas card list. Last year she had asked Bill for his address so that she could send him a card. Armed with the appropriate information, she dialed the operator again and got the number. But there was no answer on Bill's phone.

From inside the bedroom she heard a sharp metallic sound. What on earth was Jack doing? The thought slipped through her mind and vanished as she redialed Bill's number. He simply wasn't home.

Jack came out in his pajamas and bathrobe. He seemed calmer now, even though his intensity literally made the air crackle as if with static electricity. He gulped down a glass of wine and ravenously attacked the cheese plate.

"You must be starved. I've got some spaghetti sauce left from the other night." Apologetically, Nora started toward the kitchen.

Jack followed her. "I'm not helpless." He began to make a salad while she put the water on to boil for the pasta. An instant later she heard a sharp intake of breath. She spun around from the stove. Jack had cut his finger badly. Blood gushed from it. Both his hands were trembling. He tried to brush aside her concern. "What a damn fool thing to do. The knife just slipped. Nora, it's all right. Just get a Band-Aid or something."

She could not persuade him that the cut was deep; it might require stitches. "I tell you it will be all right."

"Jack, something's wrong. Tell me please. If you've lost your damn new job, forget it. We'll manage."

He began to laugh, an unmirthful bellow that came from somewhere deep in his chest, a laugh that seemed to mock and exclude her. "Oh, honey, I'm sorry," he finally managed to say. "God what a crazy evening. Come on. Get a couple of Band-Aids for me and let's eat. We'll talk later. We're both too jumpy now."

"I'll set three places just in case Bill shows up."

"Why not set four? Maybe he's picked up a blonde."

"Jack!"

"Oh, hell, let's just get something to eat and be done with it."

They ate in silence, the empty place on Nora's right a silent reminder of the unmistakable fact that Bill was long overdue. Under the flickering light of the candles, the bandage on Jack's finger began to turn a bright red shade that soon became a dark brownish stain.

The Bolognese sauce was Nora's specialty, but she found her throat unable to open. The color was so close to the blood on Jack's finger. The sense of apprehension was causing tension to turn her shoulder blades into knots. Finally she pushed her chair back. "I absolutely have to call the police and see if there's any report of an accident happening to someone with Bill's description."

"Nora, Bill makes deliveries all over Manhattan. For Pete's sake, what precinct are you going to start with?"

"Whichever one handles Central Park. If he had some sort of accident or got sick while he was working, someone would have taken him to the hospital. But you know how crazy he is with that business of walking through the park."

She called the local precinct. "The park has it's own precinct—the Twenty-second. Let me give you the number."

The desk sergeant whom she reached was heartily reassuring. "No, ma'am, no report of any problems in the park. Even the muggers are trying to stay dry tonight." He laughed at his own witticism. "Sure, I'll be glad to take his name and description and your name. But don't worry. He's probably just delayed."

"If he'd gone to the hospital because he didn't feel well, would you know about it?"

"You gotta be kidding. The only emergency-room patients we check on are the ones who come in with bullet or knife wounds or the ones we drag in ourselves. Every time someone gets a stomachache, you can't send for a cop. Right."

"Then you think I should call around to the emergency rooms on my own?"

"It couldn't hurt."

Quickly Nora told Jack what the policeman had said and realized that Jack seemed somewhat calmer. "I'll look up the numbers, you dial," he said.

They started with the major Manhattan hospitals. A man seeming to fit Bill's description had been brought into Roosevelt without identification papers. He'd been hit by a car around six-thirty on Fifty-seventh Street near Eighth Avenue. If he was Bill Regan, could Nora come and identify him? He was in a coma, and they needed to reach relatives for permission to operate.

She was sure it was Bill. "He has a niece somewhere in Maryland," she said. "If it is Bill, I can go out to his house and find her name."

She didn't want Jack to come, but he insisted. They dressed in somber silence, the still blood-wet bandage on his finger tracing outlines on his underwear, sweater, and jeans. As he pulled on his Adidas, he pointed at the bed. "I can't tell you how much I was looking forward to being in the sack with you tonight."

"Past tense?" The reply was automatic. Bill's face loomed in her mind. That dear old man, with loneliness so much a part of his expression, his need to gab and gab and gab, trying to hold someone to him, to make someone listen. *"And Nora, I said to myself, You can't stay in Queens much longer. The house is no good without May. The roof needs to be done, the shoveling's too much. A little luck and I'll be in Florida with all the other senior citizens. Maybe even a* Cocoon *kind of retirement place where I can really get to make a lot of new friends."*

They took a cab to Roosevelt Hospital. The accident victim was in a curtained-off area of the emergency room, tubes in his nostrils, his leg in a splint, an IV dripping fluid into his arm. His breathing was harsh and sporadic. Nora reached for Jack's hand as she stared down. The man's eyes were closed, a bandage covered half his face. But the thin gray strands of hair were too sparse. Bill had a thick head of hair. She should have remembered to tell them that. "It isn't Mr. Regan," Jack told the doctor.

As they turned away, Nora asked Jack to stop and have his finger checked.

"Let's get out of here," he replied.

They hurried, both anxious to get past the smell of medicine and disinfectant, the sight of a stretcher being wheeled in. "Motorcycle," an attendant was saying. "Stupid kid cut in front of a bus." He sounded angry and frustrated, as though the weight of self-imposed human misery overwhelmed him.

The phone was ringing when they got home. Nora raced to answer it.

It was the police sergeant who had sounded so jocular when she talked with him earlier. "Mrs. Barton, I'm afraid your hunch was right. We've found a body in Central Park near Seventy-fourth Street. The wallet identifies him as William Regan. We'd like to request you to make a positive identification."

"His hair. Is it thick . . . yellowish white but heavy, really full for an old man? You see, the other man was wrong. A mistake. Maybe this is a mistake too."

But she knew it wasn't a mistake. She had *known* this morning that something was going to happen to Bill. That moment when she'd said good-bye, she had *known.* She felt Jack take the phone from her. Numbly she listened as he said yes, he'd come right down to the morgue for positive identification. "I'd just as soon not subject my wife. . . . All right. I understand." He put the phone down and turned to her.

As through a shattered glass, she saw a grayish cast develop around his mouth, a small muscle that jumped in his cheek. He reached his hand to steady it, and as she watched, he winced in pain. The bandage spurted red. Then Jack's arms were around her. "Honey, I'm sure it's Bill. They'd like both of us to come down. I wish I could spare you, but they want to talk to you. Bill's skull was fractured. There's no money in his wallet. They think it was a mugger."

His arms were steel bands, crushing her. She tried to push him away. "You're hurting me . . ."

He didn't seem to hear her. "Nora, let's just get through this. Try to think that Bill had a long life. Tomorrow . . . oh honey, tomorrow, just wait and see. The whole world, everything will *seem* different . . . will *be* different." Even through the waves of shock that were washing over her, giving her the sensation of disbelief and pain, Nora was aware of how different Jack's voice was, high-pitched, almost hysterical.

"Jack, let go of me." Her own voice was a shout. He dropped his arms and stared at her.

"Nora, I'm sorry. Was I hurting you? I didn't realize. . . . Oh God, let's get this over with."

For the third time in less than two hours they hailed a cab. This time they had to wait long, chilling minutes. Twelve thousand cabs in Manhattan, and every one of them busy.

The rain was turning to sleet. Hard pelting nuggets escaped the protection of the umbrella and blew against Nora's face. Even her raincoat, which was lined with mouton from the jacket she'd had in college, couldn't keep her from shivering. Jack's raincoat had been too soaked to wear, and his overcoat was getting drenched as he futilely darted back and forth. Finally a cab with an off-duty sign stopped in front of them. The window opened a slit. "How far you going?"

"The . . . I mean Thirty-first and First."

"All right. Get in."

The cabby was loquacious. "The driving tonight stinks. I'm packing it in early. Good night to be home in bed."

By now Bill should be in his own home, that shabby little frame house that he and his May bought together in 1931. He ought to have died in his own bed, Nora thought. He didn't deserve to lie in the cold and rain. How long had he been there? Had he died instantly? At least that, she prayed.

It was obvious that the man who approached them as they entered the building had been waiting for them. He looked to be in his late thirties, with sandy hair and intense, narrow eyes. He introduced himself as Detective Peter Carlson and led them into a small office. "I'm very sure that you're going to confirm the identification when you see the body," he said. "If you think you are able to do it, I'd like to make that identification immediately. If you think that seeing him might upset you, it might be better if we talked first."

"I want to be sure." She knew he was studying them. What was he seeing? They must seem a bedraggled pair. Was he wondering why she had called so insistently to report a possible victim before he was even found? But missing-persons reports always read like that, didn't they? "*May be victim of foul play.*"

Jack's foot was tapping on the floor—a steady, annoying staccato—Jack who always seemed so calm, who had to be prodded to admit pain or worry. The day had started with her nagging him. Had she somehow cut into some sort of protective shell that he needed?

As though on cue from some hidden prompter, the three of them stood up. "It won't take long."

She had expected that he would bring them into a place where there were rows of slabs. That was the way they did it in the movies. But Detective Carlson brought them down the corridor to a curtained window. Incongruously Nora was reminded of the nursery windows in hospitals, of her first glimpse of her brother's infant. When the curtain was drawn back, it was not a lustily bellowing newborn she was seeing, but the still and bloodless face of Bill Regan. A sheet had been drawn to his neck, his mouth was taped closed, an ugly bruise covered his forehead, matting the hair that in death seemed thin and limp.

"There's no doubt," Jack said. His hands on her shoulders, he tried to turn her away from the window. For a moment she seemed frozen in place, staring at Bill's mouth. It was as though the tape had been removed, the too-bright smile had replaced it, and in her ears she heard again the rasping, hopeful voice. "I got a feeling, Nora, a feeling it's my lucky day."

Upstairs in the office, she told Detective Carlson about that conversation, about the fact that Bill really was lucky in the lottery. Several times he'd won a few hundred dollars and was always sure he'd win the big one. "When he said 'lucky day,' he meant the lottery. I'm sure of it. I think it's even possible he was one of the big winners."

"There was only one big winner," Detective Carlson told her. "As far as I know, no one has come forward." She noticed that he doodled on his pad as he took notes. "You're sure Bill Regan had a ticket."

"He told me he did."

"Well, he wasn't carrying one when we found him. But whoever robbed his wallet might have taken the ticket with the money and not even known what they had. But even suppose he was a big winner. Would he be likely to go around talking about it? Carrying a lottery ticket is like carrying cash."

Nora did not realize that a half smile had come to her face. She brushed her hair back from her forehead, feeling the curly texture that had been induced by the rain. "You look like Rita Hayworth in *Gilda*," Bill had said. She wished now that she'd told him she'd rented *Gilda* and happily realized that there was a strong resemblance. Bill would have enjoyed hearing that. But it was so hard to get a word in edgewise with him. That was what Detective Carlson had asked. "Bill was a gabber," she said, "he would have talked."

"But you tell me he wasn't specific on the phone. Just said it was his lucky day. That could have meant a raise—a big tip when he delivered something—finding money in the street. Anything, right?"

"I just think it had to do with the lottery," Nora insisted.

"We'll check around, but there has been a series of muggings in that area over the last three weeks. We'll get whoever is doing it, I can promise you that . . . and if he killed Mr. Regan, he'll pay for it."

Killed Mr. Regan. She'd never thought of Bill as "Mr. Regan."

She looked at Jack. He was staring at the floor, and the staccato tapping of his foot had begun again. And then something began to happen. The room was closing in around her. She was falling and couldn't breathe. She tried to call "Jack," but her lips wouldn't move. She felt herself slide from the chair.

When she opened her eyes, she was lying on the hard, plastic-covered couch. Jack was holding a cold cloth on her head. From what seemed to be an immense distance she heard Detective Carlson ask Jack if he wanted to call an ambulance.

"I'm all right." She could speak now. Her voice so low, Jack had to bend over to catch the words. Her lips brushed his cheek. "I want to go home," she whispered.

This time they didn't have to wait for a cab. Carlson, his manner now less formal, sent for a squad car. Nora tried to apologize: "I don't think I've ever fainted in my life. . . . It's just this awful feeling I've had all day and then having it come true. . . ."

"You've been a big help. I wish everybody was as concerned about these poor old people."

They walked to the front door, again a curiously in-step trio. Both men supported her, one firm hand under each arm. Outside, the rain was letting up, but the temperature had dropped sharply. Now the cold air was welcome. Did she only imagine that she had smelled formaldehyde inside this building?

"What happens next?" Jack asked Carlson as the squad car pulled up.

"A lot depends on the autopsy. We'll increase the surveillance of the park. Crazy that anyone would walk that distance on this kind of night. We only had squad cars out, no undercover people. We'll be in touch."

This time it was Jack who insisted she take the hot shower, Jack who was waiting with a hot lemonade and a sleeping pill when she came out of the bathroom.

"A sleeping pill." Nora stared at the red and yellow capsule. "When did you get sleeping pills?"

"Oh, at the checkup last month I mentioned that I was having trouble sleeping."

"Well, what does he think caused it?"

"A touch of depression. No big deal. But I didn't want you to be worried. Come on, get into bed."

A touch of depression. And he hadn't told her. Nora thought of all the nights she had babbled to him about the good parts she had landed—"It's only a couple days' work, but listen, Mike Nichols is directing it"—the critical reviews for her first decent off-Broadway role last spring. Jack had shared her delight, asked her if she was going to stick to him when she became a star, and gone back to the succession of jobs selling investment bonds. The novel he had finally finished had almost made it at several publishing houses. "Not quite right for us, but try us again." The discouragement in his eyes when he said, "After all day trying to sell when I know I'm not a salesman, trying to get excited when the rate goes up or some damn issue gets a triple-A rating when I just don't give a damn, I don't know, Nora, it's as though the juices are gone. I go to the typewriter and everything that I try to get on paper doesn't come out the way I want it. Yet I know it's there. I just can't find my voice knowing on Monday I'll be back in that zoo."

She hadn't really listened. She'd told him how proud she was that his first novel didn't get just straight rejection slips, that someday when he was famous, he'd be telling the tale of those early rejections; it was all part of the game.

The bedroom doubled as an office for Jack. His typewriter was on the heavy oak desk they'd bought at a garage sale. There were bottles of white-out, a handleless cup that served as a receptacle for pencils and Magic Markers, the pile of paper that was his new manuscript, the pile that she realized was no longer growing.

"Come on, drink that lemonade and we'll both take a sleeping pill."

She obeyed, not trusting herself to speak, wondering if her love for him was brimming over in her eyes. No wonder Bill had been so needing of companionship. If anything happened to Jack, she wouldn't want to wake up.

Jack slipped in the other side of the bed, took the cup from her hand, and turned out the light. His arms reached for her. "What's that song about 'two sleepy people'? If anyone had told me this day would turn out like this . . ."

Nora slept heavily and woke in the morning with the sensation of having experienced unremembered dreams. It was hard to open her eyes, her lids seemed to be glued closed. When she finally pulled herself up on one arm, it was to see that Jack was already gone. The hands on the clock were both on nine. *Quarter of nine.* She never slept this late. Trying to shake the lethargy, she pulled on her robe and went into the kitchen. Coffee was perking, Jack had squeezed fresh orange juice, another one of the dozens of small gestures that she took for granted. He knew how much she enjoyed fresh juice, even though he was perfectly happy with the frozen variety.

He was already dressed for work. He seemed to have lost none of the tension of the previous evening. Dark circles under his eyes suggested that the sleeping pill had little effect on him. When he kissed her, his lips were dry and feverish. "Now I know how to get peace and quiet around here in the morning. Slip you a knockout dose."

"When did you get up?"

"About five. Or maybe four. I don't know."

"Jack, don't go to work. Sit down and let's talk. Really talk." She tried to suppress a yawn. "Oh God, I can't wake up. How do people take those damn things every night?"

"Look, I ought to go in. There are some things I owe it to them to take care of. . . . Anyhow, you go back to bed and sleep it off. I'll get home early, not later than four, and tonight we'll . . . tonight will be special."

Another yawn and the sense of her eyes wanting to close made

Nora realize this wasn't the time to try to probe Jack. "But if you're going to be late, call. Last night I was worried."

"I won't be late. I swear."

Nora turned off the coffeepot, drank the glass of orange juice on the way back to bed, and was asleep again in three minutes. This time the sleep was dreamless, and when the phone awakened her two hours later, her head felt clear.

It was Detective Carlson. "Mrs. Barton, I thought you'd want to know. I checked with the messenger place where Bill Regan worked. He got back there about six o'clock last night, just before it closed. A couple of the other men were just finishing up. He was excited; he was happy; he did talk about it being his lucky day, but when they asked him what he meant, he clammed up. Just looked mysterious. The autopsy is scheduled for this afternoon. But our theory is that, given the blow on his head and the empty wallet, he was probably attacked by the mugger we've been trying to catch."

You're wrong, Nora thought. She tried not to sound critical as she said, "The thing that puzzles me is that if he was mugged, why wasn't his wallet taken? I don't think Bill ever carried more than a few dollars. Did he have a lot of change in his pockets or any tokens?"

"A couple of bucks in change, about six tokens. Mrs. Barton, I know it's because you cared about Mr. Regan that you're not satisfied. If a mugger has time, he'll leave the wallet on his victim. That way if he's picked up, he's not carrying it with him. The old guy had deep pockets. If a mugger checked the wallet and got what he wanted, he might not take time to go looking for change. You can't know whether or not Mr. Regan was carrying money for sure, can you?"

"No of course not. And did you check for the lottery ticket?"

Now Carlson's voice became more formal, a hint of disapproval clearly evident. "There was no lottery ticket, Mrs. Barton."

As Nora hung up, a phrase from the telephone conversation repeated itself insistently. *Not satisfied.* No she wasn't.

She heated the coffee and dressed quickly. There was something she had to do. She'd have no peace unless she tried.

You're crazy, she told herself as she hurried down the street. The weather had changed dramatically. Today was sunny, the breeze was mild, a day more suitable to April than November. It was just as well. She'd been glad she could wear her cast jacket. Her raincoat and Jack's overcoat were still damp from the trip to the morgue last night. The trench coat Jack had worn to work yesterday was still drenched.

He'd had to wear his old mackintosh this morning. A bag man was sorting out the collection of half-eaten sandwiches he had fished from the trash can. Where was yesterday's bag lady? Nora wondered. Had she found shelter last night?

At the newsstand she averted her eyes. The blind man who owned the stand must have been surprised when Bill didn't show up to help out this morning. But she couldn't bring herself to tell him about Bill now.

She took the Lexington Avenue Express to Fifty-ninth Street, switched to the RR train, and made her way to the Fisk Building. The Dynamo Express Messenger Service was in a single room on the fifth floor. The only furniture was a desk with a telephone panel, a few battleship-gray three-drawer file cabinets and two long benches, on which several shabbily dressed men waited. As she closed the door, the man at the desk barked, "You, Louey, get down to Fortieth Street. Pickup to go to Broadway and Ninetieth. Now read this to me so I know you got it right. I can't have you wasting time at the wrong addresses."

The skinny old man in the middle of the bench jumped up, nervously anxious to please. As Nora watched, he painstakingly read the instructions in halting English.

"All right. Get on with it."

For the first time the man at the desk looked at Nora. His head was covered with a badly fitting toupee. Exaggerated sideburns covered plump cheeks that were oddly at variance with a sharp, small nose. Eyes the color of grimy pennies ran up and down her body, mentally undressing her. "What can I do for you, lovely lady?" The voice was now ingratiating, totally different from the sarcastic, bullying tone of the previous moment.

As she walked toward him, lights flashed on the phone panel, and a buzzer sounded. He flipped several buttons. "Dynamo Express Messenger, hold the line." He smiled at Nora. "Let them wait."

He already knew about Bill. "Some cop was around asking questions this morning. Old Gabby, God he'd never shut up. I used to have to yell at him to quit wasting time every place he went. I got complaints."

Nora realized she must have winced. " 'Course when I say 'yell,' I mean I'd just say, Come on, Regan, the whole world don't want to know about your life's history. Say, I bet he told me about you. You're the actress. He said you looked like Rita Hayworth. For once he was right. . . . Hold on, I gotta take some of these calls."

She stood by the desk as he answered phones, scribbled information, dispatched messengers as they returned to the office. In between she managed to get in a few questions. "Sure, Bill was all excited last night. Babbled about it being his lucky day. But he wouldn't say why. I asked him if he picked up a hooker, kidding like."

"Do you think he might have told anyone else?"

"Your guess is as good as mine."

"Would you have a list of the places he went yesterday? I'd like to talk to the people he talked to. Does he usually go to offices, maybe gets to know the receptionists or whatever?"

"I guess so." Now he was becoming irritated. But he did dig out the list. Yesterday had been busy. Bill had made fifteen stops. Nora started with the first: 101 Park Avenue, Sandrell and Woodworth, pick up envelope from eighteenth-floor receptionist and deliver to 205 Central Park South.

The pleasantly matronly eighteenth-floor receptionist remembered Bill. "Oh sure, he's a nice old guy. We get him a lot. Showed me the picture of his wife once. Is anything wrong?"

Nora had expected the question and knew how she would answer it. "He was in an accident last night. I want to write to his niece. He had left a message on my phone machine saying it was his lucky day. I'd like to tell her about that, what he meant. Did he talk about that to you?"

The receptionist obviously realized it was a fatal accident, and brief concern for a man she had known slightly passed like a cloud across her face. "Oh, I'm sorry. No, well yes, actually, I was busy so I just gave him the envelope and said, 'Have a good day, Bill,' and he said something like 'I've got a feeling it's my lucky day.' "

Unconsciously, the woman had imitated Bill's voice. Nora felt a chill as she listened. "That's exactly what he said to me."

Her next stop was the apartment on Central Park South. The concierge remembered Bill. "Oh yeah, sure, he left an envelope for Mr. Parker. From the accountant, I think. I phoned up to see if I should have him bring it to the door, but Mr. Parker said to leave it with me, he was on his way down. Nah, he didn't talk. I guess I didn't give him a chance. The mail desk is busy at that time."

It seemed everyone yesterday had been too busy for Bill. A whippet-thin secretary in a Broadway office told Nora she never encouraged the messengers to hang around. "They're just like the delivery boys. Turn your back and they steal your pocketbook." Her you-know-how-it-is shrug invited Nora to share her disdain of the petty thieves she had to endure.

After that stop, she realized that she'd never get through the list if she didn't arrange her time better. Bill had crisscrossed from east to west, had made a number of stops midtown, three in the Fifties, two in the Thirties, four on lower Fifth Avenue, and two around Wall Street. Instead of following his exact pattern, she began to group the calls by area. The first two were fruitless. No one even remembered who had taken the delivery. The third, an author who had sent her manuscript to her agent, spoke to Nora from the lobby telephone of her hotel. Yes, she'd had a pickup yesterday. Certainly she hadn't engaged in conversation with the messenger. Was there a problem? Don't tell me the manuscript wasn't delivered.

At three o'clock Nora realized that she hadn't bothered to eat, that it was a worthless errand, that Jack was coming home early and she wanted to be there for him. And then she talked to the young salesman in the piano showroom.

He looked up hopefully as she came in. The showroom was empty except for the pianos and organs, which were spaced at different angles to show off their best features. A poster, MAKE MUSIC A PART OF YOUR LIFE, was directly behind a small home organ with a doll the size of a four-year-old child sitting on the bench, stubby cotton fingers resting on the keys.

The salesman's momentary disappointment that Nora was not a potential customer disappeared at the prospect of spending time with another human being. He didn't think he'd stay in the music business, he told Nora. It was really slow. Even the manager admitted that the banner years had been six or seven years ago. Everybody wanted a piano again. Now, forget it.

Yesterday? A messenger? Kind of funny-looking teeth. Oh sure, nice old guy. Had he talked? Had he ever! Been all excited. Told me it was his lucky day.

"You mean he said he *felt* lucky?" Nora asked quickly.

"No, not that. I remember he positively said it *was* his lucky day. But that was all he told me, and he gave me a big wink when I asked him what he meant."

There was only one place Bill had gone after that delivery. He had been at the piano showroom at 4:10. Just after he left the message on the recorder. And the stop before the piano showroom had been the one where the bookkeeper who accepted the delivery had told her, "Yeah, the old guy did say something about feeling lucky or whatever. I was on the phone and just kind of waved him off. I was talking to the boss and couldn't hear."

"Feeling lucky. You're sure he didn't say he had *been* lucky?"

"I'm sure he said *feeling* lucky because I remember thinking I was *feeling* lousy."

He had been feeling lucky at 3:45. At 4:10 at his next stop he had been lucky. I'm right, Nora thought, I knew it. The lottery had been pulled sometime between 3:30 and 4:00. Had Bill owned one of the winning tickets? She stopped for a quick coffee at a drugstore on Madison Avenue. The radio was on. Yesterday there had been twelve hundred winners of one thousand dollars, three winners of five thousand dollars, and one big winner of thirteen million dollars. The announcer suggested that everyone who'd bought a ticket in Manhattan check the numbers.

Just suppose Bill had won five thousand dollars. That would have been a fortune to him. A couple of times he had won a few hundred. It was crazy how some people seemed to win repeatedly. Nora reviewed the list. She could eliminate all the places that Bill had gone before 3:30. That left her with only one more to go. With dismay she realized it was in the World Trade Center. But she'd gone this far. She'd check it out and then go home.

As she entered the subway for the eighth time that day, Nora wondered how Bill had managed to keep up with that job. Had he ever admitted to himself that people didn't bother to listen to him, or had his day been brightened by an encounter with someone like the young salesman who had welcomed company.

The subway was crowded. It was a quarter of three. It used to be that middays weren't too bad, that only in the rush hour did you have to hang on to a strap or grab a pole. The heavyset man beside her deliberately leaned against her when the train swayed. She quickly moved away from him.

The ground floor of the World Trade Center was crowded with purposeful people hurrying across the concourse, disappearing into the subways, cutting across to the other buildings, diving into restaurants and shops. Most of them were well dressed. Nora lost five minutes by mistakenly going to the number-two building instead of number four.

The forty-second floor was her destination. As she rode up, she wondered why the name of the firm sounded familiar. Probably because she'd been looking at it all day.

Lyons and Becker was an investment firm. Not too large, she could see. That was good. There'd be a better chance of someone remembering Bill.

The outer office was smallish but well appointed. Behind it, Nora could see into some of the cubicles, earnest young men and women trading stocks and bonds.

The receptionist didn't remember seeing Bill. "But wait a minute, I was on my break around that time. Let me get the girl who sat in for me."

A blonde with slim legs and overly generous breasts was the replacement. For a moment, she listened puzzled, then broke into a wide smile. "Oh sure," she said. "Where's my head? Of course I remember that old guy. He almost forgot the pickup."

Nora waited.

"I was just handing it to him when he kind of looked around and spotted one of our salesmen." She turned to her co-worker. "You know who. Jack Barton, the cute new guy."

Nora felt a cold ache in the pit of her stomach. That was why this place had sounded so familiar. It was the company Jack had so reluctantly told her about yesterday. His new job.

"Anyhow, the old guy spotted Jack and he looked real surprised. Said, 'Is that Jack Barton? Does he work here?' And I said yes. Jack was just going out that door." With a nod of her head she indicated an employee door at the far end of the room. "And the old guy got so excited. He said, 'I've got to tell Jack about my lucky day.' I had to yell after him to grab the package. For Pete's sake, that's why he came here, wasn't it?"

There had to be a reason why Jack hadn't told her he'd seen Bill. What reason?

Nora tried to quell the fear that was confirmation of yesterday's uneasiness by buying a newspaper and reading on the subway ride, but the print danced before her eyes. When she reached home, the first thing she did was to go to the bathroom, where their coats were hanging on the shower-curtain pole. The one she had worn last night was completely dry, even though they'd stood in the rain for ten minutes. The coat Jack had worn to the hospital and morgue last night, his good coat, was still slightly damp. But his trench coat, the one he'd been wearing when he came in last night, was still soaked. He hadn't just walked from the subway. She remembered again the glittery excitement, the tension that crackled like currents of energy around his body, the way he'd held her and cried.

How far had he walked last night? Why had he walked? And who had been with him? . . . or whom had he been following?

"Please, God, no," she whispered. "No." He had come home, and she'd made him shower and she'd phoned the police. When he came out of the bedroom, he'd helped her make the calls. He'd looked up the numbers. But she'd been on the phone when he first came out. And before that, she'd heard that funny sound, that clunk, and had wondered what he was doing.

Like a prisoner going to an inexorable fate, she walked into the bedroom and reached into the closet for the metal safety box that held their important papers, their wedding license, insurance policies, birth certificates. She took the box to the bed and opened it. Jack's birth certificate was on top of the pile. Slowly she lifted the papers out one by one until she reached the last one, a pink and white lottery ticket. No, Jack, oh please, she thought. No. Not you. Not for a thousand dollars. You couldn't. You wouldn't. There has to be an explanation.

But when she compared the numbers with the winning numbers listed in the newspaper, she understood. She was holding the ticket that could be redeemed for thirteen million dollars.

Bill Regan had known he'd be lucky. She had known that something terrible was hanging over her. She looked around the room blindly trying to find an answer. The manuscript was by Jack's typewriter, the manuscript that wasn't going anywhere because he was burned out. Jack's sleeping pills, for "a touch of depression." Then she remembered her own unmerciful probing yesterday morning till in an embarrassed whisper he had mumbled the name of his new company and told her Merrill Lynch had let him go . . . and then added with that attempt at dignity, "Part of the overall cutback. It was just I'm one of the low men on the totem pole. It had nothing to do with performance."

So yesterday, Bill had told him about this ticket, and something in Jack had snapped. He must have watched for Bill to leave the Fisk Building and followed him into the park.

What was she going to do? With violent rejection, Nora scorned the thought that she ought to contact the police. Jack was her life. She would kill herself before she abandoned him.

It's my lucky day. Bill had wanted to go to Florida, where he could live in a retirement home with interesting people like the ones in *Cocoon.* He had deserved that chance.

* * *

Nora was sitting on the couch in the living room when the key turned and Jack came home. She had managed to concentrate on the fact that the upholstery was really shabby and that new slipcovers wouldn't conceal the sagging cushions. Even though it was only a quarter past four, twilight was setting in, and she remembered that they were only a month away from the shortest day in the year.

She got up as the door swung open. Jack was carrying an armful of long-stemmed roses. "Nora." The tension was gone now. He had grieved with her for Bill Regan last night, but this was *his* night. "Nora, sit down, wait. Oh my God, honey, wait till you see what's happened to us. I can write, you can have a maid, we'll buy this place, we'll buy a house on the Cape. For the rest of our lives we're set. We're set. I wanted to tell you yesterday when I came home. But I didn't want Bill Regan coming in on top of us. So I waited. And then with what happened it was impossible to tell you."

"You saw Bill yesterday."

Jack looked puzzled. "No I didn't."

"He ran after you when you left your office at four o'clock."

"Then he didn't catch me. Nora, don't you see? I heard the winning numbers in yesterday's lottery. And they sounded familiar. It was crazy. I just pulled them at random. You know, usually if I buy a ticket, I do our anniversary, your birthday, or something like that. And then I couldn't find the damn ticket."

Jack, don't lie, don't lie.

"I was going nuts. And then I remembered. When I was cleaning out my desk at Merrill Lynch last week, it was right on top. Unless it got thrown out, it had to be in one of the files I was putting in order. I ran over there and went through every damn one of them. Nora, I was going crazy. And then I found it. I couldn't believe it. I guess I went into shock. I walked all the way home. And then when you offered to give up your career for me, you must have thought I was nuts when I started crying. I was bursting to tell you, but when I thought poor old Bill was going to be barging in on us, I had to wait. It had to be just our night."

He did not seem to notice her lack of reaction. Thrusting the flowers at her, he said, "Just wait till I show you," and rushed into the bedroom.

The phone rang. Automatically she picked it up, then wished she hadn't. But it was too late. "Hello."

"Mrs. Barton, this is Detective Carlson." His voice was friendly. "I have to tell you you were right."

"I was right?"

"Yeah, you were so persistent that we went over his clothes again. The poor old geezer had a lottery ticket stuck in the lining of his cap. He won a thousand bucks yesterday. And you'll be glad to know he wasn't mugged. Guess the excitement was too much for him. He died of a massive heart attack. Must have smashed his head on that rock when he fell."

"No . . . no . . . no . . ." Nora's shriek matched Jack's wail as he rushed from the bedroom, the strongbox in his hand, the ashes of the lottery ticket wafting up and drifting across his fingers.

TILL DEATH DO US PART

DOROTHY SALISBURY DAVIS

Kitty found him finally. He was out on the terrace, no place to be on such a night. He stood, his hands on the parapet, his face to the wind and the strange billowing fog. At times the whole galaxy of lights that shone across the park from Fifth Avenue vanished from sight. Mark leaned over the parapet and looked down, unaware—or not wanting to acknowledge—that his wife had come out from the party to look for him. The apartment was full of guests, most of them agency clients and among those some of the most successful writers in the country, and Mark was out on the terrace.

"I've been looking all over for you. People are asking where you are."

"Who?" he said over his shoulder.

"Oh, God. You're in one of those moods. I'm sorry if I interrupted you with Jonathan, but I could see him getting restless. He has no patience. I didn't want him to leave the party."

He mumbled something she didn't hear.

"If you must know, I didn't want him hurting your feelings."

"Or me hurting his. Or isn't that possible?" He half-turned toward her. "I was going to ask him if now that he has all that money, we can call him the Root of all evil. You interrupted just in time."

"Are you drunk?" He had played upon the author's name, Jonathan Root, and referred to the recent book contract Kitty had negotiated for him, seven figures.

"Not as drunk as I'd like to be."

"You're going to catch cold out here, and we don't need it this time of year. Please, darling."

November, with all the cheerful holidays coming up, he thought. He turned and faced her, his elbows on the parapet. She looked glamorous—and was! a white beaded dress, one shoulder bare, the little sway of self-assurance, and those very blue eyes that, except for the sparkle, were to be seen only in his mind's eye at the moment. "It's you that's going to catch cold," he said. "Go in and enjoy your party."

"It's not my party. It's our party."

"No, Kitty. That mixed bag in there is all yours. I don't like to see people eating their hearts out."

"That's pure imagination, and you're wrong. Success rubs off. Believe me. Look at me! Am I not the perfect example? If you've got it, you'll get it. I'm going in now and I want you to come with me."

"In a few minutes."

"Damn you," she said and whirled around to almost collide with André Wilczynski, a young writer, mostly of poetry, who was both client and sometime employee. When he served as waiter on such occasions as this, Mark called him their poet in residence.

Wilczynski tried to hold the door for Kitty and at the same time balance the martini on his tray. He, too, had been looking everywhere for Mark. Kitty snatched the glass from the tray. "Let him come inside for it if he wants it."

Kitty swept indoors. Mark turned back to watch the fog. When the doors closed between him and the party, he could hear the singing wheels of the traffic below and the rev of a heavy motor when the bus pulled away from the stop at Seventy-fourth Street. Looking down, he could see the doorman—like a tin soldier blowing a thin whistle with a little toy taxi creeping into view.

"Shall I bring you another drink, Mr. Coleman?"

Mark did not answer, annoyed that the young man was still there.

"Are you all right, sir?"

"Bring me the drink, André. Straight up. No rocks this time."

Kitty, indoors and checking people's glasses, looked around for Tom Wilding, the agency's lawyer and Mark's longtime friend, thinking to send him out to persuade Mark in. He wasn't in sight either. There were sixty or seventy people in clusters about the room, and yet it wasn't crowded. She could see everyone. The apartment—on Central Park West—was the top floor through of a building that had gone up in the 1920s. The Colemans had kept its decor to the fashion of the day. Mark called it late Scott Fitzgerald.

Aware that her feet hurt but that she was going to have to carry things entirely on her own, she put on a jaunty air and moved among the guests. She encouraged the successful authors to hold forth and gave a squeeze to the arm of a listener who hadn't made it yet as much as to say, All this can be yours too. Among those whose careers were modest and who chose the company of their own kind, she would linger long enough to bring the conversation to where she could recount the meteoric success of an author—not present, but a name everyone recognized—who'd been living hand-to-mouth on minuscule advances until Kitty took her in hand.

Tom Wilding watched all this from alongside a pillar in the dining-room archway. He knew the script. He also saw the young man in a white coat that was too big for him take a single drink out onto the terrace. So that would be where Mark was and why Kitty was carrying herself around with a brave tilt to her chin. What an actress she was: a royal presence moving among her subjects. Kitty avoided mirrors, he thought, and never looked behind. Therefore she didn't know—or didn't have to admit to caring—what people thought of her.

In a broad sense, Wilding had been watching Kitty for a long time, almost twenty-five years, from the time, he suspected afterward, she made her choice of whom to go after, him or Mark. To admit the truth, he had been briefly attracted to her, beguiled by her vivacity and those big blue eyes. He remembered taking a long look into them on the eve of her marriage to Mark. Whatever he saw then, it was not the Kitty of today. Nor was Mark the man he liked to remember. In those days Mark was considered one of the best young literary agents in New York. His authors loved him. Even publishers loved him, which might be the key to his eclipse—if that was what it was. Wilding had always considered himself lucky to have acquired the Mark Coleman Agency as a client for the legal firm in which he was then a junior partner. He hadn't known how lucky. Today he could live on the income from it. Which was the reason he could take the gaff from Kitty that he did. He often wondered how Mark took it. But he also wondered sometimes if Mark knew what he was taking.

About to light a cigarette, he thought of going out with it and joining Mark on the terrace. Kitty hated the smell of cigarettes. Wilding smiled at his motivation, but he proceeded on his way outdoors. Before he reached the terrace, he saw a scuffle going on there, a flash of the white coat and then the crash of glass as the young man flailed, trying to get his balance. Wilding ran to help him; so did others, the whole party rising to its feet.

Both of the French doors shattered, and shards of glass seemed to explode. Wilczynski was instantly a-glitter with them, and Mark still went after him and tried to pull him up by his lapels with the manifest intention of hitting him again. He threw off Wilding's attempt to get hold of him. "Get out of here, Tom. Keep out of this!"

It was Kitty who intervened and pulled Mark away. Wilding took Wilczynski through the gaping, gasping guests to the nearest bathroom. He had several cuts on one side of his face, the slivers of glass still in some of them. On the other side his jaw was swelling, a possible fracture. "Can you talk?"

"No." Which meant that he didn't intend to, Wilding thought, not to Coleman's attorney certainly.

"We'd better get you to an emergency hospital," he said, a proposal he hoped would assuage the man. "First aid is going to do it, but let's get it from a professional." He took him through the kitchen and out by the back hall. Their topcoats were jammed among others on a rack in the foyer. Wilding said he'd come back for them later. In the cab, which crept through the fog westward toward Roosevelt Hospital, he tried again to find out what had happened.

Wilczynski took away the towel he was holding to his face. "I'm not going to sue or anything like that, Mr. Wilding, so you don't have to worry."

Wilding held up a hand to forestall his saying anything more in that vein. "My concern at the moment is to get you to a doctor, and I don't think you should think about noble gestures in your present condition."

Wilczynski didn't speak for some time. He touched his jaw tentatively and winced. Then: "When I took a drink out to him, I thought at first—he looked as though he was going to jump off the terrace. Maybe it was all in my mind, but I started to talk him away from the ledge, saying how people like me needed him, things like that. When he realized what I was talking about, he came over and told me to put down the tray. He wanted to know what I'd suggest instead of the big jump. I wasn't going to say anything, but the way she'd humiliated him in front of me, I just let go: 'You don't have to take that shit, sir.' And whammo."

"I get the picture," Wilding said.

"I guess I'm lucky not to be on my way to the morgue."

Wilding said nothing.

"He shouldn't have asked me a question like that," Wilczynski said and buried his whole face in the towel.

The attorney waited until almost noon the next day expecting Coleman to call him. Then he called Coleman. "Any word from Wilczynski?"

"No."

"What got into you, Mark?"

"He maligned my wife."

"Just what did he say?" Wilding wanted his version.

"If I could remember, I wouldn't repeat it."

"You could be in serious trouble, Mark. Twenty-eight stitches. There could be disfigurement."

"I'd hate to see that happen. He's got a nice face—homely, but a good face. And he's a good writer if he could stay with it."

"I think you ought to apologize to him, Mark."

"Kitty says no, that I'd lose face. Which is pretty funny when you think about it."

"I'd better talk to Kitty," Wilding said reluctantly.

"She's waiting for you. Hang on. I'll switch you over."

Kitty came on the phone full force. "Most lawyers I know would advise a client to stay clear of the victim, whether it's an accident case or whatever. Our lawyer, it seems, commits us to instant liability."

"Would you have had him bleed to death out there on the terrace?"

"Was there nobody in that whole crowd who knew anything about first aid?"

"Twenty-eight stitches, Kitty. That's beyond first aid."

"You made sure of it, rushing him to the hospital. Just tell me where things stand now. Give it to me in words of one syllable."

Very slowly, making sure of his own composure, he explained the situation as he saw it. He knew very well that Kitty's point did have cold-blooded merit.

"So what's the big deal? He'll apologize."

"Kitty, just in case the worst happens and he does decide to sue, I want to apprise you of the way I think it might go. If it were ever to come to trial, whoever represented Mark would have to plead him mentally disturbed. Counsel would ask leniency, and the judge might grant it on condition that he undergo psychiatric care."

"He's been seeing a psychiatrist for years."

Wilding hadn't known it. So much for psychiatry, he thought. "Well, let's see what the apology will do. The warmer it is the better. And you might ask Mark to let me know if Wilczynski also apologizes."

"He will," Kitty said. "He's jealous of me and he adores Mark. We shouldn't represent him at all, much less make a household pet of him. He's like every poet I ever heard of, arrogant as Lucifer and nothing you can do for him is ever enough." Her voice became a purr of sarcasm. "But Mark has a conscience about impoverished talent. The more impoverished, the greater the talent."

"I'll be in touch," Wilding said.

Mark, at his own desk in his office, hung up the phone after listening in. It was something he was not in the habit of doing, but neither was he in the habit of throwing punches, not since the age of thirteen. He looked at his bruised and swollen knuckles and tried to think why such a blazing fury should have erupted in him. No answer came. He had known there was no love lost between Kitty and Wilczynski, but André had kept it under cover until last night, when, Mark had a sneaking suspicion, he had deliberately provoked the boy into letting go. But to say that Wilczynski adored him was one more of Kitty's exaggerations. And yet the very idea of it made him both sad and pleased—sad that he had struck him and pleased that someone among the agency's clients still held him in esteem. So why had he struck him? Still no answer. He could ask his psychiatrist—if he had one. Kitty's lies of convenience were a commonplace, but why it was convenient for her to tell Tom Wilding that he had been seeing a psychiatrist for years was one more thing he was at a loss to know.

He wrote André a note in longhand and mailed it himself when he went out to lunch. Kitty was furious. Not even a photocopy, with the machine sitting right outside his office door. "You should have spoken to me sooner," he said.

"I thought we agreed you were *not* to apologize," she said.

"Did we?" he said blandly. "Then I changed my mind."

"So did I. But I'd like to know what you wrote."

"I apologized."

Kitty turned on her heel.

* * *

Tom Wilding went out of town that afternoon. He had already told Kitty before the party that he would be away for a few days attending his son's wedding. It was a bittersweet occasion for Wilding because it brought him together again with his former wife, whom, despite her desertion and remarriage, he still loved. During the flight he pondered from time to time how that could be, given his anger, jealousy, pain, and humiliation, the embers of which still flared up now and then. He had not even realized when it was happening. He had been on the Coast a great deal and, the children in college, Irene had gone back to school and taken her master's degree. He'd been very proud of her. There was in his musings a barely conscious comparison of his situation with Mark Coleman's. He was comparing apples and oranges, he told himself. Irene had not emasculated him, although he felt it at the time, and he had put together another life without her. The Colemans were somehow bound together in their needs. They had simply switched places. Supposing Irene had stayed with him and got a law degree? He laughed at himself and rang the stewardess for another Scotch.

The next afternoon, while the wedding party was at the church rehearsing, he and Irene sat before a fire together. She had not changed save for the scattering of gray in her soft brown hair and a few new laugh lines. There came a moment when she looked at him with warm concern in a way that made him ache, remembering. "And how is your life, Tom?"

He was all but overwhelmed by the urge to tell her of his loneliness and what her leaving had taken from him. "I'm enjoying it," he said, and the temptation passed.

Whenever he thought about the Colemans between then and his return to Manhattan, he would wind up trying to pinpoint the place and time when their rise and fall intersected, where in plain fact Kitty had taken over and Mark had let go. She had come to New York wanting to be an actress and was in acting school when Mark met her. She started in the office working part-time in the Dramatic Rights department; Mark thought it would give her confidence as an actress to learn something of the business end of things. He was jubilant when she was able and wanted to take over the department. That wasn't long after they were married. Her next step upward was becoming a member of the firm, and after that the question arose whether the agency name shouldn't be changed to include hers. She was adamant that it remain the Mark Coleman Agency. By then she might have thought she was the Mark Coleman Agency. Equality seemed never to have entered her mind. The only good word she had for the women's movement was for those of her clients who wrote about it. Wilding tried to remember what Coleman was like in negotiations at given times along the way. More and more, he could see now, Mark had left the gritty bits to him, the legal expert. Kitty, to the contrary, would tell Wilding what she expected and, outrageous as it might seem, she almost always got it. She was an exhausting negotiator. Only once recently had he been with both Colemans in the same negotiations, and by then Mark had lost much of his personal prestige and his perspective. He insisted on explaining to Kitty points that she knew better than most of the people present. She listened him out, however, and smiled with cold defiance at anyone less patient than herself. She would defend him to the death from others, Wilding thought, and then turn on him and savage him herself.

One of the first things he did when he was back in the office was to find out if there had been an exchange of apologies. He would rather have talked to Mark, but it was Kitty who had promised he would apologize. "Mark wrote him," she said, "and purposely didn't show the letter to me. What do you think of that?"

"Understandable," Wilding murmured.

"He kept no copy of it—wrote it in longhand. Is that also understandable? And no word from André in the meantime, at least according to Mark. What's going on there, I'd like to know?"

"Let them sort it out between themselves, Kitty. Give it a little more time."

"Tom, the more I think about it the more bizarre the whole situation seems to me. It isn't like Mark to engage in fisticuffs. Between you and me, I can't see him doing more than telling André to keep his opinions to himself. I suppose what I'm saying is, I don't think I was the issue at all."

"I don't know what to say to that. Why don't you give his psychiatrist a ring and have a confidential talk with him? He might find your input useful."

"I suppose I could do that," she said. "I'm glad you're home. How was the wedding?"

"All brides are beautiful. It was very nice."

That afternoon Wilding got André Wilczynski's phone number and called him. A purely personal concern, he explained.

"No complications," the writer said of his wounds. "How is Mark?"

"I wish I could tell you. I've been out of town and out of touch with him."

"Why don't you try and help him, Mr. Wilding? That man's in trouble. Do you know what he wrote to me? I haven't answered it yet, I don't want her getting hold of it and twisting what I say into what she wants me to say. That's pretty complicated, isn't it?"

"What did Mark say?"

"He said he was hitting out at himself, and I just got in the way."

"That *is* complicated," Wilding said. "A very peculiar traffic jam."

Wilczynski laughed, and Wilding was glad that he could—in more ways than one.

Coleman had surprised himself in writing as he had to André. It was almost as though he had let out something from his soul in automatic writing. But reading it over, he had known it was the truth and sent it off. When days passed and he had not heard from the young writer, he wondered if he had made a fool of himself. Or worse, if he had not compromised Kitty. When Tom Wilding called him and suggested lunch, he was sure something had gone very wrong. They had not had lunch alone together for years.

They met at the Century Club and had a drink at the bar before going into the dining room. Mark's hand trembled as he conveyed the glass to his lips, and he said again something he had already said far too many times about the first drink of the day: "It's nice to be drinking again." He turned to Wilding. "You've heard me say that before maybe?"

Wilding laughed and admitted that he might have.

"Does Kitty know we're having lunch?"

"Not unless you told her," the lawyer said. "There's nothing heavy on the platter, so relax."

Mark could feel the relaxation happening. He turned his glass around and around by the stem and said, after a moment, "I wonder if these things aren't doing me in. I forget things. I say things I don't mean. Sometimes I even say things I do mean. I flare up—as you may have noticed. I blame Kitty . . ."

"For what?"

Coleman shrugged. "For more than she ought to be blamed. God knows, she takes good care of me."

Wilding took a chance. "Is that good?"

"Have you been talking with Wilczynski?" It was said not seriously but with a twinkle reminiscent of the old Mark. Then: "I thought he might have answered my letter by this time. I suppose you know, I did apologize."

"He'll answer. He intends to."

"But when? Kitty wants to see it in writing."

At the table, when Coleman had his second drink in hand, Wilding said, "Mark, I'm going to make a suggestion. Give this thing time. Take a few days off and get away from the office . . ." He paused, seeing alarm in Coleman's eyes.

"Why?"

"I was thinking how much good it did me to get away and see the family, people I hadn't seen in years."

"I see too many people. I'm sick of people and I'm sure a lot of them are sick of me."

"Then how about this: Go up to my place on the Cape. This time of year it's nothing but sea and sand and stars. It's as pure a place as you'll find on earth."

Mark was instantly thrust back in place and time to the graceful sand dunes along Lake Michigan where he'd grown up, Carl Sandburg country, a poet all but forgotten, as were most of the poets of his youth. He blinked at Wilding across the table and said, "I've just had a short trip—back home to Indiana."

"What about the Cape?"

"I can't get away, Tom. I've got too many things in the works."

Wilding clamped his mouth shut.

"Go ahead and say it," Coleman challenged.

"You can't get away from Kitty. That's what it's all about." Wilding pulled back. "I'm sorry. I shouldn't have said that. That's for your psychiatrist to say, if anybody's going to say it."

With a smile that was almost self-satisfied, Coleman said, "I haven't had a day of psychiatry in my whole damn life."

Wilding was speechless. He felt that even the breath had been knocked out of him. After all the years of Kitty watching, he still had no idea of where her facile tongue might dart. "Might it not be a good idea, then—a few months of therapy? With the right man, of course. Or woman."

Coleman missed the unintended irony. He had scored with himself for having again told the truth instead of fudging on it to cover Kitty's lie. Then it occurred to him, causing him some anxiety, that there could have been a reason for Kitty's saying he was in psychiatry: It put a wall up around him, as it were, to protect his privacy.

"Not that it's any of my business," Wilding added. "I presumed on a long friendship."

"Psychiatry invades everybody in the patient's life. I wonder if Kitty might not take it as an insult."

"For Christ's sake, Mark. I'm talking about you, not Kitty."

"The same thing, isn't it?"

They were back to square one. Mark had stopped any censure of Kitty before it started. Wilding gave up. There was no way to help a man who would not be helped.

After lunch, which both men found a strain, Mark put the lawyer into a cab and made his own way uptown through the swarming Christmas shoppers on Fifth Avenue. Salvation Army Santas were cleaning up, so were the vendors and the street musicians, who had to blow on their hands to keep their fingers nimble. Only the blind man, whose dog lay on a mat at his feet, was missing out. On the crowded sidewalk in front of Saks, people didn't see him in time. Mark stepped off the curb, dug all the change from his pocket, and went back to put it into the beggar's cup. It was a gesture that seemed to have perfect logic—if symbolic logic could be perfect. Something had happened with Tom Wilding at lunch that at the time gave him the smear of pain and satisfaction he usually found euphoric. But the pain lingered when the euphoria wore off. He had seen a longtime friend cut loose from their attachment.

Kitty was exasperated at her inability to come to terms with the Mark-Wilczynski incident. She, who was herself one of the greatest stonewallers in a business where such talent was indispensable, was wearing down under the failure of the situation to resolve itself. She imagined all sorts of changes in Mark. For example, he was not as responsive to her in bed as she had come to expect. But that might be the booze. And if there had to be a choice between the two, she'd rather it was the booze than Wilczynski certainly.

She walked into Mark's office the day after he'd had lunch with Wilding, giving him only a moment's notice as she came down the hall. Two of the younger associates were putting up Christmas decorations, and she stopped for a word with them. Mark smiled up at her from a desk as neat as a jelly bean. The smile was false, she thought, meant to deceive, to distract her from something. It's a Christmas present, she tried to tell herself, something he'd just managed to hide. She could tell that to someone else, not to herself. On the desk in front of him was a folder advertising a survival knife, the illustration a jagged, lethal-looking weapon.

"Christmas shopping?" It sounded as false as his smile had looked.

He threw the folder into the wastebasket. "I'd like to get away for a few days, Kitty. Tom has offered me his place on Cape Cod, and I might take him up on it."

"Now?" Her mind raced to what she could remember about Wilding's beach house. In summer it was private. This time of year it would be isolated.

"I was thinking of next week."

She watched the little pulse start at his temple. All so casual on the surface. Inside he was in turmoil, she could tell. He couldn't lie to save his life. "Would you like me to go with you?" She succeeded in sounding as though she was suddenly enchanted with the idea.

"It never occurred to me that you'd want to." His voice was as flat as the floor.

"I do want to, but darling, I can't get away, and neither can you. Janet Caruthers will be here from London next week, and I'm counting on you to cope with her. You said yourself it would be disastrous to submit her manuscript as it is now. When did Tom offer you the beach house?"

"We had lunch."

"You've heard from Wilczynski, haven't you?"

"I expect to. I thought I might ask him to go up to the Cape with me. He knows more about the outdoors than most people."

She could not believe her ears. What kind of a fool did he take her for? As naïve as himself? "Mark, did he or did he not insult me? What's this business: 'He maligned my wife'? Give it to me straight out, what *did* he say?"

"Actually, it was me he insulted, only I didn't look at it that way at the time."

"*What did he say?* The exact words: spit them out."

"He said I didn't have to take all the shit."

"From me?"

Mark shrugged. Who else?

"The insolent pup. To dare to speak to you like that. Or is that among the privileges you've given him?"

"What does that mean?"

"Mark, do you see what you're doing to me? You're rewarding him for what he said."

"You're forgetting, I almost killed him that night."

"Too bad you didn't," Kitty said. "One more botched job to your credit."

Back in her own office Kitty phoned Wilding. "What in hell are you trying to do, break up my marriage?"

"That would take an act of God, Kitty."

"What about Wilczynski?"

"What about him?"

"Is there something going between him and Mark?"

"Sexual? It would never have entered my mind."

"Then think about it: You offer him a house on Cape Cod, and he decides to take Wilczynski with him."

"I didn't even know he was taking me up on the offer, Kitty."

"He's not. Believe me."

"Kitty, don't jump to conclusions. That's a really off-the-wall notion about Mark and Wilczynski. It's father and son if it's anything besides agent and writer."

"If you're holding back on me, Tom, I'll cut your heart out."

Mark had heard from Wilczynski. When Kitty left him, he retrieved the survival-knife flyer from the wastebasket by way of occupying himself until it was safe to resume what he'd been doing when she came into his office. He watched her out of sight and then kept his eye on the phone lights until he saw that she was at her desk and busy. Then he took the manuscript from the middle drawer where he had swept it out of sight on her arrival. He had heard from Wilczynski and found the communication a great deal more disturbing than not hearing from him had been. Some thirty pages and a brief outline had arrived from him that morning with a covering letter that read:

Dear Mark:

I think you know that I have wanted to divide my time and talents in such a way that I can earn my living by writing. I like the idea of poetry and the murder mystery, but until our recent bloody encounter I could find no satisfactory act of violence on which I could take off.

Please let me know what you think of these few pages and whether you would consider working with me on the plot. I've heard Kitty boast about working with her writers, so that I don't hesitate to ask. You may consider this beginning an impertinence, but if it is, it's a devoted one.

André

P.S. I am sending a letter to both you and Kitty under separate cover. It should clear the air.

The locale of Wilczynski's proposed novel, although said to be in a building on Riverside Drive with a view of the Hudson River, was plainly the Colemans' apartment on Central Park West, which André knew startlingly well. The principal characters, crudely drawn in this beginning, were comparable to the Colemans only in that they were a married couple approaching middle age. The woman was fat, long-suffering, and bland, and kept a meticulous house, nobody recognizable to Mark. The man had a Mephistophelian quality. "A cross between Mephistopheles and Svengali," André had written. Which, Mark thought, did not leave much room for character development. Mark had suddenly realized what Wilczynski was trying to do when Kitty walked in on him: He had switched the roles of the Colemans. It did not bother Mark much to see himself portrayed as a tub of lard, and under other circumstances, Kitty might enjoy the role into which she was cast. But the whole gambit disturbed him, especially with murder as its objective. However, if André could write suspense, he should be encouraged and helped to find a different vehicle. Without Kitty's knowing of this beginning. It was with this in mind that Mark had briefly entertained the notion of going to the Cape after all and taking Wilczynski with him, and had tested it out on Kitty. Patently he was not going with Janet Caruthers about to arrive. He put the Wilczynski proposal—to describe it a more advanced way than it deserved—into an agency folder and stashed it in a desk drawer. He decided to do nothing about it until the other letter André had mentioned came.

Wilding came out of a meeting to take Coleman's call. Mark hadn't said it was urgent. The sense of urgency was his own. Kitty's conjecture about Mark and Wilczynski had distressed him. She was an unpredictable woman, and he didn't like to think what she was capable of doing if something of hers was threatened.

But Mark was quite cheerful. "Kitty said you wanted to know: We now have a letter of apology from André Wilczynski."

"Read it to me if it isn't too long."

"Very brief in fact." The pertinent line read, " 'I hope you will allow me to consider my punishment sufficient to the offense.' "

"Fancy words," Wilding murmured. They did not sound at all like Wilczynski. "But they'll do as long as he signed the letter. What does Kitty say?"

"I'll tell you exactly what she said, 'Okay. Now let's get rid of him.' "

"I'd do it, if I were you. I'd get on the phone right now and tell him in the most diplomatic way possible that while you accept his apology in the same spirit as he accepted yours, you think it would be better for him to find other representation."

"No. I can't do that, Tom. And to tell you the truth, I don't see why I should."

Wilding, aware of the suspended meeting awaiting his return in the next room, could not think of a judicious way to persuade Mark in the time at hand. "It's up to you. But for God's sake, don't lose that letter."

"It's safe. It's in Kitty's hands."

Mark postponed further thought about the Wilczynski proposal until the Janet Caruthers visit. He spent most of the weekend going over her manuscript. He thought it barely literate, but he would not say that even to Kitty, abiding by his habit of loyalty to his authors. He had merely told her that it needed work, something to which she agreed on rereading it. The problem was to persuade Caruthers that she owed it to herself to do some rewriting. Her publisher might well accept the book as it was, she was that popular. Mark felt good about himself and the work he did on the script. He was able to concentrate for long stretches, which, he would be the first to admit, said something for the Caruthers manuscript as well. Kitty was right: Literacy wasn't everything.

Caruthers arrived in New York Monday noon. Mark did not see her until Wednesday evening, when, at Kitty's suggestion, he took them both to dinner at Le Perigord. As soon as he had ordered cocktails, Kitty announced, "Janet and I have made a pact: Tonight is trivia time. Not a word about *Storm over Bertram Heights*. Don't you love that title, Mark?"

He said that he did and looked around to see if they were getting his drink. It was usually mixed and chilling by the time he'd given up his topcoat and seated his guests. It occurred to him that if Kitty and Janet had agreed not to discuss the manuscript, they had probably already discussed it. "What are we going to talk about? Am I allowed to ask since I wasn't in on the arrangement?"

Kitty flashed him a warning glance. He was not to be contentious. A quick smile followed. "What?" she repeated, an invitation to suggest a subject.

"Other writers—who's in, who's out," Caruthers said. She was a big, amiable woman, getting bigger with every success. She did not like to write especially but, as she put it, she had a knack for it and she loved the little luxuries writing could buy. It turned out she had spent the afternoon at Kenneth Beauty Salon.

Which information, along with the arrival of their cocktails, cheered Mark up considerably. There was something reassuring about having a client who spent the afternoon with Kenneth.

Mark scraped his last oyster from the shell. The women were slower, having champagne with theirs, vulgar or not, as Kitty said. He found himself free-floating, as it were, adrift in their easy conversation. Kitty was the heroine of all her stories, and he marveled at the attention authors paid her, even Janet. A kind of fairy tale.

Kitty, for her part, was quite aware that he was drifting in and out of their presence, speaking only when spoken to. He was still an attractive man, she thought: They were noticed wherever they went together. And she liked it that way. His silence troubled her, as though he'd gone off secretly on his own. She wasn't sure she wanted to know where. During the clearing of the oyster shells, she pondered how to reach him. She waited until the *Rôti de Veau à la Maison* was served and their guest involved in her gastronomic adventure. Then she said to him, almost casually, "Mark, would you like me to try to place a collection of André's poems with Linden House?"

He came to instant attention. "I thought you wanted him . . ." He avoided saying the word *out* in Caruthers's presence.

"Obviously you don't," Kitty said. "And I thought you'd be pleased at the idea."

"Why Linden House?" He was shaken by the suggestion. And it was not a publisher he'd have gone to with poetry. Nor would he go to any house with as thin a body of verse as Wilczynski had so far produced. Kitty didn't even know what there was of it, much less its merit. She was putting him on, Mark decided, wanting to see how he'd react. But why? In her phone conversation with Wilding, the one on which he had eavesdropped, she told the lawyer Wilczynski was jealous of her. Now, he realized, she was jealous of Wilczynski. It boded both ill and well if she was serious about placing the poems.

Above all, it would take him off the hook in discussing with André the mystery-novel proposal in his desk drawer. To have his poems published by a reputable house would seem extraordinary to him, and the very possibility of it would melt his hostility toward Kitty.

"A hunch," she said about Linden House. "You know me and my hunches. I always play them." She laid a finger on the busy wrist of Janet Caruthers. "I had a hunch Janet would like the veal."

"I've never had an experience like it," Janet said happily.

Mark kept thinking of Linden House and who there would possibly be interested in Wilczynski. It would have to be someone in the upper echelon. Kitty always went to the decision makers. He did not want to press her. She might turn on him in front of Janet.

Then Kitty said, "Mark, stop racking your brain. I only had the idea five minutes ago, but you'd better believe I can get him a contract if I put my mind to it."

"Now who are we talking about?" Janet asked, dabbing her lips with her napkin.

"A young poet Mark is fathering," Kitty said.

Caruthers turned to him. "Is he good? He must be or you wouldn't be interested in him."

"I think he is." Then he remembered: On the terrace the night of the party Kitty and he had exchanged words about Jonathan Root, and that was the Linden House connection. Kitty had switched Root there on a million-dollar contract. She was quite capable of going back to them and squeezing out a thousand dollars more for a book they might or might not eventually publish.

But why would she do it? To lure the poet away from him? Or had she done it *for* him? He looked at her across the table. Her eyes were wide, blinking in anticipation. She expected him to say he was pleased. So he said it and added that young poets needed all the encouragement they could get.

It was a crisp, clear night, and they decided to walk the few blocks to the St. Regis, where Caruthers was staying. They paused to look at the long sweep of lights up Park Avenue and the joyous punctuation of a Christmas tree every block for as far as they could see. The tree in the hotel lobby was full of old-fashioned ornaments, and the music sounded as though it came from a calliope. Janet invited them to have a nightcap at the bar, which had a new jazz pianist, and she knew Mark loved jazz. The Colemans declined—a working day ahead, Kitty said. Janet kissed them both, thanked them, and wished them a Merry Christmas.

"I don't envy you Christmas in Los Angeles," Kitty said.

"Is it true," Janet wanted to know, "red, white, and blue Christmas trees?"

"And pink," Kitty said.

"When do you get back?" Mark asked. Somewhere along the line he had missed the information that she was going to the Coast.

"Late spring. One of you will come over to London before then. It would be super if you could come together."

"You're flying home directly from L.A., is that it?" Mark said.

Janet nodded.

"And . . . *Bertram Heights*?" He mimed a spiral with his hands suggestive of something ongoing, unfinished.

Kitty took over. "Darling, Janet had lunch with her editor and all of them yesterday. They want the book *now*. I said you'd agree—if that's how they feel, they'd better have it. You do agree, don't you?"

"The point is moot by now, isn't it? Shall we go home?"

"There simply wasn't time," she said in the cab when he had not spoken by the time they passed Columbus Circle and headed up Central Park West.

He still said nothing.

"If you must know, Janet made the decision. She's very fond of you, but she doesn't like her agent playing editor."

He turned his head to look at her. "You have such a gracious way of saying things."

"I tell it the way it is," Kitty said. "The trouble with Janet is her head is getting as big as the rest of her. She writes such awful stuff it's hard to believe how popular it is." She laid her hand on his where it lay cold and gloveless on his knee. "It would have been a waste of your time, darling."

"When I could be playing agent," Mark said.

Kitty left the apartment early in the morning, going directly to a meeting outside the office. Mark, his nerves jumpy from too little sleep and too much to drink, walked to work through the park. There was the feeling of snow in the air, and he could smell horse manure from the bridle path; the ground was hard beneath his feet. He thought of the time when, as a boy, he had tried to dig a grave for a bird the cat had killed and couldn't because the earth was frozen solid. He'd put it in a shoebox and kept it in his room. One day he smelled feathers burning. When he looked in the box, the dead bird was gone. Neither he nor his mother ever spoke of it. Where had such silence gone?

In the office he tore up his notes on the Caruthers novel and sent the copy of the manuscript to file. Left in the drawer were the folder with André's projected thriller and the advertisement for the survival knife. The knife would require six to eight weeks for delivery. André's project could stay in abeyance. He got the tearsheets of Wilczynski's published poems—as well as a few rejects—from the file and put them on Kitty's desk.

At noontime he did his Christmas shopping and then visited Herman's Sporting Goods and bought two knives, one for hunting, a long narrow blade, and the other an all-purpose survival knife. It was its description that kept getting to him. He got through lunchtime without a drink by the simple means of going without lunch as well. He called Tom Wilding midafternoon and said he'd changed his mind again. He wanted to take him up on the loan of the Cape Cod house. He'd be ready to go up in the morning.

"It's not possible," Wilding said and explained that his caretaker would have to turn on the water and get the heat up. Saturday at the earliest. "Mark, are you going alone?"

He hesitated. "Is that part of the deal, that I go alone?"

"Of course not. I was only thinking that it may get pretty lonely up there for someone as used to the city as you are."

"That's what I want," Mark said, and arranged to pick up the key the next morning.

"It's impossible," Kitty said. "There are several things during the week that we really must go to."

He cut into her recital of the holiday festivities. "You'll get along. Tom will be glad to take you—any number of people—flattered."

"It's not the same. We've always been a couple."

"Or at least one," Mark said.

"What's that supposed to mean?"

"I don't know what it means to you. I only know what it means to me. If anyone should ask where I am, just say I'm drying out."

"That'll be the day. I suppose André is going with you?"

"What gave you that idea?"

"You said you were going to ask him."

"That was a passing thought at the time."

"It's none of my business," Kitty said. "I merely wondered." She took her glass to the bar. For the life of her she could not figure out what was going on with him. "There's time for another drink before dinner. Do you want to fix it while I light the oven?"

"André's your client now. He'll be devoted to you," Mark said, getting up.

"What's this business of your client, my client? They're all *our* clients."

"If you say so, dear. But I give you my word on it, André is not going to Cape Cod with me."

"I don't want your word on it!" She started for the kitchen but paused in the dining-room archway. "And I don't want him as a client. I'm doing it for you, if you must know."

Mark didn't say anything. There was a time he had thought as much himself. He wiped his hands on a cocktail napkin. They were cold and sweaty. He mixed Kitty's Manhattan and then added a few drops of water to what was left of his first martini. The thought of drinking it gave him no great pleasure. One day at a time.

In the kitchen, the swinging door closed, Kitty phoned Tom Wilding at home and, not reaching him there, phoned him at his club. Wilding listened out her tirade against him for having suggested that Mark go in the first place—this time of year, his tendency to catch colds, his state of mind. After which she demanded that he call Mark and say the place had burned down or blown away, anything to forestall his going. She was frantic, and he thought for the first time in years there was some hope in the situation. Old Mark was standing his ground.

Finally he said, "Kitty, why don't you let him go? That's the only way to stop him."

"You and your goddamn riddles! You're two of a kind." And she slammed down the phone.

Friday promised to be the longest day in Mark's memory. He went into the office thinking that Kitty might stay home, as she often did on Fridays, to read manuscripts without interruption. She was in the office fifteen minutes after his arrival. She kept coming in to see him on a variety of pretexts, some with concern about what he was taking with him—and did he want her to pack for him? He did not. There was concern also for what he was leaving behind, unfinished agency work. It was with almost demonic intuition that she said, "What about your desk drawers? You're always sticking things away and forgetting them."

"Clean," Mark said. "I'll be leaving them as clean as a whistle." And at that point he decided that he had to take the Wilczynski proposal with him, or send it back, or take it home and bury it in his study.

On one of her sorties she announced that she had bundled off the collected poems of André Wilczynski to Linden House.

"So soon?"

"It's almost Christmas," she said, further implying the kindness of her gesture. She could not have read them; he was inclined to wonder if anyone would. He told himself that cynicism would get him nowhere.

"It will be interesting to see if you can pull it off."

"Oh, ye of little faith," she said.

When Kitty went to lunch—to ease his own mind and despite his practice of not telling an author of a mere submission—he called Wilczynski. He told him that Kitty had submitted his poems to one of the biggest houses in Manhattan.

"No kidding. You mean she likes them?"

"I like them," Mark said with asperity.

"It's great. It's just great," André said.

"It's by no means a hundred percent sure, but Kitty has a way with publishers."

"Mark . . . don't show Kitty that suspense thing I sent you. She's a smart lady."

"And I'm not smart?"

"I didn't mean that, sir." André reverted to formal address. As author to agent, he went on a first-name basis; as an employee, he called him Mr. Coleman. "I hope you'd understand what I was trying to do."

"If I understand it correctly, I'm not sure I want to encourage you with that particular vehicle. Mind you, if you can write suspense, André, I'll certainly work with you. But why don't I send this manuscript back to you? Have another look at it yourself. I'm going out of town for a few days' rest. I'll call you when I get back."

"Mark . . . the apology was all right?"

"Of course. Otherwise . . ."

"Mark, please give it another read. The people can be changed. It's the house and atmosphere and the puzzle at the end I want to hang on to. I'm very keen on it."

He wound up wishing he had not called André at all. He put the manuscript in an otherwise empty dispatch case to take home with him. In the late afternoon he picked up the rental car. He felt too edgy to drive through the midtown traffic, so he went uptown by way of First Avenue to Ninety-sixth Street, where he crossed through the park and drove south again. He made several passes at a parking place near the apartment building and finally got the doorman to guide him into it. Upstairs he put the Wilczynski manuscript on a shelf in his study with a number of others in photocopy. Kitty called his study the land of forgotten books. But that was not so. There was some material there he even knew by heart.

He packed before dressing for the evening, laying the sheathed knives at the bottom of the suitcase. Only one of them had meaning for him, the survival knife. He wasn't even sure why he had bought the other. Tom's place was bound to have every kind of knife he might need—except the survival knife. The new film he and Kitty saw in special showing was not good, but the stars were there, and congratulations flowed, as abundant and effervescent as the champagne. Everybody assured everybody else of Oscar nominations. It would have taken him several martinis to warm to the occasion, and he was drinking ginger ale disguised as bourbon and soda. Kitty asked him twice if he was really going in the morning. Even her proposals to help him get away, he realized, were meant to deter him, and the ultimate act of deterrence was the dispatch of André's poems. He was beginning to sweat with the strain of the evening, when Kitty looked at him and said, "I'd better take you home."

While he was undressing, he noticed the carton half-tucked in at the side of his suitcase: a bottle of Wild Turkey bourbon. He thanked Kitty and then, while she was in the bathroom, buried the bottle in the drawer among his socks. His sleep was fitful and dream-ridden. He dreamed of someone he called mother, only it was not his mother. But it wasn't Kitty either. Sometime before dawn Kitty left her bed and crawled in at his back. He stiffened everywhere except where, presumably, she wanted it to happen. A fierce fantasy raced through his mind: rape and he the rapist. All that happened was the sweat again, and Kitty left his bed as silently as she had come to it. He thought he heard her crying but pretended not to. If Kitty was crying, it was a last resort.

He showered and shaved and then decided not to take the shaver with him. Kitty had finally fallen asleep. He took his luggage into the vestibule before zipping it. He made instant coffee and toasted a slice of rye bread that scratched his throat when he swallowed it. He looked out at an ominous red and purple sunrise and wondered whether to waken Kitty or to let her sleep. It would be easier to get out the door by himself. He reminded himself not to forget to turn the key in the top lock: This was something that figured importantly in Wilczynski's script, he remembered. He hadn't understood it. He wasn't sure the writer understood it either. Very muddy. For a moment he thought of taking the proposal with him. He even thought of losing it. Which had to be his low point on the ladder of cowardice. He brought in *The New York Times* from the hall and turned to the obituary page. There was nobody he knew among that Saturday's deceased. He felt a little disappointed. He folded the paper neatly. If there was anything that got Kitty's day off to a bad start, it was a newspaper that looked to have been read before she got to it. He used the maid's bathroom; it wasn't used very much, their household help coming in three days a week, the cleaning crew once a month. The water, when he flushed it, looked pink, rusty. He thought at first it was blood.

When he returned to the kitchen, he took up the chalk, intending to write a note on the blackboard. But what to say? See you this time next week? See you soon? Love. He put down the chalk, having written nothing. He set out a tray with a cup and saucer, plate and napkin. And the bud vase. A large bowl of chrysanthemums stood on the dining-room table. There were always flowers there, and he would often pluck one out and put it in the bud vase on the tray. Did he do it for Kitty or for himself? He put the dishes away, pocketed the napkin, and took the tray back to the butler's pantry. He simply could not get going until he pushed himself. He took a handful of cigarettes from the box on the dining-room sideboard. It was years since he had smoked, but he remembered the comfort a cigarette used to be, a companion on a long drive alone. He could not remember his last cigarette or his last drive alone. He got his parka from the hall closet, his earmuffs, gloves, scarf, and keys. The only sound when he left the apartment was the heat starting up. In the lobby the night doorman was asleep sitting upright in a high-backed chair. A robot could have taken his place and done a better job. Mark let himself out without disturbing the man.

Kitty wakened a few minutes after eight with the feeling that she had been drugged, which was so: Valium at 5:00 A.M. He was gone, she realized, the bedding pulled down but left unmade, the heavy drapes closed, the room cold but too dry, always too dry. Another Saturday morning and he'd have brought her a tray by now—croissant if he'd been out—otherwise toast and fruit and dark fragrant coffee, Zabar's best, and almost always a rose in the bud vase. He would draw the drapes to let in the sky, as he put it, and start up the music in the radiators. Very poetic. Which put her in mind of Wilczynski. "Shit and damnation," she said aloud. She got up and went from one room to another, just to make sure he was gone, her mules clacking on the hardwood floor, then muted on the heavy rugs, then loud again and with a faint echo as of distant hammering. She was tempted to give up her Saturday morning at the health club. But why? To do what else? She rinsed his cup and used it, the jar of instant coffee on the counter where he'd left it. Not even a note on the blackboard. She phoned Tom Wilding.

"I hope I didn't interrupt anything sexual," she said when he came to the phone short of breath.

"I have better concentration than that, Kitty. What's on your mind?" He had no intention of telling her that he was bicycling in place, and he never understood why he was the recipient of her sexual innuendos. Hardly innuendos, but they certainly weren't passes either. To him she was about as sexually attractive as a camel in heat, and she could think up something as revolting to say of him, he was sure.

"Could I have your Cape Cod phone number? He's on his way, you'll be glad to know."

"I'm sorry, Kitty. The phone up there's turned off for the season."

"If you're just saying that, I can find out some other way, you know."

"I do know. I also know that with winter storms—' "

"Okay, I believe you," she interrupted. "More important—I have two seats for the Actors' Benefit of *Candy* tomorrow night. Will you take me?" *Candy* was the hottest ticket in town.

"I'd love to, Kitty—"

"Good. Pick me up at seven."

"—but I have a date," Wilding finished his sentence.

"You can break it. It's important for me to be there." She let a second of silence hang and then said, "So I'll see you tomorrow night." When she put down the phone, her hand was trembling. She had thought he was going to turn her down. Now, she decided, she would give him his Christmas present early—after the theater. Actually, she had bought it for Mark—an old English print of a court scene during the Restoration. She was sure Wilding would appreciate its worth, and it might just raise her stock with him a point or two. She would rather court than tomahawk him, but she knew she would never win him, and she didn't like herself for trying. From the day she had first trapped his eyes with hers, he had seen every black spot on her soul. He might even have seen some she did not know were there herself.

The masseuse inquired after Mark. She had met him once when she came to the apartment and thought him very attractive. Kitty wove a tale about his having gone to the north woods for a week of duck hunting. If he got his bag early, he intended to go farther north on a moose trek. There was great hilarity between the women on where to hang the moose head if he brought one home. Then Kitty admitted she was pulling her leg about the moose hunt. But she did promise her a wild duck for Christmas, thinking of the butcher shop on Madison Avenue that specialized in game.

She cabbed home greatly relaxed by the sauna and the probing hands of the masseuse. She admitted to herself that she might not know Mark as well as she had thought. He might very well come home in better shape than he had left. And, in truth, she looked forward to an evening or two with Tom Wilding. The one thing she wished she could do in Mark's absence was get rid of Wilczynski. He had become a ridiculous intrusion in their lives, a snot-nosed kid. She wondered if it was safe—legally safe—to undertake dropping him herself. She proposed to speak to Wilding about it, to have him compose the letter.

When she opened the apartment door, she smelled cigarette smoke, and that frightened her. Then she saw the suitcase, its contents spilling over the floor, shirts, shorts, socks. With the parka dropped on top of them. She found him in his study slumped in the swivel desk chair facing her, his face gray, his eyes glassy. The bottle of Wild Turkey sat on the desk unopened.

"What happened? Were you in an accident?"

"No."

"What then?"

"I couldn't go. I just couldn't go."

Her rage was explosive. She flung her pocketbook at him, the only thing at hand. "You weak, impotent fool!"

The pocketbook contents scattered on the floor. When Mark stooped to gather them, Kitty saw the knives on the desk, both unsheathed. Her fury subsided. "Mark?" She pointed to the knives.

He straightened up and swiveled to where he could pick up the knife with the jagged edge. "This one is called a survival knife. I thought it meant something. Not a thing." He threw it down and took up the other with the slick, long blade. He used it to break the seal on the whiskey bottle. "You know, it's funny—I thought you'd be glad to see me."

Kitty brought two glasses from the teacart, the portable bar. She took the bottle from his hand and poured them each a drink. Touching her glass to his, she said, "Welcome home," and threw down the whiskey. She picked up the two knives and started from the room with them.

"Leave them," Mark said.

"Where?"

He shrugged.

She put them in a manuscript box on a shelf near the door.

Mark gave her a sad little smile. "Whatever else is wrong with me, Kitty, I am not suicidal."

A few days later, on Christmas Eve, Wilczynski called the office to see if Mark was back. An office party was in progress, so that the person answering Mark's phone didn't bother to inquire whether or not he wanted to take the call. "It's for you, Mr. C.," she called out, and Mark soon found himself explaining how, at the last moment, he'd not been able to get away after all.

"I don't suppose there's any word yet on my poems?"

"It's too soon, and Kitty would have told me," Mark said. "Do you need money?"

"That's not why I called. I wanted to wish everybody a Merry Christmas."

"Thank you, André. But *do* you need money? You don't have to keep a stiff upper lip with me."

"Just read my pages again and see if we can go to work."

"I promise to do it over the holiday."

"Mark, are you sure Kitty was serious about getting my poems to a publisher?"

"Absolutely," Mark said, but even as he said it, he felt his heart drop down.

"I don't mean to be ungrateful, but I'd like to have put them together myself. The order makes a difference, don't you see? And not all of them should go in. Would you ask her? I've retyped and arranged them, and I'd be glad to bring them in on Monday."

"Call me first thing Monday morning." Mark had a terrible feeling, hanging up the phone, that Wilczynski was wiser in the ways of Kitty in this instance than he was. She had moved with impossible haste.

He kept waiting for the right moment to approach the subject. Kitty did it for him. They were home in pajamas and waiting for the delivery of barbecued spareribs, chips, and onion rings, when she said, "Did you tell André I was showing his things to Linden House?"

"I didn't mention Linden House."

"But you did tell him something?"

"I did, yes."

"Well, now you can have the pleasure of telling him I've changed my mind."

"You can't do that to him, Kitty. I can't do it. Didn't you tell me you'd already sent them to Linden House? You did tell me that."

"I told *you* that. I didn't tell him. I wanted to see if it was really good news to you. And it was. Oh, yes, it really was."

Mark was too upset to say anything.

"Don't you see, this snot-nosed kid, this two-penny poet of yours is fucking up our lives?"

"They were pretty well fucked up before he came along. Oh, Christ." He poured himself a double shot of gin and drank it straight.

"You do hate me, don't you?" Kitty said.

"Sometimes it isn't hard."

"You can't live with me and you can't live without me, right?"

He sat down, his face in his hands, and tried to think how to deal with Wilczynski. All his poems retyped, all his hopes recharged.

Kitty twisted her fingers into his hair and pulled his head up. "Get rid of him, Mark. Or I will."

He pulled away from her. "No. I've promised to work with him on a project and I don't intend to let him down on that. But I agree; he's better off out of the Mark Coleman Agency."

Wilding read the draft letter, dated January 5, to Kitty over the phone. It was much along the lines of what he had proposed Mark say to Wilczynski in a phone call. "Mark should sign it, you know."

"And if he won't?"

Wilding thought back to the day he'd advised that Mark apologize and Kitty's saying, No problem. "I thought you said he agreed to the severance. I'll talk to him."

"What I want is to sever the relationship entirely. This thing they're working on—it's an excuse. That's all. I see them out there in

Central Park, walking up and down like a pair of lions in their natural habitat. Oblivious to traffic, to weather . . ."

"Kitty, get rid of the binoculars."

"Don't be such a smart-ass. There are a lot of hungry lawyers in this town."

"God knows, I'd wish them bon appétit," Wilding said.

Kitty ignored the remark. "He's obsessed with this ridiculous person. And it's not as though he has talent. He calls himself a poet, therefore he's a poet. I couldn't submit stuff like that if I'd wanted to. And I did want to. Sort of."

"Did you read it?"

"My secretary read it."

Mark had said she hadn't, and she hadn't. There were moments Wilding could almost feel sorry for her, but they were rare moments. "I'll talk to Mark," he said.

"If you can't reach him just say your name's Wilczynski."

Mark and Wilczynski, huddled in their overcoats, sipped their tea in the drafty zoo cafeteria. Little tornadoes of dust and leaves were dancing outside the glass enclosure. André was saying that he thought he could now take the story, which he'd call *Till Death Do Us Part,* from there without Mark's help. At least till he got to the locked-room situation. "You've taught me an awful lot, Mark."

"It may turn out that *awful* is the precise word for it." He leaned back and enjoyed the realization that working with André had been a great pleasure—the quick and probing mind, the eagerness to work, to rework.

"One thing you taught me," André said, "Henry James wasn't a mystery writer."

Mark laughed and said, "Drink your tea and we'll walk back to the apartment and run through the lock business on the scene."

"Couldn't we just work it out on paper? I don't want to meet Kitty."

"She's at the office," Mark said. "One member of the firm has to support A.T. and T." He got up. "And if she were home—so what?"

André mimed cutting his throat.

They were skirting Tavern on the Green when André said, "Mark, did a publisher really reject my poems? You just said they were rejected. Was that Kitty?"

"Yes. She was wise enough to see that you aren't ready yet and to withdraw them. There's not a publisher in the city with whom your record isn't entirely clean."

"Good old loyal Mark," Wilczynski said and gave him a hug.

Kitty had not intended to be home that afternoon, but something at lunch had disagreed with her. Or else she was coming down with a bug. In any case, she wanted an instant cure, having to carry most of the office burden alone these days. Once home, she certainly did not intend to go out on the terrace with binoculars. She had acquired them after Wilding's wisecrack, a figure of speech on his part. But she did go out. It was cold and raw and windy, and she really did not care at the moment if she got pneumonia, for no sooner did she have the glasses in focus than she picked up the two men coming toward her. It was at the moment Wilczynski threw his arm across Mark's shoulder.

When they got out of the elevator, Mark illustrated his usual procedure on arriving home. He rang the buzzer—two longs, two shorts. "If Kitty were home, she'd answer and probably let me in. And vice versa if it were I who was home . . ."

"What do you mean, probably? That's not good enough."

"Don't be so fierce," Mark said. "We'll work it out. Let's say I was in the habit of forgetting my keys sometimes. And say I phoned to tell her I was on my way home and had forgotten them. She'd be sore as hell at me, but when I buzzed my two longs and two shorts, she'd yank the door off the hinges to confront me. How's that?"

"Mark, that's exactly how I had it in my first version, the one I sent you. Transpose the sexes and it goes like this: She throws the door open to you, only it's not you. It's a burglar, a killer. He'd stolen your briefcase in the park with all the notes you'd made on this thriller you were going to write . . ."

"Who then does the real job for me," Mark said. "And look . . ." He illustrated the two-lock system: "This is what's called a warded lock. You have to turn the key in it to open it and, once in the apartment, you have to turn the key to lock it behind you. The tumbler lock is automatic. Now the fact is I've been known to go out in a hurry and simply let the door lock behind me on the tumbler lock. I sometimes forget the one I have to turn around and diddle with. Kitty's right. I am careless."

"Then it's simple," André cried. "Let's say you've called her to say you forgot your keys. She tells you that she's not surprised because you left the top lock off again. You say, mea culpa, hang up and start for home in your own good time. When you get there, you do the buzzer routine, two longs, two shorts. No answer. You hang in there, thinking she may have fallen asleep. You try again. Then, really panicky, you run down the stairs, get the super, and he comes up with his big ring of skeleton keys. Right? You keep urging him to find one that's going to fit the top lock. He finds it, but—the shocker—he didn't need it. The lock was off all the time. But Kitty never, never leaves it off. Which means she must have opened the door to someone, thinking it was you, someone who afterward let himself out, with the automatic lock falling into place when he closed the door. The same as when you forgot your keys. You and the super get the door open, and there she is, lying in a pool of blood."

"Jesus," Mark said.

"Cold blood," Wilczynski said. "It's all in the script. All we have to do now is work out a time schedule."

"And write the book."

"You do know you're the major suspect till they pick up the guy who stole your briefcase?"

"I can live with it," Mark said.

In his study Mark got out the manuscript and outline—or, as he had called it then, the proposal. While Wilczynski read it aloud with flourishes and flying spittle, Mark poured each of them a drink. They toasted *Till Death Do Us Part* and set to work on timing the mayhem schedule.

Kitty came almost to the door of Mark's study in her stocking feet. She glimpsed both men, André at the desk. Mark leaning over him, his hand on Wilczynski's shoulder. She saw him give André an affectionate little poke on the chin, with André leaning back and saying, "Hey, that's where all this started!" Great laughter. She had almost forgotten what Mark's laughter sounded like. She heard her name mentioned, and that was enough. She fled to the bedroom, undressed, and buried herself in bed. Time passed. Darkness and silence. When she got up and crept through the apartment, she saw that they had gone out again. She checked the door. Typical: Mark had forgotten to turn the lock. She got her own keys and locked it. Then she went into his study, lit the desk lamp, and opened the middle drawer. A creature of habit, Mark had cleared his desk and put the work in progress in the middle drawer. She read every word of it and saw herself instantly as the cross between Mephistopheles and Svengali. She left his study as she had found it, leaving the vestibule light on, and went back to bed.

Mark was surprised to find her home. She had come in a few minutes ago, she said, and felt so miserable she decided to go right to bed. She reprimanded him for leaving the door half-locked.

"Isn't that just like me?" he said. "And do you know where I was? I went looking for a locksmith. And by the way, it's time we updated our security system." He leaned over and kissed her cheek and said he was sorry she wasn't feeling well. He even smelled like Judas, she thought, although she knew that what she smelled was the spice he chewed to cover the whiskey on his breath.

Kitty was scheduled for a breakfast meeting in Boston that Thursday. She had first intended to take the early shuttle flight but decided on Wednesday to go up that night and stay over at a hotel. She was not working well and she needed all her wits to try to salvage a contract a publisher claimed the author had violated. Going early meant she could not attend a dinner party Wednesday night for the benefit of the Writers' Colony, an annual gala event at which she and Mark were often photographed as being among its celebrities. There was a time when missing it would have grieved her. Now she felt only a twinge of anger at not being grieved. Mark said he would put in an appearance at the dinner, and she immediately wondered if that meant he would go off somewhere with Wilczynski as soon as he could get away.

She stopped home to pick up her overnight case after speaking at the Columbia University seminar on "The Business of Writing." The word *business* and Mark had wanted out. He also seemed to have opted out of the office that afternoon as well. He was at his desk, the study door open, the wire basket at the side of his chair half full of typescript, where, for the sake of speed, he dropped each page as he read it.

"Is that you, Kitty?" he called out as she was locking the door behind her.

"Who else?"

She stopped for a moment at his desk, and they exchanged a few words about the seminar, Mark rhythmically, automatically, and blindly continuing to leaf the pages of manuscript into the basket.

"That must be a great book," Kitty said.

Realizing what he was doing, he laughed and fished the unread pages out of the basket. "Monumental," he said.

In the bedroom she noted that he had already put out his dinner jacket, dress shirt, and black tie, and for an instant she was tempted to reverse her plans again. A seesaw: Her life had become a seesaw, she on one end, Wilczynski on the other, Mark the hump in the middle. She put a fresh blouse in the case for the morning and closed it. If she hurried, she could get in a couple of hours at the office before leaving for La Guardia. She was touching up her makeup when the phone rang. Mark took the call on the third ring. He was still talking when she set down her purse and overnight bag outside his door.

All she heard at first was a couple of grunts, cheerful, humorous sounds. She had no doubt at all as to who was on the phone. Then Mark said, "As long as you've got a tux, wear it. But no sneakers, hear me, boy?" He saw Kitty then and finished off: "Seven-thirty, just inside the Fifth Avenue door. Okay?"

"I'm not going," Kitty said when he'd hung up the phone.

"You're not going to Boston, is that it?" He glanced at her and quickly away.

"That's it. So you'd better call him back and tell him you're taking your wife to the dinner, not your mistress."

Mark sat for a second or two, grappling with the concept. Then: "Jesus Christ!" He got up and went to the teacart, where he poured himself a drink. He did not want to look at her, not the way she was now, her face distorted and blotched with anger. "I could get down on my knees and swear," he said. "But it wouldn't do any good. You couldn't believe, could you, that I had in mind how important it might be for him to meet the Colony trustees? He ought to try for a fellowship."

Kitty hardly knew what she was doing. A raging instinct sent her to the manuscript box in which she had put away the knives on the morning he had not been able to go to the Cape. The hunting knife in hand, she meant to force her will upon him, nothing else. "Are you going to call him?"

Mark took his drink back to the desk, still averting his eyes from her. "I'm going to think about it," he said and drank the whiskey down.

She even challenged him: "Look at me, Mark."

He shook his head.

When she came up behind him, he might have thought she would yank his head up by the hair again. Instead she plunged the knife into his back and left it there. He slumped forward onto the desk, and then when the swivel chair rolled out from under him, he fell to the floor. By then Kitty was at the door. She caught up her purse and overnight case only to set them down again twice, once to open the vestibule door and once to lock it behind her. There was no way she could stand and wait for the elevator. She ran down the stairs, floor after bare-walled floor, her knees buckling and then steadying sufficiently to carry her on. She stood at what she thought was the door entering onto the lobby and tried to pretend that it was all a nightmare, and that beyond the door she would wake up. She opened the door and found herself not in the lobby but in the basement, a few feet away from the laundry room, where she could hear the chatter of women and the raucous laughter of a neighbor whose voice she recognized. She went out the service entrance and then walked as fast as she could toward Columbus Avenue, a very long block from Central Park. The cold wind of February tore at the coat of her three-piece suit and then reached in to catch at her throat.

A crime of passion, a crime of passion: The words kept racing through her mind. I didn't want to kill him, she tried to tell herself, but she did and she knew it. The very thought of him and Wilczynski going to the dinner set her aflame again. She began to feel justified and instantly then to wonder if it were possible to escape discovery. The doorman might not even have seen her come home. She had bussed down from Columbia and entered the building while he was putting someone in a cab. And no one had seen her leave just now. Only Mark knew that she'd come home. She looked at her watch. Well under an hour ago. If only she had not double-locked the door, she might get away free. She realized it was their very script that she was going over in her mind! The top lock was to be left off as though a burglar/murderer had been admitted by mistake and after the crime had simply walked out of the apartment and closed the door behind him. She had even followed the instructions about going down the stairs and, inadvertently, out through the basement. She turned back, determined to go in as she had come out of the building. If she were seen, she would brazen it out somehow. Her writers called her the great improviser. She expected Mark to be discovered by their cleaning woman in the morning, who would arrive at ten o'clock and let herself in, noting as she did so that the top lock was off again. A born tattler, she never failed to let Kitty know when Mr. Coleman had forgotten to double-lock the door.

Wilczynski, of course, might try to sound an alarm when Mark failed to show up at the Colony dinner. By then she would be in

Boston, with only Mark and her secretary knowing where. The police would do nothing before morning.

She was unable to return to the building through the basement, because the entrance was locked from the inside. She stowed her overnight bag in one of the empty ash cans, where she could pick it up later and thus not be encumbered with it now. She went around the building to the corner of Central Park West, from where she watched with agonizing patience the doorman popping in and out. Then God—or the devil—was with her, for a school bus came and dispersed several children into his charge. Kitty went into the building by the side entrance as the youngsters were going around and around in the revolving center door. Mothers and nannies tried to snatch and sort them out. She reached the elevator ahead of all of them, pressed the number for the second floor below her own, and went slowly upward entirely alone. Entering her own vestibule from the stairwell instead of the elevator, she found it a foreign place. The naked aluminum coatrack—unused since the November party—made it seem a desolation. It would never be home again. The sorrow of it welled up in her, the tears making it difficult for her to see to put the key in the lock. She intended to go, having turned that one key, but the overwhelming feeling hit her again. She felt that once she opened the door, she would step out of the nightmare, home safe. But when she did open it, she knew the nightmare was forever: Mark, lying on the floor, had gathered himself to himself and died in the fetal position.

Kitty tried several times to dial Tom Wilding's number but got it wrong each time. Finally, she simply dialed 911.

THE LAST DREAM

LUCY FREEMAN

It was the first time Jonathan Thomas had not been at least ten minutes early. He always arrived in a leisurely manner, setting his own tempo and moving slowly into the mood of analysis. He had no need, as most patients did, to rush from crowded street to silent couch.

Dr. William Ames felt more and more worried as the minutes clicked by. Perhaps, he thought, Jonathan sat in restrained fury in a taxi, barricaded by buses, trucks, intrepid suburbanites, and other helpless cabs. Manhattan the moiling mess it is when sudden snow cripples traffic to a standstill.

Dr. Ames left his desk, walked to the window. Flakes fell lightly from a darkened sky. The maples and ginkgos lining the southern strip of Central Park South stood out black and brittle, bare of leaves. He thought nostalgically how the high wind of a summer storm tossed the city's sea of trees around like ballet dancers spinning on a carpet of grass. Thought, too, of how in autumn the park blazed with fall's fiery pyre to summer. During the silences into which patients sometimes plunged, strange park sounds reached his ears. The trumpeting of a caged elephant, the bark of a seal, reaching upward from the zoo. Or the neigh of a dilapidated horse as it clopped around a winding curve, its carriage of tourists staring at the surrounding wall of skyscrapers.

The phone rang, it had to be Jonathan explaining his delay. A strange voice, deeper, huskier than Jonathan's, asked, "Do you have a patient named Jonathan Thomas?"

"Who is this?" Such information was confidential unless Dr. Ames had Jonathan's approval to disclose it.

"I'm Detective Jack Lonegan, attached to the Nineteenth Precinct. I'm calling from the Thomas apartment on East Seventy-sixth Street."

Concerned, wondering what a detective was doing at Jonathan's home, Dr. Ames sensed this was no time for professional discretion. He said, "Mr. Thomas was supposed to be here at five. He's half an hour late."

The husky voice said, "I'm sorry to tell you this, Dr. Ames, but Mr. Thomas was found murdered in his office early this morning."

Oh my God, Dr. Ames thought. Nothing like this happens to analytic patients. They are not victims of murderers, they only have fantasies of committing murder or being murdered.

"I've been assigned to the case," the voice said. "Mrs. Thomas gave me your name, address, and phone number. She told me you were her husband's shrink."

Were. Dr. Ames winced.

"I'd like to talk to you, Dr. Ames. Could I come to your office? I'd be there in twenty minutes. I need your help."

"I can't divulge the confidences of my patient." Dr. Ames did not wish to get involved.

"Not that kind of help. A different sort."

Dr. Ames was silent, thought, What damage can it do to meet the detective, I want to know exactly what happened to Jonathan. He said, "Come right over. I'll ask the next patient to return at another hour."

After hanging up, the thought suddenly struck him, *Jonathan's dream has come true.* Unbelievable!

Two days before, Jonathan had entered the office as he usually did three times a week at five in the afternoon, with his casual smile, lowered his impeccably clad six feet to the brown tweed couch as though it offered great comfort. He had started the hour with a dream.

"Jesus, what a nightmare I had about dawn! I was on my way here. Only it wasn't my regular hour. It was midnight. The witching hour.

Hour of witches. Crazy. But I *had* to see you. I felt I was in real trouble. And I knew you were waiting for me upstairs at your desk."

He fell silent a moment, then went on, "The street was deserted. I suddenly realized a robber was following me. He wanted to kill me. He caught up with me. I saw he was big and fat, potbellied. His stomach stuck way out. He wore a black mask, but I noticed he had red hair and red eyes.

"He raised his hand and I saw a large knife in it. I tried to shout to you for help, but you were too far away. I thought, So this is what it's like to die. And when I woke up, it felt so real. Like I *was* being killed."

It was as if Jonathan knew he was going to be murdered. As if he suspected someone was after him. As if he were conveying the clues to Dr. Ames. When he asked Jonathan who he thought was the killer, he mentioned his wife, Elaine. He said, "Before we went to bed, I told Elaine I could no longer stand her nagging. She constantly accuses me of marrying her for her money. Not satisfying her sexually. Not spending enough time with her. She still doesn't understand a publisher has a lot of reading to do. I can't go over manuscripts during the day. The office is a ten-ring circus. The telephone never stops."

Then he had added, in a thoughtful tone, "I'm lucky my secretary is such a whirlwind. In her quiet, deadly efficient way she makes sure I answer letters promptly and keep appointments. Couldn't get along without her."

He had also mentioned his partner at Aragon Press, Jamey Brown, with whom he had quarreled. Jamey wanted to dream up a book and hire a writer for women's-liberation readers but Jonathan wanted to wait until a manuscript came into the house. He suggested that if none did within a few months, their current best-selling author, Norma Donn, whose book *The Female Orgasm* had made them over a million dollars, might write it.

These had been Jonathan's thoughts following his dream, thoughts that related to the images and words in the dream. A nightmare fantasy that had turned into horrifying reality. Was it a prophetic dream? Had there been some "real" danger in Jonathan's life? A danger in the present linked to the past when, as a boy, he feared his father's cruel tongue and emotional beating? Dr. Ames thought the dream showed Jonathan's deeply buried wish for revenge on the father of childhood, who had red hair. In the dream Jonathan was killer as well as victim: The dreamer plays every role—hero and villain, man, woman, and child.

Twenty minutes to the dot the office bell rang. Dr. Ames opened the door to a solidly built man with rough-hewn features, a Charles Bronson face, a man about Dr. Ames's own age, in his early fifties. The detective wore a brown tweed coat over a dark brown suit, brown hat.

Dr. Ames put out his hand and said, "Please come in. May I take your hat and coat?" He felt the dampness of melting snow on them as he hung them in the waiting-room closet.

He led the detective into his consulting room, where they took seats facing each other. The detective said, "I need your help, Dr. Ames. You probably know the people in Mr. Thomas's life better than anyone else. He might even have told you about someone who threatened him."

"In the year he's been coming here, he never said anything that would incriminate anyone as a murderer." But even as he spoke, Dr. Ames was not quite sure this was true. Maybe somewhere in the memories of Jonathan's thirty-nine years he had mentioned someone who wanted him dead, though Dr. Ames had not caught the implication.

He asked the detective, "How did it happen?"

"At six o'clock this morning the regular cleaning woman at Aragon Press, which, as you know, occupies the whole of the brownstone on East Sixty-first Street, went into Mr. Thomas's office on the third floor. She was surprised to see him at that hour sitting in his chair, slumped over his desk. She thought he'd stayed late and fallen asleep. Then she saw a knife sticking out of his back. She screamed and ran for the police. The medical examiner says he was killed between ten and midnight."

In Jonathan's dream the killer had followed him at midnight—was this coincidence or an unconscious premonition, Dr. Ames wondered, knowing the unconscious part of the mind was far more sensitive to threats to survival than the conscious.

The detective said, "The motive wasn't robbery. Mr. Thomas had fifty-two dollars in his wallet and a two-hundred-dollar watch on his left wrist. A thief or drug addict would have stolen both. The killer either had a key to the building or Mr. Thomas let him in. The front door was locked, the cleaning woman opened it with her key. The back door is boarded up solid, and there was no forced entry."

"You think Mr. Thomas knew who killed him?"

"There was no sign of a struggle. The murderer stood behind him, looking over his shoulder. Maybe at something he was writing. There was a fresh ink stain on his third finger, right hand. The killer let him have it with the eight-inch knife—right up to the hilt. One blow was all it took. Thomas never knew what hit him."

The detective went on. "His wife said he often stayed late at the office to read manuscripts and that she'd taken two drinks and gone to bed. She didn't wake up, she said, until we called to tell her we found the body. The knife was wiped clean. No prints."

"Where did the knife come from?" Dr. Ames started to feel like a detective.

"From the small kitchen on the same floor. Mrs. Thomas said her husband liked to serve lunch to authors and agents. He claimed all the good restaurants were too noisy and crowded at noon for editorial thinking. Whatever that is."

He added, "It's a small firm, as you know. Just Mr. Thomas, his partner, and two secretaries. Each has a key to the building, so each is a suspect. As well as Mrs. Thomas and Jamey Brown's wife. Then there's the writer, Norma Donn. Mrs. Thomas says Miss Donn had been involved with her husband. He could have let her in the office after everyone had left."

"How do you think I can help?" Dr. Ames asked.

"By interviewing the suspects. I think you might catch something I wouldn't. Kind of a psychological angle that would show a killer's instinct."

"We've all got the killer's instinct if our lives are threatened." Dr. Ames smiled. Then he said thoughtfully, "I'm not trained to find real murderers. Just fantasied ones."

But he felt tempted. He was furious that someone dared take the life of a man he liked and respected. A man with the courage to start looking at his inner self, no easy task. Who had started slowly to change the pattern of his somewhat indulgent behavior.

He heard himself say, "If I give you a full day, will you set up all the interviews?"

Lonegan grinned. "Thanks, Doc. You can set the time at your convenience. The shrink comes first."

"As soon as possible. Tomorrow if you can. I would think immediacy is of prime importance." A pause, then, "Tell me, who do you think did it? On the basis of a 'hunch,' as they say. Hunches come from the unconscious and often prove valuable."

"Could be the wife. She might be lying about staying home all night, conked out. The wife's often the killer if her husband cheats on her. Thinks she can get away with it. The Unwritten Law."

Dr. Ames muttered, "The mistress is a good bet, too."

"Mrs. Thomas also told me her husband had some fierce fights with his partner. And with Brown's wife, Alicia, who did minor editing at home for the publishing house."

"That gives us four suspects right off the bat. Not bad for a start, Detective Lonegan."

"Call me Jack, Doc. We're partners in this."

As the detective put on his hat and coat, he said, "I'll phone you tonight and let you know the hours I set up for tomorrow. I'll ask everyone except Mrs. Thomas to meet you at Aragon Press in the afternoon. That will make your life easy. You'll probably have to see Mrs. Thomas at her home in the morning."

"I'll cancel all of tomorrow's appointments."

This time Lonegan put out his hand first and said, "Thank you, Doc." There was a pleased look on his craggy face as he walked out the door.

Dr. Ames thought of the detective's quiet determination, of the unusual open-mindedness he showed in believing a psychoanalyst might uncover psychological clues a detective would overlook. Most police officers were scornful of analysts, thought them twentieth-century witch doctors. Well, thanks to Jack Lonegan, he would now have a new title: Shrink of the Nineteenth Precinct. He hoped his patients and colleagues at the New York Psychoanalytic Institute would never find out.

As he headed for the kitchen to make a sandwich—he had lived and worked in this apartment high in the sky since his divorce three years before—he didn't even mind, he thought, that Lonegan called him a shrink. The detective had said the word not in contempt but with a certain admiration.

At ten the next morning Dr. Ames found himself in a taxi on his way to interview Elaine Thomas. As he traveled cross-city, he thought of how much he would miss Jonathan, the manner that sometimes mildly mocked yet was always courteous. The low, rich voice women found so seductive. The scholar with a love of words and an intelligence that respected Shakespeare, Proust, Freud.

He recognized at once the woman who opened the door. Jonathan had described his wife as "a tall, hard-faced blonde with steel-gray eyes that can shoot poison darts through you." Dr. Ames knew

Elaine's mother and father had been killed in a plane crash when she was five and that her wealthy aunt and uncle had brought her up. She had given Jonathan $300,000 to start his publishing business and never let him forget it. Dr. Ames wondered if she knew Jonathan wanted to leave her for Norma Donn. He told Dr. Ames he was very much in love with Norma.

Elaine was dressed in black silk, as though already in mourning. In a clipped, controlled voice she said, "Please come in, Dr. Ames." He knew she had not approved of her husband going to a psychoanalyst, fearful it would break up the marriage.

There was the black velvet couch Jonathan had described when he had fallen across it in pain one night after Elaine had accused him of an affair with Alicia Brown, his partner's wife. Elaine had struck him in the stomach, this tennis champion of their club in Purchase, when he called her a liar. In revenge, after he became involved with Norma, he brought her to his home one evening to enjoy sex on that black velvet couch when Elaine, in another rage, had flown to her uncle and aunt's oceanfront home in Palm Beach.

On the gold brocade wall over the white piano hung a portrait of Elaine. The artist had caught both the coldness of her eyes and her bony build, not an extra ounce of warm flesh. The thick golden carpet matched the walls; it was a room of opulence.

"Would you like coffee? Or a drink, Dr. Ames?" She studied his face, the first time she had seen her husband's analyst, no doubt having heard from Jonathan much about him. Patients usually quoted their analyst to a warring spouse to justify themselves, but this only increased hostility.

"No, thank you, Mrs. Thomas. I'd just like to talk to you."

"I would be a poor sport to refuse your request." As if she would never do anything unsportsmanlike. She sat down on a white velvet chair, indicating that the black velvet couch was for him. He thought, with amusement, She is putting me on the couch, reversing the roles of patient and analyst, she wants to be in command.

He had decided that his part in the investigation—the most he could do to help Lonegan—was to try to find out how much early violence each suspect had suffered at the hands of a parent. He was convinced, as numerous studies showed, that in order to be capable of wanton murder, you had to be subjected to violence in childhood, either as victim or as witness. The maddened fury that led to murder usually had its origins in actual violence during the early years of life.

Violence became the way of getting rid of anger that could not be controlled or contained.

Before he could ask a question, she said, "I want you to know I thought Jonathan the most attractive man I ever met. But it didn't take long to realize he had an ego the size of an elephant and the emotional stamina of a dying flounder. Even the day I walked down the aisle of Saint John's Cathedral on Uncle Eric's arm, I thought, Get out of this, Elaine, get out *now,* while you have a last chance. But I was too trapped by Jonathan's charm."

"How long did you feel trapped?"

"Until the moment I heard he was dead."

And, Dr. Ames wondered, did she murder Jonathan to escape the trap? Was she telling him Jonathan's death was the only way to free herself of his lethal charm and unfaithfulness?

Her manner became more confiding, even apologetic. "I made a fool of myself recently at an office party. I got a bit high—two quick drinks on an empty stomach. I walked over to that bitch, Norma Donn, and said, 'Why don't you keep your overheated little hands off my husband and on your typewriter keys where they belong?' Jonathan was embarrassed. He asked his secretary, that mousy Susan Michaels, who does all the dirty work including arranging office parties, to take me home in a taxi. I knew I had made a fool of myself, but I felt righteously angry."

He waited for her to go on, as he would wait for a patient to choose the words leading to revelations that pictured tormenting conflicts.

"The night before he was killed, Jonathan said he had been thinking things over and wanted to save our marriage. He promised he was finished with Norma. I think he told her this the next day, and she killed him in a rage."

So the wife was accusing the mistress. Would the mistress accuse the wife, he wondered. He decided to explore Elaine's past and said, "Jonathan told me you lost your mother and father when you were five. You must have felt devastated as a little girl."

"I don't think I felt anything but numb." Her face held no expression of sorrow.

So this is what she had been "steeling" herself against all her life, he thought. No wonder the cold, detached look, the powerful tennis smash, the lack of emotion at her husband's death. Jonathan's murder would trigger the older, more devastating grief and anger she had felt when her parents were taken from her. A loss she could not accept either then or now. A loss that would have seemed like some willful and cruel assault by an evil God or fate and might be a spur to later acts of violence if she felt the threat of abandonment or rejection—the most wounding of all blows.

Elaine was saying, "I know Jonathan slept around. I even suspect him of a fling with that dishrag Alicia Brown. I wouldn't put it past her to have wanted to break up our marriage."

It takes two to cause a marriage to fail, Dr. Ames thought, but he knew Jonathan was somewhat of a space-age Don Juan, unwilling to hear the unhappy truths about himself from a woman who was supposed to love and honor him. It was difficult enough to accept those truths from an analyst who slowly and sympathetically helped him to understand them. Norma Donn had been only the last of a number of affairs. Jonathan promised little, and the women made few demands, seduced by his casual charm, though eventually they grew angry at his refusal to offer more than a small share of himself. He had a crippled capacity for emotional commitment.

Had Elaine flown into a fury when Jonathan did not come home the night before last, believing he had finally run out on her? Had she lied to Lonegan about staying in the apartment, instead rushed wildly to her husband's office, and, knowing where the kitchen knife lay, grabbed it, plunged it with all the power of her muscular right arm into the back she felt had betrayed her so many times atop another woman?

The hardest thing to do in the grip of intense passions such as jealousy or the rage at desertion is nothing. Dr. Ames was not sure that Elaine, awash in alcoholic fury, was capable of doing nothing.

A warm February sun, one of those days hinting of spring, had melted any remaining snow as he climbed the steps of the brownstone whose front door bore a bronze plate that read ARAGON PRESS. He was to have lunch with Jonathan's partner, Jamey Brown, then interview his wife, Alicia, the two secretaries, and finally Norma Donn.

Only two days ago Jonathan had walked up these steps and the morning after was carried down them, his stilled, lean body covered by the coroner's white sheet. Dr. Ames pushed the button underneath the bronze plate, a buzzer sounded, and he opened the door. He knew, from Jonathan's description, that the first floor contained only books and unused furniture. Jamey's office was on the second, and Dr. Ames climbed the staircase of the old town house taken over by Aragon. Chandeliers still hung in the halls, dark green carpeting covered the floors.

On the second level a nervous young woman typed away at a desk in the hall as though determined to carry out the day's work in the wake of murder. He said, "I'm Dr. Ames. I have an appointment with Mr. Brown for one o'clock."

She whispered, "Please go in, he's expecting you," pointing to the closed door of the floor's only large room.

A slight, aesthetic-looking man in his early forties stood up from his desk, walked over and shook Dr. Ames's hand desperately, as though only its warmth would keep him going. He said, "I'm so glad you're helping the police, Dr. Ames. We've *got* to find Jonathan's killer." He took Dr. Ames's coat and hat and hung them in a closet.

Jamey Brown wore thick glasses over alert brown eyes that kept peering into Dr. Ames's blue eyes as though to find all the answers. He had ordered roast beef sandwiches and coffee, said, "Let's talk as we eat. It will save you time. Ask me anything. I warn you, though, I'm still in shock. My partner, and also my best friend, murdered on the spot where he worked."

"Have you any idea who might have killed Mr. Thomas?" Dr. Ames asked as he sat across the desk from Jamey, unwrapping his roast beef sandwich. He did not think Jamey was the murderer, from what Jonathan had told him of Jamey, but Jamey might reveal a fact that would either implicate or clear Elaine or Norma. Or divulge another, as yet unknown, suspect.

"I don't think Jonathan had an enemy in the world, Dr. Ames. He went out of his way to make friends. Janitors as well as book-review editors. I knew him for twelve years, ever since we were editors at Macmillan together. We became close friends after Jonathan married Elaine and I married Alicia. Five years ago, when I inherited money from my father, a prosperous Wall Street broker, and Jonathan borrowed three hundred thousand dollars from Elaine's uncle, we started Aragon. For the first three years our books were financial disasters. Then Norma Donn came along, and suddenly we were solvent."

Dr. Ames said, "I'm afraid I have to be unsubtle, but we just don't have much time. Do you and your wife like Elaine Thomas?"

Hesitation, then, "It's hard to really like a woman, even though she's rather beautiful, and at times gracious, who drinks too much too often and, in an alcoholic haze, loudly and sometimes viciously denounces her husband in front of his friends. We overlooked her behavior because we loved Jonathan."

"Now a second question. What do you think of Norma Donn?"

"She's a sensationally good popular writer. I'm grateful to her for the money she brings in. But underneath that front of sweetness and charm, she's a complete bitch. Far worse than Elaine, whose bitchery is at least out in the open. I think Norma has been aching to bust Jonathan's marriage sky-high. *She* could have killed Jonathan if she was opposed. I don't think Elaine could."

Then worriedly, "Detective Lonegan asked me questions for nearly two hours yesterday. Almost as if he believed *I* was guilty. Maybe he thinks I juggled the books, Jonathan caught me in the act, and I stabbed him to keep from going to prison." A nervous laugh.

And maybe that's only your fantasy, thought Dr. Ames, your wish to be unsquare enough, just once, to cheat on your partner. But act it out? I doubt it, from what I sense about your high moral standards. And yet stranger things . . .

Jamey, still anxious, asked, "Why do you think Lonegan set up an appointment for you to see my wife? She has no key to the building. Unless"—again a nervous laugh—"she secretly had one made."

Was he hinting that his wife and Jonathan might have been having an affair? Dr. Ames wondered. Was Alicia Brown possibly a third important woman in Jonathan's life? A woman Jonathan failed to mention because he was afraid his analyst would disapprove of his affair with the wife of his best friend? It was unbelievable how patients held back the truths that would set them free because they thought the truth might degrade them in the eyes of the analyst.

"Detective Lonegan wanted me to see your wife because she knew Jonathan and Elaine so well," he explained, though he was not at all sure this was the reason.

Alicia Brown was a slight, pale woman, even her lipstick seemed colorless. Jamey left the office after introducing her to Dr. Ames, saying he would work in Jonathan's office, on the floor above, for the rest of the afternoon. Alicia insisted she keep on her mink hat and coat, saying, "I have to warm up first."

Dr. Ames asked, "Did you know Jonathan was having an affair with Norma Donn?"

"You'd need to be deaf, dumb and blind not to know." As her voice turned harsh, he wondered if she were in love with Jonathan. If so, she would be a suspect. And if Jamey knew, so, too, would he.

"Excuse me for being so direct, Mrs. Brown, but there isn't time for useless questions. Were you in love with Jonathan?"

A gasp, then, "What a thing to say! That's an insulting question, Dr. Ames."

"I ask because Elaine Thomas suspected her husband of having an affair with you."

"I don't believe it! She would have said something to me if she thought so. Never once did Jonathan and I see each other alone except to discuss editorial changes in a book. I'm sure he had no romantic feelings for me." Bitterly, "I'm scarcely a glamour girl, like the rest of his women."

"Did you have romantic feelings for him?"

She looked unhappy. "I may have flirted with him. The way married women do at times with attractive men. Jonathan made it easy for you to express feelings when you were with him. He was so open. Not like—" And she was silent.

"Like whom?"

"Like Jamey. He always has so much on his mind. He can be impatient at times. It's like walking on eggs if he is in an angry mood."

"Did you and your husband see the Thomases often?"

"About once a week. It was a social ritual."

"How do you feel about Jonathan's murder?"

"Need you ask?" She huddled deep into the mink. "I'm going to miss him. It's as if my best friend had vanished. Jamey and I will both miss him. Very, *very* much."

He felt her feelings were layered over with such strong defenses they would take months to break through. Though she and her husband were suspects, he did not believe either were murderers, nor did they seem to connect in any way to Jonathan's dream.

After she left, he was once again haunted by the dream. Every so often, like a lit buoy in a dark sea, the thought surfaced to awareness from the deeper part of his mind that Jonathan's dream held the answer to it all, an answer he could not as yet decipher.

Marie Sinetti, secretary to Jamey, appeared at three o'clock. She lost some of her nervousness as she openly expressed her terror.

"I've worked here only two months, and to have a murder so close is unbelievable," she announced as she sat down.

She stared at him in awe, then said, "This is the first time I've ever met a real live psycho—psycho—"

"Psychoanalyst."

"Thank you."

"Do you have other duties besides acting as secretary to Mr. Brown?"

"I also double as telephone operator most of the time."

"Did Mr. Thomas make an unusual number of calls to any particular person?"

"Not through me. But he could have used his private line."

"Even though you haven't been here long, do you know of anyone who hated him enough to kill him?"

She shook the tight curls of her blond hair. "Not a one. I can't understand a murder happening in a respectable place like a publishing house."

"You see everyone who enters this building during working hours. Did anyone come in during the past few weeks who struck you as especially disturbed?"

"If you want my honest opinion, I think that wife of Mr. Thomas's is the most disturbed person of all. The afternoon of the night he was murdered, she came in drunk and said she *had* to see him. He was in conference with an important author and—"

"Which author?"

"The lady who wrote the bestseller. Miss Donn."

"I didn't mean to interrupt. Please go on. What did you do when Mrs. Thomas arrived?"

"I rang his line. I told him his wife was here and insisted on seeing him. He said to tell her he was in an important conference and would see her later at home."

"What did she do?"

"She said she was too much of a lady to break into his office to find out the truth, so the hell with him. She almost slipped and fell as she rushed out the door. She didn't even say good-bye."

"Did Miss Donn appear upset when she came downstairs?"

"She was her usual sugar-sweet self. She, at least, said good-bye."

"Did Mr. Thomas seem upset when you saw him?"

"I didn't see him the rest of the day. I left at five. He was still in his office."

"What sort of people come to this office?"

"Mostly writers and literary agents. And delivery boys with manuscripts and books." She added, "No one that looked like he might murder Mr. Thomas, if that's what you mean."

That was just what he meant, but he did not, in his analytic heart, believe Jonathan had been murdered by person unknown.

After Marie Sinetti left, Jonathan's secretary, Susan Michaels, walked into the room, slowly, hesitantly, as though not sure she was welcome. She appeared far from Dr. Ames's image of the "mousy" but quietly brisk, no-nonsense young woman he had fantasied as Jonathan's "efficient" girl Friday. Funny, Elaine had described her as mousy, and Jonathan, as efficient. Dr. Ames supposed Susan could be both.

She was striking, with hair the color of copper touched with ruby, falling to her shoulders in a straight line of sheen. Full-figured in a manner unfashionable in *Vogue* but popular with many men, including himself. She stood as if waiting for his command.

"Please sit down, Miss Michaels."

She lowered herself into the chair with a tentative air, as though testing the texture. Her dark blue suit had an expensive look in fabric and cut, as did the navy patent leather pumps. She did not seem the ordinary secretary, she possessed a finishing-school look.

"When did you start work here, Miss Michaels?"

"A year ago." Her low voice was also slightly hesitant, like her stride.

"Do you like working here?"

"Very much. It's informal and so—so—comfortable."

He thought that an odd word to use about an office, perhaps she referred to the comfort of the kitchen for providing food and coffee, or the chandeliers and carpeting, homey remnants of former town house tenants.

"You were Mr. Thomas's secretary?"

"Yes."

Unlike Marie Sinetti, she did not speak of his death, horrified by it. He asked, "How did you and Mr. Thomas get along?"

"Very well." For a moment her eyes looked sad, as if she were lost to an unspoken sorrow.

"Was he a thoughtful employer?" He could not imagine Jonathan otherwise.

"He was always very thoughtful, very helpful. He even gave me special time off I needed for an emergency."

"What was that?"

"Not the crisis kind. I mean like an appointment to see a doctor."

"Is something wrong with your health, Miss Michaels?"

"My health is fine." The brown eyes turned away and stared out the window, though he sensed she did not see the street. He rebuked himself for so prying a question, one that might have pointlessly alarmed her. What could the state of her health have to do with Jonathan's murder?

He returned to what he hoped was more pertinent inquiry. "Do you know anyone who held a grudge against Mr. Thomas?"

After all, in terms of hours, she had spent more time with Jonathan during the past year than anyone, including his wife. If Jonathan had an unknown enemy, she might well be the one to know.

She shook her head negatively. "No one held a grudge against him that I'm aware of."

A veritable Greek chorus, he thought, except for Elaine, who hated Norma Donn and accused her of the murder.

"What about Mrs. Thomas?"

The brown eyes flickered. "I know little about her except the sound of her voice when she called to speak to her husband on the office line if his private wire was busy. She might phone several times in one day. Or not for a week."

"Didn't you once ride in a taxi with her after an office party for Norma Donn?"

The hesitant voice. "I believe we were in the cab only ten minutes."

"What did you talk about?"

"She asked about my background. Where I went to college."

"What college did you attend?"

"Barnard. Majored in English literature."

"Are you from New York?"

"I was born here. My father's a surgeon. On the staff of New York Hospital."

She looked as if she needed a rest, as though she had worked too hard. Or perhaps Jonathan's murder had struck her more deeply than she was revealing. He said, "Thank you for your time, Miss Michaels," and watched her walk out as she had entered, in that tentative manner.

Another dead end, he thought. One more suspect to go.

Norma Donn, the whirlwind upsetting the lives of Jonathan and his wife, was prompt for her four-o'clock appointment. The woman who flung open the door of Jamey's office was petite, her piquant face framed by black ringlets curled high on her head. The face looked familiar. Dr. Ames realized he had seen it in advertisements on the book page of *The New York Times*.

She held out a soft hand. "I'm so happy to meet you, Dr. Ames. Jonathan loved you." Her voice was just this side of breathless. The welcome given him by Jonathan's latest mistress was quite different from that of the cold Elaine. And there was a startling physical contrast between the two special women in Jonathan's life. Norma, tiny, fragile, jet-black hair. Elaine, tall, athletic, Viking blond.

Norma took off her Norwegian-wolf three-quarter-length coat, revealing a demure black wool dress and black cardigan buttoned close to her, like a shield. Her cornflower-blue eyes were wide, naïve. Such an aura of innocence would have been part of her appeal to Jonathan.

"Thank you for coming here," he said as they sat down. "Detective Lonegan suggested I interview everyone who knew Jonathan Thomas closely."

"Does that mean I'm a suspect?" The soft eyes looked wounded.

"Nothing personal, Miss Donn. Nor official. I'm not a police officer. I'm only trying to help Detective Lonegan, if I can. As you know, Jonathan Thomas was my patient."

She said, "Do you want me to speak freely, Dr. Ames? As if I were on your couch, no verbal holds barred? Jonathan said the only crime on the couch was not to say everything that came into your head."

"A psychoanalyst is never offended by words. Only by the omission of them if they have occurred to the patient's mind. It makes the work of analysis so much harder and it *is* self-defeating for the patient. I imagine that's what Jonathan meant. Please say anything that comes to mind, Miss Donn. It can only help us find Jonathan's murderer." He thought, Unless it is you and you tell lies.

"In the first place, I can't believe Jonathan is dead. I look up from my typewriter and think I see him standing in the door. Or the outline of a coat tossed on the bed suddenly takes his shape. I miss him so much." She hunted for a tissue in her sweater pocket, daintily wiped away tears.

"Did you know Jonathan well?"

"In one way. Not in another."

"What do you mean?" That was a curious way to put it.

"I knew him well sexually and as a fine editor. But he would never talk to me about his past. As though there were something mysterious in his life. I thought he would tell me if he felt like it. But he never did."

"What do you mean by 'mysterious'?" Nothing in Jonathan's life had seemed a mystery to Dr. Ames.

"I really don't know. He never mentioned any specific mystery." Bitterly, "Except the mystery of why he married the un-fair Elaine."

She went on, "To me, Jonathan seemed confident one minute, shy the next. That split was part of his spell. I knew he had played around but I also knew he was ready to leave Elaine for me. He told me, 'When I'm with you, I feel alive. When I'm with Elaine, I feel dead.' With Jonathan and me every moment was precious because of its forbidden-fruit quality."

"You seemed honest with each other about your feelings."

"Jonathan was never a hypocrite. Especially about sex. With him there were no taboos. When you loved, you loved fully. I had never felt that way about a man. With other men, sometimes I couldn't bring it off—have an orgasm."

Probably one reason, he thought, she had to create a book called *The Female Orgasm*. Writers unconsciously often chose those topics that expressed their conflicts in an effort to solve them.

"Tell me about your parents, Miss Donn. What does your father do?"

"He's a physicist, teaches at Harvard University. He walked out of the house when I was ten. Mother never married again. She cursed my father for her fate. He still has to support her, in addition to his second wife and two children."

"How did you feel when your father left?"

"Relieved."

"Relieved to lose a father?"

She stared at him, then said, "Why not? He and Mother hated each other. She told me he hadn't slept with her for four years, that he made it with every call girl in Boston. And Boston is the tenth largest city in the country." Ironic laugh.

"How did you feel when she told you this?" Only an emotionally disturbed mother would try to enrage a daughter with stories of her father's sexual escapades, he thought.

"You're asking for the truth, aren't you, Dr. Ames? Truth I may never have faced before." Her eyes lost the little-girl look, hardened. Another contrast to Elaine, who had started off acting tough, then softened.

"We're both looking for the truth, Miss Donn. You as a writer and me as a psychoanalyst."

Her next words came with a chilling intensity. "That bastard! I hated him! He knew about esoteric formulas for gases but nothing about loving a child." Tears came to her eyes, as though the ten-year-old girl inside was watching her father walk out of the door forever.

He reminded himself she was not on his couch, that he was there to find the murderer of Jonathan. He asked, "Miss Donn, did anyone ever hurt you physically when you were a child?"

She wiped away the tears with another tissue from her sweater pocket. "Only me, myself. I fell down ice-skating and broke my arm. My mother and father may have wounded me with words but they never struck me. Nor did Jonathan. Never, *never* Jonathan."

Then she asked, "Are you going to his funeral? The paper said it's at Campbell's, noon tomorrow."

"I'll mourn for Jonathan in my own way." He had been mourning for Jonathan since the detective's first call.

"That's how I feel too."

He asked, "Miss Donn, who do you think might have killed Jonathan in such a savage manner?"

Again the hidden snarl, the sound of fury in her. "Who but that uptight, possessive wife!"

"Why do you think so?"

"He tried to leave her for half a year. She held him by threatening to sue for divorce and tell the papers all about us. We knew it would ruin our reputations, particularly mine. As well as hurt the sale of my books. So Jonathan stayed with her."

Perhaps also, Dr. Ames thought, Jonathan did not want to cut himself off financially from Elaine, since he still owed her the $300,000 that had helped start the publishing house.

"Why would Jonathan's wife want to murder him at just this time?" he asked.

"Because he told her, the night before he was murdered, that he intended to move out. No matter what threats she made." Norma sounded as though this proved Elaine's guilt.

Jonathan had told him, in discussing the dream, that he felt he could not stay with Elaine much longer, even though Elaine herself had reported he had changed his mind and wanted to work at the marriage. Was Elaine lying to save her pride, perhaps her reputation, if she were the killer? Was Norma lying when she claimed Jonathan was leaving home? One of these ladies was lying. Jonathan may even have lied to his analyst, afraid of his disapproval. Or possibly Jonathan, who consciously hated to hurt a woman but unconsciously hurt every woman who loved him by deserting her, had been confused.

Had not known which woman to choose and told each a different story, the one she wanted to hear.

He decided to try a final question. "Jonathan fought recently with his partner about whether a certain book idea should be pursued. Do you know if there was deep animosity between the two men?" A book could, if successful, bring in as much as a bank heist.

A trill of a laugh. "Those two men admired and respected each other deeply. No matter how often they argued about a book. Jamey could never have lifted a finger against Jonathan, though he fought with words at times."

Dr. Ames needed to think. He felt as though the day had been filled with analytic hours. He could not afford to feel weary, he had to use every remaining moment to try to pinpoint the killer. He would not give up until midnight, the "witching" hour Jonathan had mentioned in the dream.

He stood up and said, "Thank you, Miss Donn. You have been very helpful."

"If I contributed anything, I'm happy." Then anxiously, "I don't think Detective Lonegan believes my alibi. I went to the movies, but I can't produce my ticket. Threw it away. And the ticket seller can't identify me. Says I'm just a face in the crowd."

He had not thought of alibis, that was not part of his line of inquiry. At the moment he felt himself on the thin edge of turning in his amateur-detective standing and returning happily to the simple frustrations of psychoanalytic treatment.

There was a knock on the door. It was Marie Sinetti. "Detective Lonegan wants to speak to you on the phone, Dr. Ames."

He helped Norma Donn back into the Norwegian wolf, watched her slip away, picked up the phone.

"How are you doing, Doc?" Lonegan sounded even huskier than usual, as though he, too, had had a hard day. "I figured you were about finished."

"I wish I had something to contribute, Jack. But I haven't found out a thing." A sigh.

"I got some news." In a happier tone.

"I'm glad one of us has."

"I spent an hour this afternoon with Mrs. Thomas. She broke down and admitted she lied about where she was when her husband was murdered. Her maid threatened to tell the police, so Mrs. Thomas decided to confess. She said she left the apartment about ten for a walk in Central Park. She didn't dare tell us because she was afraid we would suspect her of going to her husband's office and killing him. She swears she did not see him that night."

"Do you know whether she was sober or drunk when she took the walk?"

"She says she was high when she started out. Sober when she returned."

"What are you going to do?"

"I need more proof to arrest her. But it's a start." Then, "Are you going home now, Doc?" As though worried that he needed sleep.

"I may stay here for a while. Try to sort through what I've heard today."

"Will you let me know if you have any ideas?"

"Of course. Up until midnight?"

"Even after if you get only a wisp of a clue." He added, "Psychic clue, of course."

Dr. Ames hung up, feeling utterly frustrated. As he did when a patient's session yielded little he could interpret to the patient and thus help him understand more about himself.

Jamey walked in to reclaim his office. He also asked, "Did you find out anything?"

"Very little. But thank you, Mr. Brown, for the use of your office. It made my task easier."

"Happy to help you. Though it felt weird to try to work up there." He shuddered, raising his eyes to the ceiling as though expecting to see blood seep through from Jonathan's office directly above.

Then he asked, "Would you like a lift home? The day's about shot. My car's parked down the street near Third Avenue."

Not aware why, except that he felt if anything more were to be learned, it would be on the spot where Jonathan was murdered, Dr. Ames heard himself saying, "Do you mind if I sit here and unwind?"

"Stay as long as you want. The front door locks automatically when you leave." He winced. "As I suppose it did behind the killer." Then worriedly, "Are you sure you'll be all right? Everyone's left by now."

Dr. Ames knew what Jamey meant. Jonathan had thought he was safe alone in the building. Might not the murderer return to the scene of his crime if he suspected Jonathan's analyst had picked up some lead to his identity during the day of questioning?

"I'm not worried about an attack on me, Mr. Brown," he said. "Only my patients want to kill me. And then it's only in fantasy—I hope."

Jamey took his black overcoat from the closet, slinging it across his left arm. He shook Dr. Ames's hand as though loath to let go and said, "I'm sure you'll come up with something."

"I wish I were sure."

"Call me if you want anything. My home number is in the book. Sutton Place South."

Jamey's words trailed after him and his footsteps faded as he descended the marble stairs. There was the slam of the front door.

He was now alone in the building where Jonathan had been viciously stabbed two nights before, no chance to defend himself. Jonathan had been sitting at his desk, perhaps writing as Lonegan suggested, when someone stole up from behind, raised the sharp knife, and struck it deep into his unsuspecting back. Dr. Ames felt a sudden surge of fear, the ancient instinct of self-preservation. He fought it, telling himself that no one was out to kill him, the murderer was doubtless miles from the spot, and he should not let himself be haunted by his own murderous wishes, turned on himself because of guilt.

There was now one thing he had to do. The act he had avoided all day. The chief reason he had stayed on alone. He *had* to walk upstairs and see Jonathan's office. No one had suggested he do this, so he had spent the hours closeted in Jamey's office, except for the time spent briefly in the men's room at the rear of the second floor.

He walked out into the hall, chandelier-lit in the winter's early dark, then looked to the right and saw steps curving upward. He forced himself to climb what seemed a marble mountain. He clicked on the wall light at the top of the stairs. Desk, chair, and files filled the hall. This was where Susan Michaels worked.

He entered the one large room on the floor, Jonathan's office, turned on the light. The room was paneled in pine, books lined two walls from floor to ceiling. A six-foot wooden table was piled high with manuscripts. An emerald-green tufted couch with three thick pillows, matching the green carpet, ran the length of a third wall.

He walked slowly to the teakwood desk, lowered himself into the brown leather chair where Jonathan had sat over the hours, the days, the years. He visualized Jonathan puffing at a pipe. He never smoked in his analytic sessions, but here on his desk stood a rack of pipes of different shapes and woods. It was an austere room, no photograph of Elaine or anyone else. Which of the two women closest to him had preferred Jonathan dead? Which of the two had carried murder in her heart from the days of childhood? Elaine, mother and father taken violently from her when she was five, would feel murderous all her life. No matter how deep the love of her aunt and uncle, it would never be enough, she would always rage at her devastating loss. Norma, who openly hated her father for deserting her, would have wished to kill if Jonathan repeated the original heartbreaking abandonment.

Suddenly he heard something creak in the hall, something alien to that office, something unfriendly to Jonathan and to himself. And at once he felt foolish as he looked for a possible weapon. There was a letter opener on the table with the manuscripts, sharp and shaped like a scimitar. He took it up and, with a courage he knew to be false, walked into the hall. Empty. Should he stalk through the whole building to make sure no killer lurked in a corner ready to spring at him? Ridiculous. He was acting like a feeble, fantasy-ridden old maid.

Again the creaking sound, this time louder. It came from the room at the rear, the kitchen, the room that once held the murder weapon. Holding the letter opener tightly, he tiptoed into the kitchen. He switched on the light, but the room was empty except for stove, sink, refrigerator, cupboards, and the rack over the sink. The rack, now empty too, that once held the knife.

The creaking noise again. At the window. He looked out, the bare branch of a tree was brushing back and forth against the pane in the February wind. He smiled, shook his head. Still looking for an outside assassin, when you know perfectly well you are your own executioner, Ames, he thought. After all those years on the couch.

Chastened, he walked back to Jonathan's office and sank again into the leather chair. He told himself, Make one last try before you give up the psychic ship. Lean back in the chair, the chair in which Jonathan was murdered, close your eyes, relax, let your thoughts flow, as you're always telling patients to do. Maybe if you don't try so hard, the deeper part of your mind will help you discover a clue.

Just as he listened to a patient, waiting for a key word or phrase to highlight the truth, so he allowed his mind to roam over what he had heard in the past hours from Jonathan's loved and not-so-loved ones. One thought kept hovering—the thought that most of what he had heard was insignificant, that the real clue would be found in something Jonathan had said in that final session, either in the dream or in his thoughts about it, or both. Or might there also be a clue in the very room where he was murdered? A room that held so much of him.

Dr. Ames opened his eyes and looked around Jonathan's office. Was there something in it, something of Jonathan, that might reveal the murderer? He thought of Charcot's words to Freud: "Look at the same things again and again until they themselves begin to speak." Perhaps there was some "thing" in this room, some slight clue Jonathan had left him, that would speak. He had the sudden feeling, almost a foreknowledge, it would be the desk. The very spot on which Jonathan had been so brutally destroyed.

Why the desk? He remembered "desk" had appeared in Jonathan's account of the dream. Jonathan spoke of knowing, as the murderer stalked him, that Dr. Ames waited for him upstairs at his "desk." No accidents or meaningless images or words in a dream. The word *desk* was there for a purpose.

The top of the teakwood desk was clear except for the pipe rack. If anything else had been on it, the police had taken it as evidence. There were only three places to search. Two drawers on the right side, each about seven inches deep, and the horizontal drawer to the left, about three inches deep, extending the remaining length of the desk, with space underneath for Jonathan to stretch his long legs.

Dr. Ames opened the upper drawer on the right. It was stacked neatly with letter paper, imprinted with Jonathan's name and the name of the publishing house. He opened the drawer under it, which was filled with rows of envelopes to match the letter paper, plus four unused notepads and a dozen sharpened pencils. Nothing in either drawer to serve as a clue.

Then he opened the long, narrow drawer to the left, the third and last place to search. He whistled in surprise. This drawer was in complete contrast to the other two, far more like the private Jonathan. Here he had apparently relaxed, tossed in odds and ends to form a glorious potpourri of trivia—stray stamps, paper clips, rubber bands, broken pipes, tubes of glue, a tape measure, a nail file, a slide rule. Could such disorder have a purpose? Did it convey a message? Was Jonathan consciously or unconsciously trying to tell anyone who looked through his drawer that it held a lead to his killer?

He pulled the drawer out of the desk and carried it to the green couch. There he emptied it and looked and looked at its contents, as Charcot had told Freud to do, hoping the inert jumble would speak to him. But it told him nothing. He sifted through the contents, thinking that perhaps one "thing" contained a hidden message. Not everything was fantasy. Fact had to emerge to give a core to the fantasy. He picked up the items one by one, carefully examined each, and replaced it in the drawer. They all seemed innocent enough, serving their special function.

Wrong again, he thought. It was *his* fantasy, his wishful thinking, that the desk yield a clue. The desk, heart of Jonathan's life. Not women but work was his life. Work could never be untrue to you, berate you, make demands you could not meet.

He lifted the drawer off the couch, walked back to the desk, and bent over it, drawer in hand. He found himself staring into the empty space the drawer customarily filled, staring as though mesmerized. What am I doing? he asked. He shook his head, as though to clear away the strange paralysis, started to slip the drawer back into its proper place.

As he did so, at the very back of the empty space he saw what looked like a small scrap of paper. It had evidently slipped out of the overflowing drawer and remained stuck to a corner in the rear. He stretched his right arm into the space above the wooden ledge that supported the drawer. He gently dislodged and pulled out the scrap of paper.

It was the stub of a check. It carried the date February 6, 1985, in Jonathan's handwriting. A handwriting Dr. Ames knew well from the checks Jonathan gave him each month. This was February 8, which meant that Jonathan had made out the check the day he was murdered.

The check was for $1200. Jonathan had identified the payee by the initials S.M.

A chill of sudden knowledge beyond all doubt seized Dr. Ames as Jonathan's dream again flashed into mind. At last he understood the dream. The identity of the killer lay in Jonathan's dream, as Dr. Ames had suspected but could not decipher. A dream often used symbols to designate a person, and those symbols now seemed clear.

The red hair of the assassin. "Red" also in the assassin's eyes, reddened perhaps by tears. Red for hair, red for tears, red for blood. And the very hour the dream took place, midnight, the "witching hour," Jonathan had said. Then called it "the hour of witches," as though referring to a woman. And midnight, twelve, shorthand for twelve hundred dollars.

He could see Jonathan writing out the check to the murderer, then hastily scrawling the initials on the stub and stuffing it into the debris of the drawer in order to leave a tangible clue in case something he feared actually did happen.

In his thoughts about the dream Jonathan even mentioned the

name of his murderer. Used the word *deadly* about her. He pictured her in the dream not only as his killer but as a "robber." He must have felt she robbed him of the $1200. Was the money blackmail? A loan? A gift?

Dr. Ames wondered if he should call Lonegan and tell him about the stub. Then he decided she was more likely to speak freely if he were alone. He turned to the M's in the telephone directory. Her name was listed, she lived only three blocks from the office. He thought of phoning to tell her he was on his way, then realized a call might alarm her, she might slip out. He could only hope she would be home. If she were not, he would eat dinner and return again later. He felt a strange exhilaration. The feeling of revenge upon the killer who blacked out Jonathan's life.

He placed the check stub in his wallet and returned the long drawer to its rightful place. He turned off the light in Jonathan's office, then in the hall, then downstairs in Jamey's office after taking his hat and coat out of the closet. Then he walked down the last flight of the marble staircase, opened the front door, and stepped out into the freeze of the February night. He heard the door lock behind him.

On the last step to the street, the seventh step, he turned and looked up at the third-floor window. He had the momentary fantasy that Jonathan stood there, shy smile on his face, waving.

She lived in one of those squat red-brick apartment houses that dot the body of Manhattan like the measles, he thought. In the outer lobby he pressed the buzzer beside her name.

Her low voice over the intercom: "Who is it?"

He felt relieved, she was home. He would not have to spend hours watching the doorway for her return. "It's Dr. William Ames. May I come up?"

"Oh." Silence. Then, "Fourth floor to the rear. Four-G."

The elevator, empty except for him, wheezed its reluctant way to the fourth floor, where the door jerked open. He stepped into a cheerless hallway, turned to the rear, and rang the bell of the door marked 4-G. It opened in slow motion, as though the occupant were not sure she would let him in.

She stood there, red hair streaming to her shoulders. She looked far smaller. She had shed the high heels and, still in the dark blue suit, wore battered silver bedroom slippers. Her eyes were almost unseeing, as though she were walking in her sleep.

He placed his hat and coat on a small wooden table in the one large room that served as bedroom and living room. The Castro couch made that clear, as did a large bureau on which stood three bottles of perfume and an earring stand. There were no paintings, no photographs, it was as characterless as a hotel.

He sat down on the straight-backed chair, leaving her the more comfortable chintz-covered armchair. He asked, "Do you mind if I ask a few more questions, Miss Michaels?"

She shook her head in assent, almost as though she had expected him. She seemed to be pulling herself awake.

"How did you get your job as secretary to Mr. Thomas?"

"My father is an old friend of his. He called Jon—Mr. Thomas—and asked if by any chance he needed a secretary. Mr. Thomas said he did, that his secretary was just leaving to join the Peace Corps. I wanted to learn all about the publishing business and I was advised this was the way to start. That secretaries got promoted to editors."

"You told me your father was a surgeon. What's his first name?" Knowing it before she answered.

"Charles."

Of course. Charles Michaels, a former classmate of Dr. Ames at Harvard Medical School. More than that, it was Charley who had recommended Dr. Ames to Jonathan when he asked for the name of a psychoanalyst. Dr. Ames recalled that Charley, as a young surgeon, had taken care of Jonathan's mother during her terminal illness, as Jonathan had reported on the couch. There were psychic wheels within wheels in this tragedy.

Dr. Ames asked, "When did Jonathan first meet your father?"

"About twenty years ago. My father was called in by the Thomases' family doctor to find out if Mrs. Thomas had cancer. He operated, then told them there was no hope."

She seemed willing to tell the truth. She could have lied, said an employment agency had sent her to Aragon Press, and he might never have known otherwise. He hoped she would tell the truth all the way. He tried to picture her plunging the kitchen knife into Jonathan's back. He had to hear the facts. It was hardly legal proof of guilt that Jonathan had a nightmare in which his killer's hair was red. The courts would laugh if that were offered as evidence.

He decided to be direct, there was no time to circle the truth. "Why, on the day he died, did Jonathan make out a check to you for twelve hundred dollars?"

No answer. Only the eyes, now sad, staring at him.

"Were you blackmailing him?" He hoped he sounded not accusatory but firm, a tone he used with patients in trying to help them face some terrifying truth.

Her left hand flew out helplessly in an arc. "I wasn't blackmailing Mr. Thomas. I'm no blackmailer."

"I didn't think you were." It was hard to believe Charley Michaels' daughter would need to resort to blackmail. "But how do you explain the twelve hundred dollars?"

She pulled at the strands of the red hair as though in pain. Then, in that hesitant voice, "You were Jonathan's analyst." She had dropped the "Mr. Thomas," he noted. "Didn't he tell you?"

"Tell me what?" Puzzled. What had Jonathan concealed about *her*?

"What *did* Jonathan tell you about me?"

"He said you were a marvelous secretary. He seemed very grateful to you for being so efficient." He omitted the adjective *deadly* Jonathan had used to precede *efficient*. An adjective, Dr. Ames now realized, that had been a very important psychic clue.

"That's all he told you?"

"That's all, Miss Michaels."

"Why would he hide it from you?" She looked astounded.

"Hide what?"

"That he got me pregnant?"

Dr. Ames felt his second shock in two days. First, Jonathan's murder. Then this revelation. He suddenly realized the phrase Jonathan used to describe the murderer stalking him—"a fat robber with a potbellied stomach" that "stuck way out"—had been another clue. A pregnant woman with shiny red hair, disguised as a robber, who wanted to kill him when he probably demanded she have an abortion. The dream revealed Jonathan's deep, primitive fear she might well kill him for his treachery. His refusal to marry her when she became pregnant for he obviously had his hands full with his wife and Norma.

He asked, "Miss Michaels, when did you first meet Jonathan?"

"When I was six and he came to our house for dinner with his father during the Christmas holidays. He was a sophomore at Princeton, and his mother had just died. My father wanted to cheer up Jonathan and his father. I didn't see Jonathan again until the day I went to work for him."

"Did he remember you?"

"When I walked into his office he stood up with a surprised look and said, 'Little Susu!' That was my father's nickname for me. Jonathan walked over and took me in his arms. He hugged me, kissed me on the lips, and said, 'Welcome, Susu. It isn't always a man can kiss a new secretary hello.' He asked me to call him Jonathan, not Mr. Thomas."

"You must soon have found out that, in addition to being unhappily married, Jonathan was having an affair with Norma Donn. He didn't seem to hide that from anyone."

She sighed. "When we fell in love, Jonathan told me the affair with Miss Donn had ended. He said he didn't want to hurt her feelings and break it off too quickly. He assured me I was not taking him from his wife. He said he hadn't slept with her in over a year."

She added pleadingly, "I tried to fight my feelings for Jonathan. But he was such a loving, sweet man."

She did not need to tell him that, he would not be sitting in this sad, suffocatingly small room with her if he, too, had not fallen somewhat under the charm of Jonathan Thomas. The charm that was Jonathan's undoing. He had courted one too many women and sought his own destruction by not being able to remain faithful to one.

She tried to defend herself further. "Jonathan and I both fought our feelings for months. Then one day we worked late, and he asked me to dinner. I started to put on my coat, and the next thing I knew he was kissing me passionately. He pulled me over to the couch, set me down on it, and we didn't leave for two hours."

There were tears in her eyes. "After that, we had sex several times a week for nearly two months. Then I found out I was pregnant. I didn't want the abortion. I had a friend who died from one. But Jonathan said there was no way out, that he couldn't marry me."

Dr. Ames asked, "Did you seek help from your father? He certainly would make it easier for you."

She looked panic-stricken. "He would kill me! He sometimes hit me hard when I was little and did things he didn't like. Once when I was five and wet my bed by mistake, he spanked me viciously. And again when I was twelve and he caught me reading *Ulysses*."

So she had known the touch of violence when she was small, from her father, the surgeon. Dr. Ames recalled studies reporting that a number of surgeons sublimated their violent impulses by slashing and cutting up people in acts of "mercy," relieving pain and saving them from death. What Freud called reaction formation. Without which there would be no good deeds on anyone's part.

Susan Michaels had never broken the too-close emotional tie to her father. A tie especially strong because the violence was a kind of seduction. Charley was as seductive and charming and, in his way, just as cruel as Jonathan. Susan had chosen unconsciously as father of her baby a man much like her father, which all women do to some extent.

He asked, "Miss Michaels, do you intend to have an abortion?"

"Of course. I couldn't bring up a baby alone."

She stared at Dr. Ames as though trying to make up her mind how far she could trust him. Then she said slowly, "I suppose you want to hear about those last hours with Jonathan."

"I would." That, at least, she owed him, she who had senselessly slaughtered his prize patient.

"The day before it happened"—the *it* obviously referring to the murder—"Jonathan ordered me to arrange for an abortion and said he would give me the money the next day. That night I dragged myself home, lay on the bed, and cried for hours. I felt nobody wanted me. Not even a man who made such passionate love that it created a baby."

The reddened eyes of the robber in the dream, the tears. Jonathan would have known she would shed them.

"The next morning Jonathan called me into his office before I started to type his letters. He was sitting at his desk, the checkbook in front of him. He wrote out the check, handed it to me, and said, 'If you need more, let me know.' I wanted him to take me in his arms. Tell me it was all a nightmare, that he had thought things over, loved me, and wanted to marry me. Or at least tell me I meant *something* to him. That he understood the torment I would go through, physically and emotionally, to get rid of the baby."

She bit her lips. "Instead, I felt he couldn't wait to get rid of me. That even though he would not fire me, he would like me gone forever. I took the check as if it were a poisonous snake and said, 'Thank you, Jonathan.'

"Somehow I got through the day. Then, about four o'clock I saw Norma Donn walk up the stairs. I wanted to push her back down. She was the main reason Jonathan wouldn't marry me. He couldn't afford to toss her aside because of the money she was bringing the firm. She barged into his office, not even asking if he were free. Jonathan closed the door behind her. It stayed shut for forty-five minutes. I counted each second."

She stopped, mired in the misery of her memories. Then sighed and went on. "Suddenly the buzzer on my desk sounded, calling me into the office. I knocked, then opened the door. The two of them were sitting close on the couch, talking in low voices. She looked radiant, like I did after sex. I knew Jonathan had probably had sex with her in those forty-five minutes. Just like he did with me some nights and a few lunch hours."

Jonathan had certainly created chaos that day, Dr. Ames thought. What with Elaine, drunk and storming into the office, Norma visiting him in the late afternoon, and Susan, increasingly desperate at the idea of the abortion.

Suddenly Susan's voice took on a firmness Dr. Ames had not heard before. "Jonathan looked at me coldly, like I was an unwanted stranger. He said, 'Miss Michaels, will you get the latest royalty statement on Miss Donn's book from the files?' He had never, since I was six, called me Miss Michaels. I was furious! It was a dismissal from his life."

In mounting anger, she said, "I was the woman to whom he had just given twelve hundred dollars to get rid of the baby he put inside me. The woman he made love with naked on that very couch. I ran downstairs to get the royalty statement from Marie. I took it back to Jonathan. He said, 'Thank you, Miss Michaels.' They kept the door open after that. When Miss Donn was leaving, she stood on her toes and kissed Jonathan. Really kissed him, I mean. I heard her say, 'At ten this evening?' And Jonathan said, 'If I'm late, wait up.'

"After she left, Jonathan came out of his office smudged with lipstick and said, 'I want to give you all next week off'—for the abortion, he meant—'so will you stay late this evening and take a batch of letters?' "

Jonathan asking for his death sentence, Dr. Ames thought. He must have known the fury he fomented in Susan's vulnerable mind.

"He dictated letters for two hours. We didn't exchange one personal word. When he finished, about eight, he said, 'Will you make us some sandwiches and coffee? There's ham and Swiss cheese in the kitchen, left over from lunch.' I was starved, I'd felt too sick to eat lunch, I couldn't even keep coffee down at breakfast. I brought a sandwich to Jonathan and then managed a few bites at my desk.

"Jonathan said he would stay while I typed, that he had reading to do, but would leave about ten-thirty. All the time I was typing, I was thinking how after he left me, he would go straight into the arms of Norma Donn. Never mind that I had his baby inside. It was still there, I wasn't a murderer yet."

She stopped. He was almost afraid to breathe, knowing the slightest movement or sound might break whatever mood was allowing her to relive the moments that led to murder.

"About ten I finished typing the last letter. There were thirty-two in all. I brought them to Jonathan to sign. Then I picked up the dirty plates and coffee cups. I carried them down the hall to wash them so that the place would be clean before we left. I felt as if I were living on two separate planets. I didn't know what I was doing, and at the same time I was so aware of every move, it felt like slow motion.

"I put the last dish away. Then, as if someone else were telling me what to do, I took the kitchen knife off the wall over the sink, where it hung on a rack. I walked back to Jonathan's office. He was sitting at his desk in his shirt—he keeps the room very warm—signing the last few letters. He shook the pen, it didn't seem to be working."

Lonegan had been right about the ink stain on Jonathan's third finger, right hand. He had been using a pen as he was killed.

"Jonathan acted as if he didn't know I was there. I walked over to him. He didn't look up, kept signing his name. I walked around his desk. I stood behind him, the knife in my right hand. I watched him sign the final letter.

"I thought, He doesn't want me or the baby he made with me. If it's all right to kill his baby, why isn't it all right to kill him? I didn't want him to have a baby with another woman.

"I raised the knife and brought it down with all my strength into his back. I was surprised how easy it went through the white shirt. He didn't say a word. There was a kind of moan. Then he fell over on the desk.

"I knew enough to wipe my fingerprints off the handle of the knife, as they do in the movies. I used the hem of my dress. I took the letters out to my desk, slipped them in the envelopes I had typed, and left them in the wire basket to be stamped and mailed the next morning. I put on my hat and coat, turned off the lights. Then walked down the two flights of stairs and out into the cold. I knew I had to come back the next day, otherwise they would suspect me. I sat at my desk and watched them carry Jonathan out. His body was so quiet under the sheet."

Then, in a complete change of mood, like the sudden crash of thunder across a calm blue sky, she burst into sobs. Harsh, racking sobs, tinged with wailing, primitive cries. A young woman mourning her soon-to-be-murdered baby and her dead lover. Mourning, too, he thought, her own madness at killing a man she loved who had abandoned her. A love as fierce as her hate.

He handed her his handkerchief. When she quieted down, he said, "I'm sorry, Miss Michaels. I know you've suffered greatly. But I'm afraid you'll have to tell your story to the police. The sooner, the better." She would welcome the easing of her conscience: Guilt, both real and imagined, was the cruelest of psychic burdens.

She stood up. "I'll put on my shoes and get my hat and coat. Will you stay with me at the police station? I'll need your help to say it all over again."

"Of course," he said.

She had courage, but then she would—she was Charley Michaels' daughter, which made her self-destructive behavior all the more tragic.

On the street he told the taxi driver, "153 East Sixty-seventh Street." Added knowingly, "That's the Nineteenth Precinct headquarters." He had looked up the address of Lonegan's precinct headquarters.

"You're telling me, buddy?" The driver's voice was belligerent at this assault on his professional knowledge of city streets. "I been hacking thirty-three years, and there ain't a precinct I don't know. You're going to where Frank Sinatra played in that movie *The Detective*. You a detective?"

"No." Dr. Ames settled back in the seat, Susan Michaels beside him, huddled in her dark blue woolen coat, the matching hat covering most of her flaming hair.

The driver gave up his questioning, and Dr. Ames turned to his own thoughts. He finally understood why Jonathan had set up his own destruction and why he had to keep secret from his analyst one of the most important experiences of his life.

Jonathan could not tell him the truth because the truth was too dangerous. The truth was too near home. Jonathan had seduced the daughter of the man who had recommended Dr. Ames as psychoanalyst. Also the daughter of the man who had taken care of Jonathan's mother and had shown sympathy to Jonathan and his father when she died.

In Jonathan's misery at facing an unhappy choice between Elaine and Norma, not really wanting either, he had sought a third alternative, as a way out, in the waiting arms of his young, red-haired secretary, whose father had known Jonathan's mother. Susan must have stirred up memories of his beloved mother. It was all too incestuous for Jonathan to dare speak of. For his transgressions, both actual with Susan, and in fantasy, with his mother, he had to punish himself as

Oedipus did, but fatally. Also, the loss of his mother when he was only a boy meant he could never trust a woman to stay with him and, in defense, he always deserted them first.

His unconscious, in that final dream, sensed that Susan was mad enough to murder him, literally "mad" for the moment. He must have known her anger was of murderous intensity because of what she felt to be his callous cruelty—she obviously wanted him and the baby desperately. He also must have known how intensely he provoked her that last day of his life. First, by handing her the check, the go-ahead for the killing of the baby. Then, by shutting the door while he stayed secluded with Norma. Then, by calling Susan "Miss Michaels" to prove to Norma that Susan did not exist. Then by kissing Norma in front of Susan and, within Susan's hearing, making a date with Norma for that evening. Susan needed his wholehearted support at that moment, but instead of helping her through the crisis of her young life, he fanned to full fire her smoldering wish for revenge. Jonathan could never understand how he provoked women to highest rage.

Dr. Ames thought of an important fact. Jonathan had told him that though he had tried over the years, he had never been able to father a child either in marriage or affairs. At least the year of analysis had enabled him to be less afraid of being a father as he became aware of his hostile feelings toward his own father. But then Jonathan had to destroy the baby and emotionally destroy the mother. He could have divorced Elaine to marry Susan but, instead, sought his own destruction.

If only he had been able to speak more openly to Dr. Ames, less afraid of what his analyst would think. Dr. Ames thought he might have helped save Jonathan's life, helped him be more responsive to Susan's anguish, reduce her violent feelings. Jonathan had felt too much a criminal, though he was guilty of only one crime: what he had described to Norma as the only crime on the couch—not speaking his thoughts, no matter how shameful, fearful, or embarrassing. It was a crime against himself. Dr. Ames was there not to judge but to help.

The taxi stopped. They were in front of precinct headquarters. The driver said, "Here you are, buddy. The Nineteenth."

Dr. Ames paid the fare and helped Susan up the steps into the station house. A young policeman sat at a desk just inside the door. Behind him on a raised platform two older policemen at their desks talked on telephones.

"May I help you?" The young policeman was as polite as if they were arriving for high tea at the White House.

"I'm Dr. William Ames. I'm helping Detective Lonegan on the Jonathan Thomas case. May I phone him at home as he asked me to do?"

"I'll get him for you." The policeman dialed a number and handed the phone to Dr. Ames.

"Hello." Lonegan's voice.

"It's Bill Ames, Jack."

"Glad you called. Have you broken our case yet?" A joke.

"As a matter of fact, I have. I'm phoning from the Nineteenth Precinct headquarters. I'm with a young lady. She's just confessed to Jonathan's murder."

"You *mean* it?" Disbelief.

"Come over and find out. You'll have to take it from here. She's willing to tell the police how it happened."

"Be right there. Tell them to give you both coffee." He hung up, and Dr. Ames could see him flying out of the room.

Two hours later psychoanalyst and detective walked up Lexington Avenue in search of a bar. Dr. Ames felt sorry to leave Susan at the station, but she had called her mother and father and they were headed for precinct headquarters and would take over. He did not want to see Charley Michaels at the moment, perhaps at a later time. He wanted to recommend psychoanalytic help for Susan, necessary if the rest of her life was to be any happier.

"Want to stop here?" Lonegan peered through murky glass into the bleakness of the ubiquitous avenue bar, this one named Barney's.

"It's as good as any," Dr. Ames said.

They headed into the warmth of whiskey cheer, finding an empty booth in the rear. As the detective lifted his rye, he said to Dr. Ames, about to taste his Scotch, "How did you know it was Susan Michaels?"

"Did you examine Jonathan's desk thoroughly?"

"We sure did. Just a pile of junk inside."

"Did you take the three drawers out of the desk?"

"Anderson did. I saw him lift them out and dump everything on top of the desk. Why?"

"Did he examine the rear of the thin wooden ledge on which the long thin drawer on the left slips in and out?"

"He was supposed to go over the whole desk." Worriedly, "Did you find something we missed?"

"A very small something. It slipped out of the rear of that overcrowded drawer into the empty space behind. It was hidden when the drawer was in place. You had to look very carefully to see it. Even when the drawer was removed. You'd have to look and look." Pause. "Until something spoke to you."

Lonegan peered at Dr. Ames. "Are you okay, Doc?"

"I'm fine. It's been a long, long day and evening."

"What did you find in that drawer that we overlooked?"

"The stub of a check for twelve hundred dollars with the initials of the payee. S.M."

Lonegan looked at him in admiration. "So you played both shrink *and* detective. Good going. I knew you had it in you. You're going to get all the credit for this."

"I can't take any. You'll have to accept it. My name must not be mentioned. Professional reasons. I might lose my license."

"It doesn't seem fair. You deserve the praise."

"I'm satisfied if I have yours."

"You've got that in spades." Lonegan grinned. "Do you know I'll probably get a promotion thanks to you?"

"You deserve it. You persuaded me to help you."

"But your psychological expertise solved the case."

"Not really. I just had a theory about the cause of violence. That its roots lie in childhood." He mused, "You'd think someone orphaned at five, as Elaine was, or someone like Norma, deserted by her father as a child, would be angry enough to kill. But it was the one who grew up with both parents who proved angriest of all."

"Why was that, Doc?"

"Susan's parents evidently weren't as loving as Elaine's aunt or uncle, or Norma's mother. We all feel the same primitive violent wishes as we grow up, and parents can make the process of learning control easier—or harder. Susan's parents made it harder. Much harder."

Lonegan took several swigs of rye, then asked, almost shyly, "How about you and me sort of pooling our talents when there's a murder? Kind of keeping the team together. You could make New York safer for your children."

Dr. Ames laughed. "My daughter, Carol, is eighteen and living with her mother in Greenwich. Anyhow, I'd back Carol against Jack the Ripper. She's a jujitsu champ."

"You don't think working together is such a hot idea?" The detective sounded rejected.

"I think it's a great idea. Freud would have loved it. Maybe someday every precinct will have a staff psychoanalyst. But it's not exactly my bag, as they say. I helped you because I was angry. Angry that someone had wantonly destroyed a man I liked and respected."

"Well, if you ever want to try your hand again, Doc, just let me know. I can find plenty of victims you'd like and respect. They're not all Mafia or drug addicts."

He looked at Dr. Ames fondly. "I never thought I'd wind up friends with a shrink." Then, sympathy in his voice, "You miss Jonathan Thomas, don't you?"

"At moments like this, I wish I'd been a Mississippi riverboat gambler like my great-grandfather."

"Aren't you somewhat of a gambler to tackle your profession?"

"You'd better believe it." Philosophically, "But we can't expect to win 'em all. On the street, where you work. Or on the couch, where I work."

And they clinked glasses.

BIRDBRAIN
JOYCE HARRINGTON

The room looked like an aviary. There were birds everywhere. A bright red parrot roosted near the ceiling. Two toucans gazed soulfully at each other over their outsize beaks. A bronze owl brooded on a pedestal. Near one window, a flight of hummingbirds dangled from fine, clear nylon threads. And more. Everywhere you looked, there were birds of wood, papier-mâché, ceramic, metal, cloth, and even some with feathers. A few were so lifelike, Evangeline almost expected them to sing.

And there were plants. In tubs, pots, and window boxes. Leaves sprawled, vines entwined, ferns drooped juicily. The only ones Evangeline knew by name were the geraniums in the window. Pink they were, not red, and flowering mightily. The room was warm and humid, with a dank, damp, earthy smell. The windows were closed.

Tiny Phoebe sat hunched on a floor pillow, weeping. She looked a bit birdy herself. Her blond curls were tied up into a feathery topknot with a blue chiffon scarf, and she wore a creation best described as wispy. It was neither dress nor robe nor even jumpsuit, but something combining elements of all three, with bluish, purplish layers of sheer, shiny fabric overlapping and flapping whenever she moved. Her long-taloned fingernails, painted bright fuchsia, *rat-tatted* on the polished wood floor with each spasm of sobbing.

"I've got to get out of here," she moaned.

"There's the door," the ever-practical Evangeline pointed out. "I just came through it not ten minutes ago."

Evangeline was shocked at the appearance of her friend, and at the storm of tears her visit had provoked. Phoebe had always been a little bit ditzy, but she'd been a cheerful little sprite, laughing and burbling at the world and all its dangers. They'd been friends since their first day at the High School of Music and Art, when someone had stolen Evangeline's lunch and Phoebe had shared her own brown bag full of mysterious vegetarian goodies. But they'd lost touch with each other in recent years.

"You don't understand," Phoebe moaned. "I can't just *leave*. He'd find me in a minute. He's uncanny that way. Sometimes I think he's got people watching me. Sometimes I think all these *birds* are watching me. He always knows what I've been doing. Oh, Vangie, what'll I *do*?"

Evangeline kicked another floor pillow next to her friend and squatted down on it uncomfortably. There wasn't a regular chair in the place. She put an arm around Phoebe's shoulder and felt the heavy weight of the feathery head droop against her breast.

"You could come home and stay with me for a while," she said. "There isn't much room, but we could manage."

Phoebe's head shook violently, and Evangeline felt her tears soaking through her MOSTLY MOZART T-shirt. "Hey, now," she soothed. "You can't cry and think at the same time."

She found a wad of tissues in her jeans pocket and tried to mop up Phoebe's streaming face. Mascara and eye shadow turned the tissue black and blue.

"I can't think, *period,*" Phoebe wailed. "You were always the thinker. Can't you think of *something*? I don't want to leave him, but I can't keep on living like this. If I leave him, I'll be all alone, and I don't think I could stand that. I can't even work anymore. All this belongs to Victor. How would I live?"

Evangeline felt a growing impatience with her friend. Phoebe had lost what little independence she'd ever had. Her own life was hard, and she didn't have very much, but what she had was her own. She didn't owe her existence to anyone. But it wasn't fair to feel superior to poor Phoebe over that. No man had ever offered to whisk her out of her artistic poverty. Who knows if she'd be able to resist such an offer if it ever came her way? She might be just as much a pushover as Phoebe had been for Victor.

"Well, now," she said. "Let's go back a bit. I never met this Victor of yours. I don't know anything about him."

"He's not this Victor of mine," Phoebe interrupted. "I'm this Phoebe of his. That's the way it is, and I don't like it."

"Well, you must have liked it once. How long have you been living with him?"

"Six months. But it wasn't like this in the beginning. There weren't all these *birds* around." She lowered her voice and whispered close to Evangeline's ear, as if the birds could overhear her. "He knows I don't like birds. He knows I'm afraid of them. He keeps threatening to bring home a *live* one."

"So what if he does?" said Evangeline. "It might do you good to have a pet. Something for you to take care of instead of dwelling on your own misery. Birds can't hurt you."

"Oh, yeah?" said Phoebe, more her own old self. "Haven't you ever heard of parrot fever? People die of that. Suppose he brings home a parrot and it bites me? Vangie, if I die of parrot fever, you'll know Victor killed me. Promise me you'll go to the police."

"I'll promise nothing of the kind. Oh, Phoebe, you're not going to die of parrot fever or anything else. I can't believe that you're in any kind of danger, from Victor or from birds. I think you're dreaming it all up because you haven't got anything else to do."

"Vangie, did you ever see that old Hitchcock movie? The one where the birds take over a whole town and start killing the people?"

Evangeline nodded. "*The Birds*. It was a good movie."

"Victor thinks so, too. He's got it on videotape. He watches it all the time. He makes me watch it even though he knows it scares me. Vangie, please believe me. I think Victor wants to kill me. Am I being silly?"

"Silly?" Evangeline considered the question. She *did* think Phoebe was overwrought, blowing things all out of proportion, but she didn't know enough about how things were between her and Victor to know whether Phoebe had crossed over the line into unreality.

"I don't know," she said. "Have you thought about seeing a shrink?"

"Yeah, but I can't. Victor wouldn't let me. He doesn't believe in them, and I haven't got any money of my own. Anyway, he's the one who ought to be getting shrunk. Believe me, Vangie, he's *crazy*."

Evangeline sat quietly for a while, hugging her old chum, who had stopped crying and sat with her head resting on her drawn-up knees.

After a while, Phoebe murmured, "I liked the birds at first. When there were just a couple of them. I thought they were cute. Then he started talking about how I was his little bird. I didn't mind that either. At first. Isn't that what English guys call their girl friends? Birds? It was love talk, I thought."

"Nothing wrong with that," said Evangeline. "People in love say some fairly stupid things to each other." And how would I know about that? she asked herself. Nobody's ever called me his little bird. Or little anything else. How could they? Six feet tall and built like a telephone pole. It was always cute little bird-brained Phoebe who had the boys flocking around. If they went out with me at all, it was because she'd set it up. She always thought I didn't know that. And she always came to me when things went wrong. Like now. Calling me up in a panic after more than a year of nothing. Typical Phoebe.

"Nothing wrong, maybe," Phoebe was saying. "But then he started bringing home these things for me to wear." She tugged at her wispy garment. "He said I didn't know how to dress to my best advantage. Well, I grant you I was pretty much into jeans and T-shirts, like you and practically everybody else. But I had a few nice things. He threw them all away."

"You look terrific in that," Evangeline said. "It's gorgeous. Victor has good taste. I wish I could wear outrageous clothes." I wish I could afford them, she thought. That thing must have cost a mint.

"Oh, you *could,* Vangie," Phoebe burbled. "You're so tall and slender. I've always envied you that. You could get away with *anything.*"

"Thanks. I'll stick to basic black for jobs and jeans the rest of the time. That's me. That's my style."

"Still playing your flute?" Phoebe asked.

"I'm in a chamber music group. We play snooty parties when we can and once a week in a coffeehouse in SoHo. The rest of the time, I tour the subway stations. People throw quarters at me."

"Oh, Vangie!" Phoebe gazed up at her with brimming eyes. "You're so good. You deserve better than that."

"Sure. I ought to be playing Lincoln Center. Me and about two hundred other flutes around town. But I'm not, and don't you start clouding up over that. I'm doing okay. I just have to keep at it, and sooner or later my chance will come. What about you? Are you still painting your flowers?"

"No. And that's another thing. Victor made me stop. He said watercolor was too wishy-washy. He said flower paintings were for little old ladies. But, Vangie, people were *buying* them. Maybe I wasn't a *great* talent like Victor, but I was getting along. I was doing greeting cards and designs for sheets. Now I don't do anything."

"Tell me about Victor's work."

"Oh, he's an artist with a capital *A*. But his stuff is creepy, Vangie. Really sick-making. I don't know why people pay so much money for it. It's all birds now. It has been ever since I met him. But birds like you've never seen before. Nobody has—except for Victor, in that weird mind of his. Bird bodies with women's heads. Women's bodies with bird heads and feathers all over them. Birds with sharp teeth biting into women's flesh. And worst of all, women eating live screaming birds." She lowered her voice again and whispered into Evangeline's ear. "He makes me pose for him. I hate it. I'd show you, but he keeps the studio locked when he's not here."

The two women huddled together on the floor pillows, absorbing Phoebe's outburst. Evangeline yearned to leave. The stuffy room and Phoebe's insoluble predicament had turned the bright summer afternoon into a steamy hothouse where strange emotional growths flourished. She'd already offered Phoebe a place to stay. There wasn't much else she could do. She was curious about Victor, though. Knowing Phoebe as well as she did, she had to allow for a certain amount of exaggeration. Times before, when she had intervened in Phoebe's affairs, at Phoebe's invitation, there'd invariably come the moment when her practical advice was scorned and she was told to butt out. If Victor was as obsessed as Phoebe made him seem, she could conceivably be in some danger. But that was hardly likely. To Evangeline, it sounded as if Phoebe had been attracted by Victor's talent, dedication, and success, to say nothing of the easy life he offered her, and then found she couldn't cope with being a lesser light. But there was no way she could tell Phoebe that without destroying what little remained of their old friendship.

"Where's Victor now?" she asked.

"He teaches a class on Thursday afternoons over at the New School. That's how I met him. I was in his class. I'd seen some of his early bird things in a gallery. They weren't nearly as weird as the things he does now. Just regular birds. Orioles and cardinals and robins. Very pretty, very exact. And I thought it would be nice to paint some birds among my flowers. It would be good for the greeting-card trade." She sneaked a sly glance at Evangeline, who was looking slightly cynical.

"So, all right. I admit it," Phoebe said with a smirk. "The gallery had a photo of him hanging on the wall. He's gorgeous. So I went to his class on purpose to meet him. And I pestered him for advice until he paid attention to me. Don't look at me like that. You *know* how I am. And it worked. It always does. You ought to learn how to do it, Vangie. You flatter them and make them feel important, and then they won't leave you alone. But this time, I think it worked too well. It backfired on me. I'm trapped. I can't get out. Sometimes I feel as if I really *am* a bird and I'm in this cage and I'll be here forever and ever until I *die*."

Evangeline struggled to get up. Her legs were cramped, and both her feet tingled with pins and needles. She stamped around the room trying to work out the cramps and get her circulation going. "Phoebe," she said as she marched, "you've always had a wonderful imagination. Are you being fair to Victor? Could it be that you're reading something into this that simply isn't there?"

Phoebe, sitting cross-legged on the floor pillow, looked amazingly like a bird roosting on its nest. "Oh, no," she said earnestly. "I knew you'd think that. You're always so down-to-earth, and I've always been so flighty. That's why I didn't call you sooner. But I'm desperate now, and you're my oldest, dearest, closest friend. There's nobody else I could tell all this to. Do you know what he wants me to do? He's got a ladder in there. A real tall one." She nodded toward what Evangeline surmised must be the locked studio door. "He says he's going to teach me to fly. He makes me climb up the ladder, all the way to the top, and jump off with my arms spread out like wings. There's a mattress on the floor, but, Vangie, I don't want to learn how to fly. I can't. It scares me. I'm perfectly happy down on the ground. I've always been afraid of heights. I've never even been in an airplane."

"Maybe he's just trying to help you get over your acrophobia."

"Is that what it is? I never knew it had a name."

"Lots of people have it."

Phoebe's head drooped. "Vangie, please. Don't try to put me down. I know you're a lot smarter than I am. That's why I thought you'd be able to help me. Tell me what I should do, Vangie. I swear I'm not making this up."

"I can't help you if you won't help yourself."

Phoebe sighed. "Yes. I guess you're right. It's my problem, and I'll have to deal with it. If I can. I shouldn't have bothered you."

She looked so pitiful, Evangeline decided to give it one more try. "Would it help if I met Victor?" she asked. "Then I'd be able to see for myself if there's really anything for you to be afraid of."

"Oh, would you?" Phoebe scrambled up, her clothes flapping around her, looking suddenly bright-eyed and capable of flight. "I didn't want to ask you to do that. It could be dangerous for *you*."

"Nonsense," said Evangeline firmly. "What could happen to me? Do you think he'll try to turn *me* into a bird? Can't you just see that? What kind of a bird would I be, Phoebe? A stork?" She stood on one leg, flapped her elbows awkwardly, and uttered a raucous screech.

Phoebe laughed, and Evangeline laughed with her. The best medicine, Evangeline thought. Laugh your troubles away. "Let's do something, Phoebe," she urged. "It's a beautiful day. We could go over to Washington Square Park and get some sun."

Phoebe flopped back down onto her pillow and hung her head. "I can't," she murmured. "Victor should be home soon."

"All the more reason to go," said Evangeline. "If you're always here waiting for him he'll get bored with you. I don't need to tell you that."

"Do you think so?" Phoebe asked plaintively. "Sometimes I wish he would. Sometimes I wish he'd let me go and find some other girl to be his bird. But then I get frightened of what it would be like without him. Oh, Vangie, I guess you've never been in love like this."

Love, Evangeline thought. If this is love, I want no part of it. Phoebe may have been a birdbrain before she met Victor, but at least she was happy and making the most of her little talent. Now she's miserable and useless. If that's what love does to you, I'll take chop suey. "No," she said, "I guess I never have."

Once again, Phoebe's mood shifted. She stood up and became the perfect hostess. "What am I thinking of? Vangie, I haven't even offered you a drink. Or would you like some tea? I think I forgot to have lunch. Let's have a little feast."

"We could go out," Evangeline suggested again, still hoping that she could convince Phoebe to leave the apartment. "There are plenty of restaurants around here, even some vegetarian places."

"Oh, no," said Phoebe. "No need to do that. There's plenty of food in the kitchen. We can have a picnic on the floor. Wouldn't that be fun? Anything I want, I can call down for it. They send it up. Victor has charge accounts all over the place."

"Phoebe, are you trying to tell me that Victor won't let you go out? Has he actually told you that?"

"Something like that." Phoebe wafted away from her. "Come and see this kitchen, Vangie. You've never seen anything like it in your life."

Curious, Evangeline followed Phoebe down a short passageway and into an astonishing turquoise and black kitchen. Every surface gleamed and reflected back. It was like walking into a maze of semi-precious stone. "You mean you actually cook in here?"

"Oh, yes," said Phoebe. "It's got all the latest equipment. Microwave oven, food processor, coffee machine. You name it. It's here. Victor designed it himself. It's been in *New York* magazine and *House Beautiful*. Victor does most of the *real* cooking. He's very good at it. I just piddle around."

A paragon, this Victor, Evangeline thought. And why can't I ever meet someone like that? As she watched, Phoebe got down shining black plates and opened the huge marbled turquoise and black refrigerator. She got out yogurt, fruit, and granola and started arranging these in pretty patterns on the black plates. She got out a jar of sunflower seeds. Evangeline couldn't help thinking, bird food, although Phoebe had always eaten these things. And so did everyone else these days. She also couldn't help thinking that Phoebe had really lucked out. The kitchen and what she'd seen of the apartment so far fairly shrieked of money. It was a far cry from her own tiny studio in Chelsea, where she'd lived ever since she'd graduated from Juilliard and started trying to make a living with her flute.

"You could always go home," she said, realizing she was being mean.

"Huh?" said Phoebe, absorbed in creating a flower pattern out of sliced peaches and raspberries.

"If you're so unhappy here, you could go back to your parents' place, couldn't you?"

"To Brooklyn?" Phoebe laughed. "Are you nuts?"

"It was just a thought."

"Would you get down one of those trays? I can never reach them."

Evangeline obligingly reached into a shelf over the refrigerator and brought down a lacquered tray with a swirling peacock tail design in turquoise and black.

Phoebe poured apple juice into stemmed goblets. "All ready," she said. She picked up the tray and led the way back into the bird room.

"Don't you guys have any tables or chairs?" Evangeline asked.

"Oh, sure," said Phoebe, nodding vaguely toward the possibility of other rooms. "But this is more fun, don't you think?"

"I guess so," said Evangeline, lowering herself cautiously to the floor pillow and arranging her long legs in the least uncomfortable position.

"I'm feeling better already," said Phoebe, nibbling at her food. "You're such a good influence on me. It's just like when we were in high school and I would get all upset over something. You could always see right to the core of the problem and come up with a practical answer."

"You didn't always like what I told you."

"Well, no. Of course not. But I always *thought* about it. You were the only one who was ever honest with me. Or took me seriously. Everyone else thought I was some kind of birdbrain." She looked around the room and laughed. "I guess I am. Look at me now."

"Why don't you get a cat?" said Evangeline, chewing hard at a mouthful of granola and yogurt.

"Whatever for?" Phoebe asked.

"Oh, I don't know. Just to counteract the effect."

"Oh, I get it. Cat is a natural enemy of birds." Phoebe nibbled and made a major effort at thought. "It wouldn't have to be a real one, would it?"

"Probably not."

"One of those cute little stuffed ones that look almost real. Because I don't think I could take care of a real one. All that cat food and kitty litter and trips to the vet. Ugh!"

"It was just an idea."

"It's a good idea. I'll have to ask Victor."

"No, you don't!" Evangeline exploded. "Dammit, Phoebe! How did you turn into such a wimp? Can't you do anything for yourself?"

Tears began falling into Phoebe's granola. "You don't understand," she wailed. "I thought you would understand, but you don't."

"Oh, cut it out," said Evangeline. "Look. I'm sorry. But, honestly, I hate to see you like this. If you really want my advice, you'll get back to doing your own Phoebe things. Paint your flowers if you want to. Don't let Victor overwhelm you. Get rid of all these birds if that's what's bothering you."

"Shut up," said Phoebe, dabbing at her eyes with her napkin. "I hear the elevator. That's probably Victor. Do I look all right?"

"You look fine," said Evangeline, not looking at her but turning expectantly toward the door.

The man who came through it was not at all what Evangeline expected. He was not dark, sinister, or hawklike. He did not have hypnotic eyes. He exuded no menace, nor did he seem to be blessed with an overpowering amount of personality. He didn't even look like an artist, in the way that artists are conceived to be scruffy and unkempt because they're too busy painting to care much about how they look. He wore a perfectly ordinary tan summer suit, and his tie came from Brooks Brothers, no doubt about it. The first word that popped into Evangeline's head when she saw Victor was *clean*. And the second one was *healthy*. And to top it all off, he was even more handsome than Phoebe had led her to expect. Evangeline felt herself smiling idiotically.

"Hello *there*!" Victor said enthusiastically as he strode into the bird room. "You must be Vangie. Phoebe said she might invite you over. Boy, am I glad she did. My little bird-child could sure use some company these days." He spoke with a faint southern drawl.

"Evangeline Rivers. Nice to meet you." She scrambled up to shake his hand, a movement that was complicated by the fact that he carried a shrouded birdcage in one hand and a large grocery bag in the other.

He put the birdcage down on the floor and managed a left-handed greeting. From beneath the dark cloth hood on the cage, a few muted whistles were heard.

"What *is* that?" shrieked Phoebe, scuttling on her pillow as far away from the cage as she could get without knocking over several of the tall potted plants.

"Just what you've always wanted, dear heart," said Victor. "We'll have the unveiling just as soon as I unload our dinner." His smile was blindingly white and boyishly eager in his smooth tanned face. He turned to Evangeline. "You'll stay for dinner, I hope. I brought enough for an army."

"Well, I don't know," said Evangeline, warily watching Phoebe's fright and Victor's apparent indifference to it. "Phoeb and I were just having a little snack."

"Oh, I know all about Phoebe's little snacks. Not enough to keep a bird alive. No. I brought some real food. Phoebe can eat all the nutburgers she wants, but I refuse to be converted. Please say you'll stay. It would do Phoebe good to have a real long visit with you. I'll get out of your way after dinner. I'm getting ready for an exhibit, and there's plenty for me to do in there." He glanced longingly at the closed studio door.

"I'd like to see your work," said Evangeline.

Victor frowned. "I don't know," he said. "I don't usually let anyone see it until the exhibit. Except for Phoebe, of course. She's the best model I ever had." But he was examining Evangeline with calculating eyes, her long legs, her slender arms, her neck.

Evangeline felt a sudden chill and put a hand to her throat. Why was she thinking that the nicest compliment anyone had ever paid her was to tell her that her neck was swanlike? She glanced down at Phoebe cowering in the shelter of a pair of broad, drooping leaves. Could a mania be contagious? Was she catching Phoebe's bird fixation?

"Well, I'll stay," she said. "But not too late. I have to get up early. I want to catch the morning rush-hour crowd in the subway. Business is always better in the morning. Sometimes people drop dollar bills into my flute case."

Victor shook his head sympathetically. "What a life!" he said. "This country doesn't know how to treat its artists. I've been very lucky. Listen. I'll be right back. I just want to put this food away." He stopped to peer through the leaves at Phoebe. "You hear me, honey? I'll be in the kitchen for a few minutes. I wish you'd come out of there and visit with your friend."

Phoebe made not a peep.

Victor whispered to Evangeline, "See what you can do." Then he disappeared with the grocery bag into the turquoise and black splendor of the kitchen and thoughtfully closed the door behind him.

As soon as he was gone, Evangeline raced over to Phoebe. "Come on out of there, you little idiot," she whispered, tugging on Phoebe's arm. "What's the matter with you? He seems perfectly normal to me. Better than normal. He's polite and clean and darn good-looking. And he obviously cares about you. It sticks out all over him. You're the one who's acting crazy."

Trembling, Phoebe crawled out of her shelter. "I know. I know," she wailed. "I can't *help* it. What do you think he's got in that cage?"

"Some kind of bird, of course. A present for you. Can't you tell he's so proud of it, he's ready to burst? Come on now, stand up and be a sport. Tell him you like it, even if you don't. Don't spoil it for him."

"Okay. Okay. I'll stand up," said Phoebe, "but I won't be a sport if I don't feel like it. And I know I'm going to hate it, whatever it is. Stop pulling at me. I can stand up by myself."

Evangeline let go and watched Phoebe get shakily to her feet and smooth her ruffled garment. "Feel better?" she asked.

"I'm okay," said Phoebe grumpily. "So you think he's just a normal person?"

"So far," said Evangeline. "Where's he from? He sounds kind of southern."

"Somewhere down there. He told me once, but I forgot. Some little town in Kentucky or Tennessee. Does it matter?"

The kitchen door opened, and Victor stood beaming at them. "You ladies like some wine? I've got some chilled Chardonnay out here."

"Yes, thank you," Evangeline said, while Phoebe made a nasty face.

"Just keep right on visiting, you two. I'll be with you in a minute." He closed the door again.

"He knows I don't drink wine," Phoebe whispered. "I don't drink any kind of booze."

"Well, when did you get so virtuous?" Evangeline asked. "I seem to remember certain six-packs that disappeared in your vicinity."

"That was then," said Phoebe. "I have to be careful now. I can't let my guard down for a single minute. You noticed, of course, that he didn't even kiss me when he came in."

"Maybe he's too polite to do that in front of a stranger."

"Yeah," said Phoebe. "Maybe."

"Well, I didn't see you leaping up to welcome him home. You were too busy having hysterics and hiding in the jungle."

"I was frightened." She glanced warily at the covered birdcage, from which faint scratching sounds came. "I'm still frightened. What if it's a parrot?"

Victor came out of the kitchen, grinning proudly over a tray of wineglasses and a plate of amazingly professional-looking hors d'oeuvres. "Compliments to the chef down the street. All I did was pick them out. Takeout food has come a long way since two egg rolls to go." He crossed the room and put the tray down on the floor near the birdcage. "We could go into my den," he said to Phoebe, "and be comfortable. Vangie might like to sit on a couch instead of the floor."

"I like it in here," Phoebe pouted.

"As you wish, sweetface." He passed the wineglasses around.

Evangeline noticed that Phoebe took hers without hesitation.

"Today," Victor proclaimed, raising his own glass high, "is a day of importance. An historic occasion. And, Vangie, I'm glad you're here to share it with us. Today is our sixth anniversary."

"Is it?" said Phoebe sullenly.

Evangeline felt like kicking her. "Congratulations," she said, clinking her glass against both of theirs.

"Yes, indeed," said Victor. "Six months ago today," he put an arm around Phoebe's shoulder, "this sweet little bird flew into my humble nest."

Phoebe drifted out of his embrace and swallowed deeply from her wineglass.

"Not so humble, if you ask me," said Evangeline.

"Thanks," said Victor. "I'm glad you like it. It wasn't always like this, though. I've had some hard years, but this is no time to be remembering them. I'm truly grateful that Phoebe came into my life and that I'm able to give her the pretty things she deserves. And now, in honor of the occasion, I would like you both to meet Mickey. Ready for this?"

Phoebe skittered back a few paces and closed her eyes.

Victor whipped the cloth off the birdcage and said, "Say 'hello,' Mickey."

Phoebe screamed, "It's a parrot! I knew it! What did I tell you, Vangie?"

The bird, black with a bright yellow beak, cocked his head and said, "Hello, Phoebe. Pretty Phoebe. That's a nice girl."

Evangeline laughed. "It's not a parrot. It's a myna bird, isn't it? How did you get him to say that?"

Phoebe stared at the bird. "It's a black parrot," she insisted. "It's the same thing as a parrot."

Victor glowed with pride. "They've been training him for me at the pet store. Listen to this." He spoke to the bird again. "Who does Victor love, Mickey?"

"Vicky loves Phoebe. Mickey's hungry. How about a peanut?"

"He never did get that just right. He knew how to say the last part before."

"Amazing," said Evangeline.

"Do I have to feed that thing?" said Phoebe.

"Oh, Phoebe," said Victor, at last displaying a touch of disappointment, "I thought you'd really like Mickey. You always said you wanted a talking bird."

"What I said was, if I had to have all these birds, I'd rather have one I could talk to."

"Well, here he is. You can teach him to say anything you like." To Evangeline, he said, "Has Phoebe shown you around the place?"

"Not yet. Only the kitchen. Fantastic."

"Well, come on. Let me show you. I hope you won't think I'm being house-proud, but if you could see the way I lived before, you'd understand. I had nothing but a dream when I came to New York ten years ago, and now my dream is coming true. I've been one of the lucky ones. Phoebe, sweetheart, will you excuse us for a few minutes? See if you can get Mickey to say some of his other things. He's got quite a vocabulary."

Phoebe shrugged and sipped her wine. Evangeline noticed that her glass was almost empty. She tried to catch her eye, but Phoebe, staring at the myna bird as if hypnotized, ignored her.

Victor led her into a cozy room, lined with books and stuffed with a comfortable leather couch and armchairs. "Sit down a minute, please, Vangie. I've got to talk with you." Worry marked his handsome face, and his eyes were bleak. "I'm so glad you're here. You've known Phoebe a long time. She's talked about you a lot, and she respects you. Have you any idea what's going on with her? Has she ever acted like this before?"

Evangeline considered her reply carefully. She didn't want to betray any of the things Phoebe had told her, but she was concerned for her friend and now for Victor, who seemed genuinely distressed. "She's always been . . . um . . . sensitive. She picks up on things other people don't seem to notice. And sometimes she exaggerates things. She seems to be a little unhappy about all this bird stuff."

"Well, that's what I don't understand," said Victor. "She's the one who started it. It was a joke at first. She brought a silly papier-mâché parrot with her when she moved in with me, and a Boston fern. I guess I teased her about it, and maybe I shouldn't have. But I didn't mean any harm. From there, the whole thing just grew. Believe it or not, I once had a living room just like anybody else's. Well, not exactly like anybody's. I'd decorated it myself and chosen all the furniture. But Phoebe didn't like it, so I let her do what she wanted. And that's what she wanted—plants and birds and pillows on the floor. Sometimes I think she thinks she's a bird. She says one day she's going to fly. And that's kind of scary. I don't know if she means it literally, as in fly out the window. Or if she means she's going to leave me."

"Hum," said Evangeline, not knowing how to reconcile the two opposing stories. "She told me you paint a lot of birds."

"True enough. For some reason I'll never understand, the stranger I paint them, the more people want them. I'd really rather be doing something else, but I'm not about to quarrel with success. Lately, Phoebe's been insisting on posing for me. She wants me to paint her as a bird. She's not a very good model, too fidgety and really too pretty. You'd be a better model than she is. There's something so calm and serene about you."

Evangeline felt far from calm and serene. What was Victor suggesting? That she take Phoebe's place in his studio? And where else? But his next words reassured her that he had no such intentions.

"You know, she used to do such pretty little watercolors of flowers. I wish she'd do more of them. But she hasn't picked up a brush in over three months, no matter how much I try to encourage her. I really don't know what's gotten into her. Did she give you any clue?"

Victor was so earnest, so down-home honest, Evangeline decided on the spot to trust him. She wouldn't be betraying her friend. She'd be trying to help her. "Phoebe tells it the other way around," she said. "According to her, you're the one behind all this bird business. You made her give up her painting. You make her pose for you. You make her jump off a ladder and try to fly." Even as she spoke, Evangeline realized how ridiculous it all sounded, but she plowed ahead. "She says you won't let her go out. Is that true?"

"Oh, gosh, no!" Victor exclaimed. "She can go out any time she wants. She won't even go out with me holding her hand, let alone by herself. Do you think she has some kind of phobia? I tried to get her to go see a doctor about it, but she won't."

"Could be," said Evangeline. "Why did you bring home the myna bird? Didn't you know it would upset her?"

"Well, I worried about that. But she said she wanted a talking bird. So I planned it as a surprise for her. I'd get that sweet little lady a whooping crane if that's what she wanted. I just don't understand why she's acting so strange. Vangie, I love her and I don't know what to do."

He looked so puzzled and forlorn, Evangeline longed to pat him on the shoulder and tell him everything would be all right. But it wouldn't, unless Phoebe snapped out of her funk and became once again the blithe young woman she used to be. And she didn't know how to make that happen.

Victor sighed and got up. "Thanks for listening," he said. "I wish Phoebe had invited you over sooner, before things got to such a state. Let's go back and see how she's making out with Mickey. To tell you the truth, I'm not crazy about having a live bird around the place, but if it makes her happy, I'm all for it."

When Evangeline stood beside him, she was pleased to notice that he was at least an inch taller than she was. "Maybe I can get her interested in something," she said. "Maybe you'd both like to come over to the coffeehouse some Saturday night when I'm playing."

"We can only try," said Victor, but he didn't seem very hopeful.

The birdcage stood empty when they returned, its door hanging open and Mickey the Myna nowhere to be seen. Phoebe lay facedown on the floor with a pillow over her head.

Victor rushed over to her. "Sweetheart!" he cried. "What happened? Where's the bird?"

Phoebe muttered something, but the pillow muffled her words.

"I can't hear you, darling." He tugged at the pillow, but Phoebe clung to it. "Please sit up," he begged. "Tell me what happened. I won't be mad at you. Honest I won't."

Phoebe flung the pillow aside and bolted upright, her face red and contorted with anger. "The damn thing attacked me!" she shouted. "It tried to peck my eyes out!"

"This window's open," Evangeline remarked. "It wasn't open before."

"You stay out of it, busybody!" Phoebe screamed. "If it's gone, good riddance."

Victor cuddled Phoebe in his arms and pressed her head onto his shoulder, making soothing noises while she whimpered.

Evangeline closed the window and began searching the teeming shrubbery for the bird. "I don't understand how he got out," she said. "You must have let him out, Phoeb."

"Ssh," said Victor. "Don't upset her. She feels bad enough already."

"But that bird must have cost a bundle," Evangeline protested.

"Doesn't matter," said Victor. He turned his attention back to Phoebe, petting and stroking her ruffled hair and assuring her that he still loved her no matter what had happened.

Evangeline found no living bird among the house plants. "A bird like that won't be able to survive in the city," she said. "You should put an ad in the *Village Voice*. Offer a reward." But no one paid her any attention.

After a while, they set out the food that Victor had brought home. It was all delicious, but no one had much appetite. Phoebe scarcely said a word. Evangeline tried to entertain them with stories of her life as a street and subway musician: the blind woman who always stopped for a while to listen and gave her a dollar whenever she played Mozart, the children who snitched quarters from her flute case, the territorial claims of all the street musicians trying to coexist around the city. Victor listened and commented, but he was clearly distracted by Phoebe's somber mood.

At last, Phoebe, who had drunk at least three glasses of wine, said, "I'm tired. I think I'll go to bed."

"I'll be going, too," said Evangeline.

"Don't you want to see my paintings?" Victor asked. "I don't mind showing them to you."

"You shouldn't miss that," Phoebe said venomously as she drifted away to another part of the apartment.

"Well, all right," said Evangeline. "But then I've really got to go."

Victor fished a set of keys out of his pocket and unlocked the studio door. "You must think I'm paranoid to keep this locked up. But Phoebe took a knife to one of my paintings once, and I can't afford to let that happen again."

Evangeline followed him into the darkened room. Before turning on the lights, he took her hand and led her a little distance into the darkness. His hand felt smooth and strong in hers.

"Stand right there," he told her. And then he left her alone in the inky blackness.

When the lights came on, Evangeline gasped. Whatever else Phoebe may have distorted in her mind and in her tales about Victor, she had been utterly truthful about his paintings. They were more than weird. They were disturbing, violent, fantastic portrayals of birds and women, melding into each other, consuming each other, becoming each other. It was as if the fairly pleasant room they'd left, with its tame house plants and its pretty representations of birds, had shown its other, primal face. Horror was here, superstition and idolatry. Evangeline's eyes darted from one huge canvas to the next of the twenty or so that were lined up around the room. She did her best to quell a feeling of revulsion and was alarmed to realize that this was accompanied by a morbid fascination. When, at last, she turned to face Victor, she groped for something to say.

"They're . . . stunning." She meant that she was stunned, struck, changed, pierced, and exalted.

"Yes," said Victor softly. He was smiling.

"And Phoebe . . . ?"

"There she is," said Victor, pointing to the unfinished canvas on the easel where a fierce-eyed bird glowered over a human baby cradled in its wings. The bird had breasts bulging with milk, but it was hard to tell whether it was preparing to nourish or devour. In the lower foreground, there was a broken, bloodstained eggshell. The cruel human face of the huge bird bore a faint resemblance to the sweet pretty face of Phoebe.

"People buy these?" Evangeline stammered. "I don't mean to be insulting, but I'm afraid they'd give me nightmares."

"I can't turn out enough of them. Every time I have a show, it's cleaned out within a week. And the price keeps going up. Not bad for a country boy whose hero was Audubon. I've come a long way since then."

"Yes," Evangeline whispered. "Thank you. I think I'd better go now." She fled from the room, noticing as she stumbled through the door a tall ladder propped up against the wall.

Victor followed her, turning off the light and locking the door. "I hope you'll come back. Phoebe needs you. I need you."

Again, that look, remote but intense. Hungry. Or was she imagining it? It was gone in an instant, and he was once again a simple, friendly, handsome young man, with a worried, preoccupied air about him.

"Say goodnight to Phoebe for me," Evangeline said as she shook his hand. "I'll call her tomorrow. I'll call her every day. There's got to be something we can do to help her."

"I'm sorry tonight was such a disaster," he said. "But next time will be better. I'll make sure of that."

All the way home on the subway, Victor's visions interposed themselves between Vangie's eyes and the ordinary underground sights of weary passengers and graceless graffiti. She tried to reach some rational conclusions about her evening with Victor and Phoebe. No doubt that Phoebe was disturbed, but was she telling the truth? Phoebe had been known to tell lies in the past, when it suited her purpose of the moment. But never anything as bizarre as this, and she'd always given herself away by the air of sublime innocence she'd put on for the occasion. Phoebe was not a good liar. That alone gave Evangeline room for doubt. On the other hand, Victor seemed so normal, so nice, so solicitous of Phoebe. Wouldn't it be wonderful, she thought, to have someone like Victor just aching to indulge your every whim? That myna bird, for instance. Parrots cost thousands of dollars, and mynas couldn't be far behind. They might even cost more if they were rarer. Mickey the Myna could have paid her rent for several months, and now he was out flying around the city, big bucks on the wing, while she scurried home to her dingy little room with nothing to look forward to but begging, that's what it amounted to, begging for change on a subway platform in the morning. Cut it out! she told herself. You're jealous, and that's not nice.

And then there were Victor's paintings. Evangeline shivered in the stifling underground heat of the subway car. Imagine living in the same apartment with a flock of those horrible birds. Even though they were locked up in the studio, even though they were nothing but paint on canvas, they were enough to send the strongest, sanest mind round the bend. And Phoebe was, as she'd told Victor, sensitive. Fragile. Easily influenced. Evangeline herself, practical as she was, had to admit to being fascinated by the painted beaks, the talons, the glistening feathers of Victor's bird-women. A mind that could produce such visions had to be a little bit on the kinky side.

Her thoughts teetered, first one way, then the other. Victor and Phoebe. Phoebe and Victor. Which one was right? Who was telling the truth? Or were they both obsessed, with each other and with the whole idea of birds? It was too complicated. She wished Phoebe hadn't called her, that she hadn't gone to see her. It was impossible to make any sense at all of what she'd seen and heard. And underlying all of it, she was sharply aware that she found Victor attractive. The way he'd said, "I need you," echoed in her mind. She thrust the thought away as disloyal.

Once safely home, she collapsed onto her daybed. It wasn't late, but she was exhausted. Yet she knew she wouldn't sleep. She got up and put on a recording of James Galway playing Japanese melodies. The simple, lilting music and the precise, clear notes of the flute soothed her. After a few moments, she got out her own flute and tried to accompany the record. If she could play even a fraction as well as Galway, she could leave the subway platforms and street corners behind forever. When the record finished, she played on alone. She'd never doubted that she had the stamina, the staying power, to conquer the world with her flute. But now, after seeing Phoebe, she wondered. Phoebe had caved in, given up. She'd traded in her minor talent for a life of luxury and ease, and it was probably that that was bothering her more than anything else. Evangeline was made of stronger stuff. If *she* were in Phoebe's shoes, she certainly wouldn't allow herself to go all limp and looney. That notion she had about Victor wanting to kill her was so far off-the-wall Evangeline didn't even want to think about it. Victor was too simple and honest and too much in love with Phoebe to do anything to hurt her.

She drifted away on a tide of Telemann sonatas until her fingers wearied and her lips grew dry. Then she put her flute away and ran a hot bath, extravagantly using up the last of her fragrant bath oil. Soaking in the hot water, Evangeline felt her eyelids grow heavy and her mind blissfully blank. Later, in bed, she promised herself she would keep out of their troubles. There was really nothing she could do.

The next morning, early, she set out for work, as she called it. The subway station at Seventy-seventh and Lexington was always good for twenty dollars or so during the rush hour, so long as she didn't appear there too often. She hadn't been there for at least two weeks. It was another bright, sunny summer day, not too hot yet. And it was a Friday. People would be feeling good, looking forward to the weekend. They'd be generous to a tall young woman who cheered them on their way with sprightly music. Her own mood had lifted. Nothing terrible could happen so long as the sun shone and the quarters and dollar bills fell into her flute case. Depending on how the morning went, she might even treat herself to that Guatemalan shawl she'd been admiring in the window of a SoHo boutique. It would go a long way toward brightening up her dreary wardrobe. Nothing like Phoebe's fine feathers, but it was certainly colorful, and she could wear it with just about everything she owned. And then tonight, there was rehearsal with the oboe and the violin. The oboe was from West Virginia and the violin from Montana. They were good people to make music with, but they wouldn't understand what she was talking about if she tried to explain Phoebe and Victor to them, let alone her own feelings. There was no one she could talk to.

On her way to the subway, she passed a newsstand, glancing, as she always did, at the headlines to see if there was any news worth scrounging a newspaper out of the garbage for. The headline on the *Post* caught her eye: VILLAGE WOMAN LEAPS TO DEATH. Beneath it was a photo of the building on West Tenth Street where Victor and Phoebe lived, with a dotted line swooping down from a window that might have been theirs.

Evangeline bought a paper. She stood on the street corner reading the story while people hurried past her, jostling her in their hurry to get to work. Yes, it was Phoebe and, yes, it had happened shortly after she'd left last night. The story didn't say much more than that. It sniggered over the fact that poor Phoebe was naked when she fell and that she and Victor weren't married. It alleged suicide. It quoted Victor as saying, "She'd been depressed over her work."

And Evangeline wondered. If she'd stayed a little longer. If she'd been more sympathetic to Phoebe, even insisted that she leave and come home with her. If Victor hadn't brought home that myna bird. If Victor hadn't . . . tried to make her fly, Phoebe wouldn't have jumped out the window. Evangeline was sure of that. She was too terrified of heights. What had happened after she'd left?

There was only one way to find out. She tucked the paper under her arm and marched determinedly to the subway station. She intended to face Victor with her suspicions. She would stand right up to him and say, "Look, Victor. I knew Phoebe too well. She would never have jumped. So what really happened? Did you push her?"

And if he said, "Yes." If he said yes, what on earth would she do? Go to the police? But he wouldn't say yes. Not so easily. If the newspapers were saying it was suicide, he'd probably already convinced the police that Phoebe had been deranged enough to take her own life. With his open, honest manner and his handsome, clean-cut, all-American face, that wouldn't be hard to do. He'd probably wept a few sincere, manly tears.

On the subway platform and on the downtown train, she wrestled with the problem of how to confront Victor. Should she be the distraught, sorrowful friend, overcome with the news and in need of consolation? That wouldn't be an act; she was all of those things. Or should she ooze sympathy for Victor, the bereft lover? That was probably the best tactic. If she could get him talking, he might give something away.

It even occurred to her that the best and safest thing to do would be to stay away altogether and simply go to the police with her suspicions. If Victor had killed Phoebe, he might have no qualms about doing it again, to anyone who threatened his security.

But not so soon, she reassured herself. That would be too suspicious. The police couldn't fail to take notice if two women died violently in two days in Victor's vicinity.

When she emerged from the subway on West Fourth Street, the sun was still shining, but Evangeline felt that she walked under a cloud. Usually, the shop windows of Greenwich Village intrigued her with their displays of antiques, jewelry, and expensive clothing, none of which she could afford to buy. But this morning, she passed them without a glance. There was only one shop where she paused and stared. In its corner windows, bright birds slept on their perches or peered sleepily at her as she gazed back at them. There were parrots, cockatoos, lovebirds, and toucans. Nothing so commonplace as a canary. And there in the corner was a pair of mynas. She wondered if one of them might be Mickey. He could have returned to the place he knew best. She had no doubt that this was where Victor had bought the bird, and she would have inquired, but the shop was closed. She could have disarmed Victor totally, given him a jolt, by arriving with the bird in hand.

But nothing could bring back Phoebe. She trudged on grimly, still wondering what approach she would take with Victor. When she arrived at the apartment building, she gave her name clearly to the doorman. If anything happened to her, she hoped he would remember it and that she'd asked for Victor's apartment number.

When she got off the elevator, Victor was waiting for her with the door open.

"I knew you'd come," he said. The strange, intense look was there in his clear blue eyes, and his boyish grin seemed suddenly evil. "I'm glad you brought your flute. Will you play for me?"

"Yes," said Evangeline, "but what about Phoebe? Did she . . . ? Did you . . . ?"

She trembled as Victor took her hand. She allowed him to draw her into the apartment. His blue eyes, hungry eyes, never left her face.

"Hush," he said. "Don't ask questions. You'll soon know everything." He locked the door behind her and led her toward the open door of his studio.

The painted birds flocked around her. Distantly, she heard their shrieks and caws. They were calling her.

Closer, a compelling whisper in her ear, she heard Victor say, "I need *you* now."

"Yes," she answered. "I know." And she bent her swanlike neck.

AN ELEMENT OF SURPRISE

WARREN MURPHY

"Is this Alex Garth?"

"No, moron. It's Bonnie Prince Charlie. I always stay at the Budget Six Motel when I'm in Boston. Who is this?"

"That's one thing I like about you, Garth. You've got a sense of humor."

"Shrinking by the minute. Who is this?"

"Who's not important."

"Just what I was thinking," I said and hung up the telephone. It started ringing again while I was walking into the dingy little motel bathroom. I took my time. I wiped my hands on my pants. It was still ringing when I came back out, so I picked it up.

"You've got twenty seconds," I said.

"That's another thing I like about you, Garth. You've got a lovely temper."

"Fifteen seconds and counting."

"All right," he said. "They're going to punch your ticket when you get back to New York."

"Who's they?"

"Some of the people you work for. Something about some snow that stuck to your shovel."

"I don't know what you're talking about," I said.

"Suit yourself, pal. I was just trying to do you a favor. Forget it."

"Hold on," I said. I paused for a moment, then figured what the hell. "This hit. Who's supposed to do it?"

"Charlie Cletis."

"You know when?"

"When you get back. This weekend. I don't know exactly."

"Why are you telling me this?" I asked him.

"You did me a favor once. Now we're even."

"Who is this?" I said.

"Sorry. Your twenty seconds is up."

Click.

Sometimes you do stupid things. Like I just stood there for a minute, looking at the phone, as if it could tell me who had called. Then I put the phone down and plopped back on the unmade bed.

One large puzzle. Who had called? I didn't recognize the voice and he said I did him a favor once. That just didn't ring true because I couldn't remember ever doing anybody a favor. Not when I was a cop in New York and not when I was trying to make a living off that crummy private-detective agency. Especially not since I've been taking a lot of money to kill a lot of people for people who often want other people killed.

Who had called? That was the only puzzle. The rest of it was easy. Some snow stuck to my shovel. That was in Philadelphia, my last job, and the guy I bopped had a kilo of pure cocaine in his room and I took it. And somehow they had found me out. All right, a mistake, but I wasn't going to let it turn into anything serious.

I stood up and saw the gun on the end table next to the telephone. Dammit, I thought, I should have gotten rid of that before. I took it into the bathroom and used toilet paper to wipe it clean. Then I wrapped it inside the paper bag they used for a liner in the waste basket, those cheap bastards, and I stuck it inside my jacket pocket. I went over to the motel office.

On a job, I always traveled light, paid cash in advance for my room, and got my change when I was leaving. Simpler and no records.

The clerk was this college cretin with pimples. "How was everything, Mr. Johnson?" he asked me.

"Fine. I think you're growing a better brand of roach since the last time I was here," I said.

"Roaches?" He put this big concerned face on. He ought to be concerned about his complexion, I thought. "I'll call our exterminator right away."

"This place doesn't need an exterminator," I said, pocketing my change. "Try a demolition team."

"What do you mean?"

I just sighed. "Forget it, will you?" I said.

Another flea, another fleabrain. The world was filled with them; it really *could* use a good exterminator.

Outside the sun was shining its ass off—I read that once in some sappy detective novel—so I put on these big wide wraparound sunglasses that I like. I wished I hadn't when I looked back and saw Pimples was looking at me through the office window. But then, I figured, aaah, to hell with it. Everybody looked alike wearing sunglasses.

Two blocks away I bought a newspaper from some dork who seemed more interested in telling me to have a nice day than in taking my money, and another block later I took the wrapped gun from my pocket, put it inside the newspaper, and dropped the whole package in a litter basket.

Another block away I flagged down a cab.

"The airport," I said.

The guy looked into the backseat and said, "Logan, right?"

"You know any other airport in Boston?"

He turned back. "Logan it is. Wicked hot, ain't it this summah?"

I always hated New Englanders and their stupid accents. They talked like cretins and, to boot, were absolutely the worst drivers this side of Mexico City.

"Just can the chatter and get me to the freaking airport in one piece, will you?"

I watched this imbecile drive and figured that directionals must be outlawed up there. To make a right-hand turn, he pulled into the left-hand lane, then leaned on his horn and swerved across two lanes of traffic into another street. It was Charles Street, and all the shops seemed to have signs that read, "Ye Olde" this and "Ye Olde" that. I thought if these people love England so much, they ought to try visiting Ye Olde London, where the people had to be the stinkingest on earth. I had been there about two years earlier, and Ye Olde soap bar and Ye Olde deodorant hadn't seemed to be real big hits.

The cab lurched to a stop at Logan, nearly loosening my teeth, and

Idiot Boy says, "That's fourteen dollahs." So I dropped a ten and a five through the front window.

"Keep the change. Use it for remedial-driving school."

I had a few minutes, so I stopped in the lounge for a drink, and the television was filled with news reports on "the gangland-style killing" of a young attorney that morning. He had been shot by an unknown assailant as he left his home for work. The only description of the killer was that he wore dark sunglasses. I thought it was probably a little late, but I took off my sunglasses anyway. The lawyer left a wife and three small children, and they had an interview with the wife, who was crying and wailing and wondering why someone would kill her husband, who didn't have an enemy in the world.

Wrong, lady, I thought. He had at least one enemy, somebody who hated him enough to pay me to kill him. What the lawyer had done, I didn't know and didn't care. He was just another day's work.

When the shuttle to New York was airborne, I drank a Chivas Regal on the rocks, then figured maybe I ought to walk back to the bathroom to see if there was anybody on this plane that I recognized.

There wasn't, so I hunkered down in my seat with another Chivas and thought about that phone call again. So they were going to try to kill me, all over a stinking 2.2 pounds of cocaine, a stinking pile of degenerate powder for stinking degenerates who wanted to kill themselves.

I had taken it only for the money. That much blow was worth more than a quarter of a million out on the street, and I wanted it. I remembered thinking, Take it, Garth. You're fifty-four years old, and it's your "screw you" money. With that kind of bankroll, you can turn down a job or maybe just pack in the whole business. That's what I thought. So it was a risk, but I took it, and then they'd found me out and gave Charlie Cletis the job of killing me.

That kind of made sense in a rough kind of way. Fifteen years ago, I had been forced out of the police department when some reform bastard came in and decided cops shouldn't shake down bookies anymore. Then I found out I couldn't make a living from a ratty private-eye business, and my first solo contract had been on the guy who recruited me and tried to teach me about the hitman's trade.

So I thought it was poetic justice that they gave the job of kissing me off to somebody I had trained. It was the way the people I worked for liked to plan: neat, tidy, no loose ends. Except there was already one big loose end that they didn't know about. I knew that Cletis was going to try to kill me, and I had no intention of lying down and playing dead.

I was thinking it all through when this red-headed bimbo stuck her nose in and said, "Another drink, sir?"

"When I want another drink, I'll ring your bell," I snapped. She got uppity, the way they always did when somebody didn't fall for their big phony I'm-staying-at-the-Plaza smile, and stalked off, so I just nursed the Chivas and weighed my options.

Option one: I could run away.

Option two: I could kill Charlie Cletis.

Option two was better. If I just ran, the contract would stay open, and anyone could collect on it. I had this image of what my life would be like . . . a marked man, looking over my shoulder, sleeping with a bazooka under my pillow, owning a freaking toy poodle who barked at raindrops, just to make sure that nobody sneaked up on me.

I figured that if I killed Cletis, though, it would be different. Then the old peppers who ran the organization would have to vote again on whether or not to issue a new contract on my life, and chances were they wouldn't. I had worked for them for fifteen years and I knew them. They didn't like untidiness or risk, and despite all that crap about imitating Marlon Brando and Don Corleone, if they were faced with a man who fought back, they would just wash their hands of him. They'd accept their losses, let me know that I was expected to be quiet, and I'd go on my own sweet way. With the cocaine. Maybe they'd even give me a gold watch for my faithful service. Anything rather than risk being shot themselves.

It was the only way to go, I thought, so that left Charlie Cletis to get rid of, and I figured that wouldn't be any problem at all.

I put on my sunglasses and tilted the seat back and tried to take a nap, but I couldn't get Cletis out of my mind. He wasn't the kind of guy you would forget, six feet six or so, less than 150 pounds, a big shock of hair that looked like straw. I could picture him, an automatic in each hand, dimwitted lout, firing out whole clips at random.

It wasn't a bad memory, because Charlie Cletis just hadn't been too bright, and he had something else going against him too: He had lost the surprise factor, thanks to whoever that was who called me. And that was the sure way to die.

I had warned Cletis about it when I broke him in . . . hell, it had been six years earlier. We were at one of the organization's properties in New Jersey, one of those big isolated warehouses they build to keep the garbage dumps from running into each other. I had been asked to show Cletis the ropes as a favor to some organizational friends in Chicago. He hadn't impressed me much, but I tried to do the job. No skin off my nose; my territory didn't reach all the way to Chicago.

So I had tried my best. I sat down this big scarecrow-looking thing and I told him the truth.

"Nothing is important except surprise. Look at political killings. The ones that work are always surprises. The easiest hits are where you just walk up to the target and blow him away. If you don't have to, don't even take the gun out of your pocket; just shoot him right through the cloth. The target doesn't even know he's a target. That's how it works best. Surprise. Surprise is the key, because without that, it's just another even fight, and who the hell wants an even fight? You're not getting paid to win half the gunfights at the OK Corral."

But Cletis just looked at me, and I could see contempt in those watery-blue eyes of his. I knew it right then. He was some kind of throwback to the merry days of Al Capone and the twenties, the type who'd use a submachine gun when a .22-caliber target pistol would do the job. His teeth were too big for him to be smart.

He didn't have much future, I thought, but I tried one more time. "Goddammit, Cletis, did you hear anything I said?"

Cletis smiled and gave me that soft southern drawl, the way they talk when their mouths are filled with sheep turds, and he said, "Raht. Suhprazz."

Christ, I hated southerners. They wouldn't recognize an idea if it jumped up and fastened its teeth on their corncob pipe.

"That means, 'Right. Surprise,' doesn't it? In English?" I said.

"Raht. Suhprazz," and then he walked off to shoot another hundred rounds into a stationary target.

So that was that, and Cletis was off to Chicago. For a couple of months I scanned the papers most days, expecting to hear about him dying in some dumb shoot-out, but he must have gotten lucky, because I never saw anything about him and I put him out of my mind.

Until that phone call and I was on my way back to New York and I thought, Charlie, you've been lucky till now, but your luck is running out. I'm going to have a surprise for you.

And then I dozed off until the plane touched down in New York. At the airport, I walked around for a while, making sure I wasn't being followed, then I took a cab to this private parking garage in Queens where I always stashed my car when I went out of town.

But I didn't go back to my apartment. Instead I checked into a fleabag hotel on the other side of Fourteenth Street, then called my own telephone number and used a beeper to get the messages from my tape machine.

There was only one.

"Hiya, ole buddy. This is Charlie Cletis. Long time, no see. How 'boutcha give me a buzz when you get in?" He left a phone number.

I could feel the sweat starting on my palms as I asked the hotel operator to get me the number. It was a good feeling. It was starting.

"Hello, Cletis. This is Garth."

"Axe, ole buddy. Nice message ya have there on your answering machine. Most folks do leave some kinda message, you know. Not jus' thirty seconds of dead air."

I hated him. I hated the way he talked, the way he sounded talking to a man he was planning to kill. I hated him for thinking he was good enough to take me on. I hated it that the dumb rebel bastard couldn't pronounce Alex and always called me Axe.

But all I said was, "You know me, I don't care much for chitchat. You want something?"

"Jus' in town for a couple of days R and R," Cletis said. "Thought we maht get together for a drink."

"You run out of shitkickers to drink with?"

"No, but 'tain't often I get a chance to drink with my mentor." He pronounced the last word slowly, men-TORE. " 'Course, iffen ya don' wanna . . ."

"No, sure. What the hell," I said. "Let's get lunch."

"Fahn. When? Where?"

"Let's meet at my office tomorrow," I said. "I get in around eleven. Meet me there, and I'll take you to a good restaurant. Real food. Not that catfish crap you people eat."

"Eleven o'clock? You come in at eleven o'clock? Business must be good to work banker's hours."

"Not that good," I said. "It's just my schedule. Saturday mornings, ten o'clock sharp, I get my car cleaned at the car wash down the block from me and then I go to the office to check the mail. Like clockwork."

"You always was like clockwork," Cletis said with a dry chuckle. "Ah'd be careful at that carwash, was I you."

"How's that?" I asked.

"You still driving that old blue clinker?"

"Yeah."

"Well, the dirt's the only thing holding it together."

"I like my cars slow," I said. "Only my women fast."

"Fast women, fast ponies. That's what I remember about you," Cletis said. "Ya been away?"

"Out of town a couple of days. Business."

"But you're home now," he said.

"Hey, pal. Home is an empty apartment. Right now I am where the welcome is warm and so is the company," I lied.

"Ole dog," Cletis said. "Ya gonna get married and settle down is what ya gonna be tellin' me next."

"Not a chance," I said. "Listen. This lady is anxious, and so am I. Tomorrow, after I get the car washed, I'll meet you at the office. Anytime after eleven."

"Look forward to it, Axe," he said.

"Me too," I said, but after I hung up the phone, I said out loud, "You stupid shitkicker, who do you think you're jerking around with?" So I had some gray in my hair and at fifty-four I was a little thicker around the middle than I used to be. So what? I was as good as ever and I found it, well, I'll tell you the truth, I found it kind of insulting that the people I worked for could think that Charlie Cletis was good enough to take me. Not a chance, not on the best day that rebel ever lived.

It would be the car wash. I knew it because Cletis was just too damned obvious about it. I figured I'd have to plan a little surprise for him, so I left the room to go for a walk. It was cooler, and the night air always helped me to think.

One way or another, I wound up going toward Fourteenth Street, and as I walked across the big east-west drag, I saw the mostly burned-out lights of Alphabet City stretched out in front of me.

Alphabet City. It's this ugly slash of New York, running south from Fourteenth Street, and sliced up by Avenues A, B, C, and D. That's where it got its nickname. There and maybe from the fact that most of the people there couldn't recite the alphabet. More than Harlem, more than Times Square, it was New York City's combat zone. Drug dealers ran wild. The streets weren't only unsafe at night; they were unsafe at high noon. Gary Cooper would get his ass shot off walking down these streets. Every kind of lowlife and degenerate seemed to drift into the area sooner or later, and once in a while the cops would put on a show for the newspapers and send in extra manpower for a couple of days, but as soon as they left, it went right back to what it had been before.

I called it home. It's where I lived, among the orange-hairs and the leather boys and the girls who wore tire chains around their neck and T-shirts with holes cut in them so their nipples stuck out. It was where I wanted to live. No one asked any questions and no one cared what you did, and that was all I wanted from a neighborhood. And Alphabet City would stay that way too, because the scum of the city would always need a place to collect. That made me feel sorry for the trendies—young women mostly—who had moved into the area because the rents were low and then they found out they had just leased a cage in the city zoo.

I saw one of them coming toward me down the street, a tall, thin woman, flanked by two woolly dogs with heads big enough to belong to grizzly bears.

I almost laughed aloud. These dumb women, they faced torture and murder on the streets, but rather than move someplace sensible, they decided to buy large guard dogs. I never could understand the logic. Granted, this dumping ground was about the only place in the city where human beings could afford to rent an apartment. Not like the rest of the city, where leases are handed down from generation to generation like the family jewels. But what was the point of saving money on rent when you had to spend all that you saved to buy hundred-pound dogs and tons of soup bones and Alpo beef chunks by the case and wee-wee pads the size of mattresses? I just call that stupid.

The woman was getting close and she smiled this nervous smile at me. Not smart, I thought to myself. Never let the enemy know you're afraid of him. I smiled back but I couldn't resist it. Just when she got near me, I jumped in front of her, waved my arms, and yelled, "Boo."

Well, she shrieked, and those two stupid Japanese dogs whimpered and hid behind her legs.

"Hey, lady," I said. "Why don't you move the hell out of here and go someplace nice? Before you and your doggies get hurt?"

She mumbled under her breath and yanked the dogs along with her. Just for good luck, I reached out and patted her rear end as she walked away.

Guard dogs. I thought maybe in Harlem, lady, maybe to scare off blacks, but not around here, not in Alphabet City. The violence here wasn't black. It didn't belong to anybody. It was like a fog and it swirled around everybody and touched everybody. To survive down here, you needed luck and brains, but most of all, smarts. Smarts kept you alive down here, not some yuppie guard dogs that you had to hand-feed sushi to.

Smarts taught you things. You learned how to walk the streets, how to make eye contact with a stranger. Just long enough for him to know you weren't afraid of him, but not so long that it looked like you wanted to pick a fight. You learned to survive and you'd better because in Alphabet City there were only three kinds of people: smart people, dead people, and candidates for dead people. I was one of the smart ones and I laughed aloud on the empty street. It felt good to be back home. Down here, I said to myself, Charlie Cletis would be dog meat.

I turned toward the river, then stood across the street from my tenement building. There were no curtains in my windows, and I could see the bare bulb hanging from the ceiling. I never could see spending money on decorating. Ponies and women. That was all I wanted to spend money on.

I used my key to let myself in and I walked up the dark steps to my floor. I listened at the door, but it was quiet inside. I felt at the top of the door for the piece of Scotch tape I always stick there so I can tell if anybody was in my apartment after I left. The tape wasn't there, and for a moment, my heart thumped hard and the breath caught in my throat. Then I remembered I had run out of tape and didn't put any there when I left for Boston.

I unlocked the door, pushed it open, waited awhile, then went in. I had come for a gun, but just like that, a plan started forming in my mind, and I took a few pieces of clothing from a pile in the closet and stuck them inside an old gym bag. There was a wastebasket under the kitchen table, and I picked it up and from the bottom took a .32-caliber revolver that was taped there. It was loaded, so I put it in the holster on the back of my belt under my jacket. It was a clean gun, no record of it anywhere, and it was the gun I figured to use on that stupid Charlie Cletis.

Back on the street I felt better, feeling the weight of the gun under my jacket, and a few blocks away I stopped in a bar called the Stinking Parrot. I'd never seen it before, but that didn't surprise me because in that neighborhood, a guy opened a saloon, used it as a front while he sold a million dollars' worth of drugs, then took his money and got out and sold the joint to somebody, who changed the name and started it all over again.

When I opened the front door, the smell from the place almost made me gag. It was this mixture of urine and smoke and alcohol and sweat, and it was lethal. I thought that somebody someday was going to light a cigarette in there at the wrong time and the place was going to explode in a fireball. I stood at the corner of the bar and put the gym bag on the floor between my feet.

"Get you something?" this fireplug bartender yelled at me over the noise.

"Chivas, rocks," I said.

"Pretty fancy for in here," the bartender said.

"Not for me."

"Why not?" he asked.

What I wanted to say was that I was a Lithuanian princess in disguise, looking for a suitable husband. What I said was that I hit a pony and would he please get me my drink.

I gave him the three dollars and looked around the place. It was lit like a pinball machine, and I wondered how much money a person could make in a dive like this. I spotted the big man at the bar right away. He was this big noisy black dude wearing a black leather jacket and dirty white painter's pants, and even in the middle of July, he had a ski cap on.

The plan for the whole thing was coming together in my mind, but I had to work it out carefully. No slipups. I thought I had been careless a couple of times already that day. Taking too long to dump the gun in Boston, wearing sunglasses watching that stupid news report looking for a killer in sunglasses. I even waited too long before checking to see if anybody dangerous was on that plane. No tape on the door. Little mistakes like that, I knew, could cost you, and when I went after Cletis, I didn't want any mistakes.

I was swirling the drink in my hand, watching the black man's mouth move, and wondering again why the organization would send someone like Cletis after me. Christ, they could've hired Martino. He was a wop, but at least he was a professional. I realized my pride was hurt that somebody would think that Cletis could take me.

"Yo' be havin' trouble wif yo' eyeballs?"

I blinked and saw the big guy was yelling at me. I had been staring at him. I looked away, but it was too late; he came down the bar and stood alongside me.

"Ah ask you, somefin' wrong wif yo' eyeballs, you starin' at me like dat?"

On a different night, a different place, I might just have said, "No. Actually I was mesmerized by your mastery of the English language." But not this night.

So I just said, "Sorry, mister. I'm just leaving."

"Yo' leaves when ah says yo' leaves."

The bartender was hovering around, so I leaned over and said softly, "Get this tree climber off my back, will you?"

"Hey, Uncle Joe," the bartender said. "Let him be. He's leaving now."

"Ah makes sure o' dat," the baboon said.

I grabbed the gym bag in my left hand and headed for the door. I could feel the black guy walking behind me and I knew what was next. As soon as I got outside, he'd slam me in the back, cold-cock me, drag me into the alley, and lift anything I owned.

I had the gun in my hand before I was out the door and I sensed when he was starting his punch, so I pulled away, spun around, and let him see the gun aimed at his face. He still had his fists clenched together, in front of his head, but now he separated them slowly.

"Hey, bro. No need fo' dat," he said. Then he smiled. Then I smashed the heel of the gunbutt into his nose. He dropped like a wet sock. I knelt alongside him and slammed his face again with the butt of the gun. What there was of his nose went soft under it.

"You're lucky, Bomba," I said. "I'm busy tonight or I'd just love taking you apart." He groaned and his eyes rolled back into his head, so I picked up my gym bag and took off at a trot before any of his buddies came out looking for him.

I walked back to the hotel feeling good. I might be getting older, but I wasn't old yet. Not yet.

Later, I was lying in the bed in the fleabag, and the picture of my father jumped into my head. The old man had left home when I was fifteen, and nobody missed him. He was a heavy-handed juice-head who talked all the time, just to hear himself talk. But once in a while, he had made some sense. I knew that, even when I was a boy. So I remembered something he told me once when he was crying into his whiskey glass at the kitchen table.

"Alex," he had said. "Listen to me." I had nodded but I stayed out of his reach, just in case. "There's nothing better for a man," he said, "than that his enemies should underestimate him. Remember that, boy."

I nodded again, but he had already forgotten that I was in the room. But I knew a good piece of advice when I heard one and, lying in the bed, I realized that it was exactly what was happening to me: My bosses had underestimated me and they were sending Charlie Cletis after me, this half-a-retard who was as slow and dopey as a housefly in November. Well, their tough luck.

I stayed awake for two hours, carefully working out the trap I was going to set. When I finally rolled onto my side to get to sleep, I knew it was dead-center perfect. I closed my eyes wondering again who it was that had called me in Boston. Why would somebody want to help me? And in those last few seconds before sleep, the answer popped into my head. It had to be somebody who hated Cletis even more than I did, somebody who had a score to settle with the redneck rube. It was a good reason and it solved the puzzle, and I slept like a baby.

Nine o'clock the next morning, I parked my car in front of a small luncheonette two blocks from my apartment. The neighborhood was ripe today, I thought, as I stepped from the car. The hot July sun was already baking the garbage on the sidewalks, and the sweet stench of decay hung in the air.

Through the window, I saw a beefy gray-haired man behind the counter, and when I went in, he said, "Hey, Al. How's the private-eye business?" His name was Benny, and he thought he was my friend.

"Looking good. I need a favor."

Naturally, he looked away without answering. In Alphabet City, favors were the kind of thing that generally got you thrown in jail.

"Nothing serious," I said. "I need you to drive my car through the car wash down the block."

"Yeah?"

"That's it," I said. "There's twenty bucks in it for you. Ten minutes' work."

"Can I get some kid to do it?"

I shook my head. "No, Benny, it's got to be you."

"Why?" He was suspicious again.

" 'Cause you look like me a little. I'm playing a joke on somebody."

"Just go get your car washed?"

"At ten o'clock. That's all," I said.

"This isn't dangerous, is it?"

"Come on, Benny, for Christ's sake. I'm talking about a car wash. I tell you, it's a joke. I'm planning a surprise for somebody."

"Twenty bucks." Benny hesitated. "All right. What the hell."

"It's got to be ten o'clock sharp," I said.

"No sweat. Louie can watch the counter."

I took three ten-dollar bills from my jacket pocket. "Here's your twenty. The extra ten's for the car wash."

"What do I do afterward?"

"Bring the car back here," I said. "I'll pick it up later."

"Okay."

"And be sure to wear these." I took off my snap-brim hat and my wraparound sunglasses and put them on the counter. I tried my smile on Benny. "Part of the joke," I said. "A disguise for you."

"So I should look like you," Benny said.

"You should be so lucky, fatso," I said and grinned at him. Like a friend would.

In the men's room of a saloon on the corner, I took a bottle of black shoe polish from the gym bag, put some on my fingers and dabbed it on the hair on my temples, changing the gray to black. Then I washed my hands, put the shoe polish back into the bag, and changed from my suit jacket into an old baseball warmup jacket. I put on a New York Yankees baseball cap, then folded my suit jacket and put it inside the gym bag. On top of that I put the .32-caliber revolver.

When I walked away from the tavern, I felt the churning in my stomach that I always felt when a job was near. I guess some people might have found that sensation unpleasant, but not me. For me, those were the moments when I was most alive. Draw up a good plan, execute it well, and bingo. It was what life was about. And death.

There was the usual Saturday morning line at the car wash. A couple of old winos and other assorted debris from last night's drinking lay cluttered around the apartment buildings on the block.

Like trees lining the entranceway to some estate, mounds of green plastic garbage bags decorated the entrance to the Kleen-Kwik Kar Wash. In other parts of the city, garbage piled up only when the sanitation men went out on strike. In Alphabet City, it was always there, a municipal monument.

At one minute to ten by my watch I saw my car pull into the end of the line and I saw Benny behind the wheel, although with the snap-brim hat and the big sunglasses, I really couldn't recognize his face.

Almost time, I thought. I still hadn't seen Charlie Cletis, but I knew he had to be around. He had tipped it all off last night on the phone when he started showing so much interest in what kind of car I was driving. My father's words came back to me again: "Nothing better for a man than that his enemies should underestimate him."

Charlie Cletis, I'm the last person you'll ever underestimate, I told myself.

Benny was now only two car lengths from the car-wash entrance, so I opened the gym bag, took out the revolver, and stuck it in my belt under the jacket. I stashed the bag behind a garbage pail where I could pick it up later and started strolling down the street to the Kleen-Kwik.

It happened just like I knew it would. As Benny pulled the car up to the entrance, the door of another car parked on the street opened, and a gangly tall man with straw hair stepped out. He left the door open and walked toward Benny in the car. He had swallowed it, I thought. Hook, line, sinker, and fishing rod.

I was only a few steps behind him and I thought, They should have known better, Charlie, than to send somebody like you after somebody like me.

The thin man stopped next to the car Benny was driving. He put his hands on the car roof and leaned over to look inside the passenger's window. I remember thinking it was strange that his hands were empty, but before he could reach for a gun, I stepped up behind him and put my hand on the gun inside my jacket.

"Hello, Charlie," I said. "Sorry but somebody dropped a dime on you."

I wanted him to turn around, to see my face as I shot him. The man turned. It wasn't Charlie Cletis. Somebody else but not Charlie. What was happening? I didn't know.

My hand squeezed the grip of my gun. Hard. The man said, "You Garth?"

I nodded. "Who are you?" I asked. He looked so much like Charlie Cletis.

He said, "I've got a message for you. I was told to tell you that another thing I like about you, Garth, is that you're so predictable."

That's what he said just now and I don't understand it, but I know if I have a minute or two, I can figure it out. Everything is flashing through my mind right now, like a super-speed slide show, everything I've said or thought or done since yesterday in Boston. But what's he mean? I'm not sure. Give me just a minute and I'll figure it out. Just a minute.

Do I have a minute? Maybe not. I feel something now against the back of my neck. It's hard and it's cold and I know what it is. It's the muzzle of a small gun.

I don't have time to turn around. I just hear a voice, this soft southern voice, and it's saying . . . what's it saying? . . . it's saying:

"Suhprazz, Axe, ole buddy. Suhprazz."

THE VALENCIA ORANGE MURDER

BERNARD ST. JAMES

Do you remember way back, when the Mystery Writers of America had its headquarters at the Hotel Valencia on East Twenty-ninth Street? No, of course you wouldn't remember that, you weren't a member then. In fact, I'd just joined the organization the last year we held our monthly cocktail parties there. That was when one of those incidents occurred that could only happen in real life. If you tried to work it into fiction, no reader would buy it. There we were, about forty or so mystery writers (and an equal number of guests and fans) gathered at a party, unaware that while we were celebrating, a real murder was being committed in the hotel. Correction: One person there was aware of it.

I'd sold two short stories, one to *Ellery Queen*, the other to *Mike Shayne*, and I was sitting on top of the world. Here I was, rubbing elbows with people whose work I'd admired all my life, and even though I was really a beginner, they treated me as an equal. Here were writers who were legends in their own time.

That was where I first met Jeffrey Merritt, truly a legend in his own mind. I'd heard his name when I was a kid, yet it never occurred to me that such a person really existed. I mean, that the author was a flesh-and-blood human being. We tend to think of writers as creatures who inhabit another planet, and movies encourage this belief. They show writers doing everything but writing. Of course, there's one mandatory scene where the guy's sitting at a typewriter. He pecks away desultorily for a few seconds, then pulls out the sheet of paper, crumples it, and throws it across the room. That tells us he's a *writer.*

But show me the movie where our writer hero plants his ass on a chair and sits and slaves away all day, week after week, month after month. Hell, no. This guy spends most of his time solving a real-life murder and chasing after the girl of his dreams. Yet somehow, his books get written.

Oh, yeah, one more thing. Especially on television, a first novel is always, always a bestseller—even before publication. I sold those two stories right after I got out of college, and it took me years before I sold another piece of work. That was my first novel, and it died an ignominious death.

I started to tell you about the Hotel Valencia. Surely you must have passed the place. It's an old building in the ornate style of a bygone era. It was built in 1905, with another section added on years later. In the days of its glory there was a posh restaurant downstairs, off the lobby, and Caruso used to dine there regularly. Legend has it that Harpo Marx was once a bellhop there. Anyway, by the time MWA had its suite in the hotel, the place had gotten pretty seedy. Faded and worn carpeting, wallpaper peeling in some places, dim lighting in the hallways. You know what I mean. Atmospheric as all hell.

That was in 1970, and Jeff Merritt used to come to the cocktail parties frequently. Not every month, but most of the time. I think he came mainly for the cheap drinks. Admission at the door was a dollar, and a generous shot of whiskey was seventy-five cents. And there stood Jeff, boozy, weaving, and always amiable.

Jeff was of medium height, sandy-haired, and indeterminate age. He could have been anywhere from forty into his late fifties. Sometimes he brought a lady friend with him, but most of the time he'd pick someone up at the party. Someone told me (maybe it was Jeff himself) that there were very few of the younger women he hadn't taken to bed.

Jeff Merritt, you see, was a "celebrity." He wrote short stories about private-eye Bill Hoehner, originally in the pulps. The stories really caught on, and he sold his later ones to the slick magazines—

Liberty, *Collier's*, and the *Saturday Evening Post*. They were reprinted in a hardcover collection, and later in paperback. In the late forties *Bill Hoehner* became a weekly radio show, and in the mid-fifties a series on TV. I was just a kid, but I remember that series in what must have been its last season. It wasn't on too late, eight o'clock, and my parents used to let me stay up to watch. I liked the action and Bill Hoehner's wisecracks. We all repeated them in school the next day. My mother thought the actor who played Bill was cute. What was his name again? Warner Stevens, that's right.

You know, for all their popularity, the stories—I mean the printed stories—didn't rate all that highly with the critics or with the *mavens*. Read today, they come across as competent but standard hard-boiled private-eye stuff. If you want to be less than charitable, you could describe the writing as warmed-over Hammett and Chandler. Still, the stories were successful, and Jeffrey Merritt was undeniably a successful author.

And the damn thing is—and this is the whole point of my story—Jeffrey Merritt actually did get involved in a real-life murder case. . . .

Jeffrey Merritt made his way up Fifth Avenue toward East Twenty-ninth Street. It was the second Friday in December, only two weeks before Christmas, but the weather was crisp and clear, not at all cold, and Jeff had walked from his home at Twelfth Street and University Place in the Village. Only the fact that it was already dark, at a few minutes past seven, marked the season as winter. The atmosphere wasn't at all Christmasy.

When he reached the corner of Twenty-ninth, he turned right and headed toward Madison. The party had been under way for two hours. Normally, those things broke up at eight, but this being the Christmas party, it would probably run on somewhat longer. He hoped he'd find someone interesting there. Why the euphemism, he asked himself. By "interesting" he meant young, female, pretty, and available.

The reason for his lateness, aside from his decision to walk, was that he'd been on the phone most of the afternoon with his agent. They'd been reviewing the situation regarding the TV series. Ever since the series was canceled, following its fourth season, it had been in almost steady syndication around the country. It had also been popular abroad (which, in turn, had given a nice boost to foreign sales of his books).

Now, however, things had taken a turn, and not for the better. Only a very few small independent stations still carried the *Bill Hoehner* series in the United States. The villain, and the only one *Bill Hoehner* couldn't defeat, was color TV. *Bill Hoehner* was in black and white. The programs were still being shown overseas, where some countries' systems had not yet converted to color, and those that had simply couldn't afford to buy that much color product. But for how long . . . Oh, come on, Merritt, snap out of it. It's Christmas. Well, almost Christmas. Anyway, a Christmas party. And who knows, perhaps the most beautiful woman in the world . . .

He entered the lobby of the Hotel Valencia, with its faded grandeur. The red carpeting was indeed worn and faded, and what looked like the original chandelier still hung there, but it wasn't polished and it was no longer lighted. A few lamps, scattered around the lobby, now provided rather dim illumination, and the elegant restaurant had long ago been replaced by a coffee shop.

The Valencia did cater to transients, but most of its clientele were resident guests, some of whom had been around for decades. There were always a few of these seated in the lobby. Tonight was no exception. Why should it be? There was also a family of out-of-towners at the desk, getting material from the clerk about things to do and see in New York. They were a middle-aged couple, their adolescent son, and their preteen daughter. They sounded as if they came from the Midwest.

Jeffrey Merritt was to remember all of these details clearly later, for although he didn't know it yet, this evening would prove to be one of the most memorable of his life. He took the elevator up to the fourth floor, and as soon as he stepped off, he realized that something was up. The hallway was filled with police, both uniformed and plainclothed. Obviously, something was going on in Room 412. The flashes told him the police photographer was at work, and a man carrying a medical bag was just coming out of the room. MWA's suite was just around the corner, their party was in full swing, and it was entirely possible that no one there knew about this.

Jeff went up to one of the uniformed policemen. "What happened?" he asked.

"Somebody died," the cop answered.

"Natural death? Accident? Homicide?"

The cop looked noncommittal. Jeff decided it had to be homicide. Even with an accident, there wouldn't be that much activity, or that many plainclothesmen involved. He decided to voice his observation.

"Say, you're a real detective, ain't you?" the cop said. The truth was that he had nothing much to do and was amusing himself. "Read lots of mystery stories, do you?"

"Yes, I do read lots of mysteries," Jeff replied, "and I also write them." This last statement was certainly no falsehood. It was merely the tense that was incorrect: He hadn't written anything in years. "I'm Jeffrey Merritt," he added.

The name seemed to mean nothing to the police officer.

"I write the Bill Hoehner private-eye stories."

The policeman's attitude changed from one of gentle mockery to genuine admiration. "*Bill Hoehner!* I used to watch that show on TV. That was my favorite program. What are you doing here, Mr. Hoehner—I mean, Mr. Merritt?"

"Mystery Writers of America has a suite in this hotel. Right around the corner on this floor, in fact. They're having their Christmas party tonight, and I was on my way there."

"No kidding. Boy, is that ever a coincidence. Hey, Sarge," he called out to another uniformed officer who had been talking to one of the plainclothesmen. "Do you know who this is? This here's Mr. Merritt. He writes the Bill Hoehner stories."

The sergeant was an older man who must have been nearing the retirement age. He remembered the radio series as well as the TV shows, and the name Jeffrey Merritt did mean something to him. He'd been a fan of the detective magazines and had probably read some of the original stories. "Are you really Jeffrey Merritt?" he asked.

Jeff took out his wallet and showed him his MWA membership card. No question about it. The sergeant was impressed. He shook Jeff's hand and said,

"Pleased to meet you, Mr. Merritt. We could sure use Bill Hoehner on this case. It's a lulu."

Jeff was interested. He was excited. He was intrigued. The sergeant had as much as told him it was homicide, and he wished he could get in on this case. Bill Hoehner's cases always involved murder, even if they didn't start out that way, but he'd never been part of a real homicide investigation. Perhaps the sergeant read his mind, but more probably he got carried away by his own enthusiasm. He went off to find Inspector Janssen, who was in charge of the investigation.

Inspector Arne Janssen was a big, blond, solidly built Swede who looked to be somewhere in his forties. He was well over six feet in height and broad as the proverbial house, so that he dwarfed even the sergeant, who was by no means a small man. He looked tough, or rather as though he could be tough, but he seemed to be in a congenial mood. Perhaps it was the Christmas season.

"So you're Jeffrey Merritt," he said, pumping Jeff's hand with his huge paw. "This case is right down your alley. In fact, it looks like something you could have written. Are you sure you didn't arrange this little puzzle for us?"

Jeff decided the inspector was kidding. "Word of honor, Inspector," he said, raising his right hand. He was by this time fairly bursting with curiosity.

"The sergeant tells me you're on your way to a party, Mr. Merritt. I wouldn't want to keep you from it, but this is what you'd call a classic mystery puzzle. Doesn't the victim in stories always leave a clue, with his dying breath? Well, this time he really did. He wrote out a message, or tried to."

Oh, God! Jeffrey thought. Please let me in on this. I promise I'll never deflower a virgin again. (Besides, I'm getting too old for that anyway.) I'll only pick on women of experience.

Aloud he said, "Did he write it in his own blood?"

"No, he used a pad and pencil. I know you want to get to your party—"

"The party can wait," Jeff said magnanimously.

Hallelujah!

"Then come in, but don't touch anything," Janssen said. "But I don't need to tell you that."

The patrolman opened the door for them as Janssen led the way, Jeff following behind the inspector's broad back. Room 412 turned out to be a suite of rooms, decorated in a hideous shade of orange. The inspector turned around and was still effectively blocking Jeff's view. There was a lot of activity going on around them. One man was dusting the room for fingerprints. Another came up to give Janssen a written message, and the inspector made the introductions.

"This is my assistant, Sergeant Henry. Mike, this is Jeffrey Merritt."

He and Jeff shook hands.

"The victim's name is Louis Morturier," Janssen began, "according to his passport a French citizen. He's been here at the Valencia for a week. A bellhop discovered the body. Morturier had earlier ordered up several bottles of Scotch, vodka, orange juice, an ice bucket, and four glasses. The bellhop had to go out to buy the liquor, as there's no bar in the hotel. That was around three o'clock. He came back at six to take out the wagon and the ice, as he'd been asked to do. The door was unlocked, he found Morturier dead and went and told the manager, who in turn called us. We came in through the service entrance, and only the manager, the bellhop, the desk clerk, and the switchboard operator know about this."

"You work fast," Jeff noted, with more than a little admiration.

"We do our best," Janssen said modestly. "Morturier had an ice pick stuck in his chest, but he still managed to drag himself to the writing desk and get hold of a pad and pencil. Incidentally, that ice pick tells us the killer hadn't originally intended to commit murder. He didn't bring his own weapon. The ice pick belongs to the bucket."

"And the message?" Jeff asked. "What did Morturier write?"

"You can see that for yourself," Janssen told him. "We haven't removed it yet. The body is still lying as the bellhop found it, the writing pad clutched in his hand, the pencil lying next to it."

The inspector stepped out of the way, and now Jeff saw the body clearly for the first time. There was a bloodstained trail on the carpet, leading from about the middle of the room over to the writing desk, which was at the window. The chair in front of the desk was overturned. The Frenchman was lying partly on his left side, partly on his stomach. His head was resting on his left arm, and his left hand still clutched the pad. The pencil had evidently rolled out of his right hand while he was trying to write, his life's blood ebbing out of him.

Jeff tried to swallow and became acutely aware of how dry his mouth and throat felt. Bill Hoehner had found lots of bodies in his time, but he, Jeff Merritt, had never before seen anyone who'd died violently. The biography published with his book stated that he'd served with the U.S. Army Air Force during the Second World War. That was true enough, as far as it went, but in fact he'd held down a desk job in Colorado throughout the entire war.

The ice pick was still embedded in the Frenchman's chest. The front of his sport shirt and jacket were covered with blood, and there was a great rust-colored stain on the brown carpet where he lay. Jeff gingerly made his way around the corpse until he could see the pad clearly. There was only one word or, more specifically, part of a word, written on the blood-smeared pad in an understandably shaky scrawl.

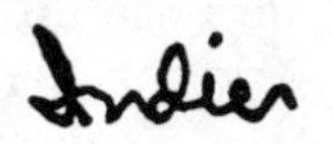

"I need a drink," Jeff said, to no one in particular. He knew where he could get one. He stumbled out of the room, miraculously not bumping into anyone or anything. Once out in the hallway he straightened up, took several deep breaths, and made his way around the corner to the familiar suite. The noises of a party came at him through the closed door.

Closed, but not locked. The place was jammed, as he had expected it to be. Jeff must have been white as a sheet. He felt white as a sheet, but no one seemed to notice, for the lighting here, too, was dim. He fought his way over to the bar and got himself a good, large shot of Scotch, straight up.

The whiskey felt good going down. It warmed him, and he felt the color returning to his face. He became aware for the first time of other people, of faces both familiar and unfamiliar, of conversations carried on in loud voices, of laughter, of smoke, of a Christmas tree at the other end of the room.

"Jeff! How are you?"

It was Moshe Hirshbein (a.k.a. Selena Romance).

"Fine, Moish. Just fine. And you?" He seemed to have reentered his own body.

"I'm fine, Jeff."

"Got any new Regency romances coming out next year?"

"Two of them."

"Same plot?"

"Same plot."

No question about it. He was almost his old self again. Strictly through force of habit he looked over the room. He spotted Tatiana Haynes, who'd sold her first stories while she was still in school, who looked like the young Vivien Leigh, and who was probably still a virgin. (She sure as hell wrote like a virgin!) He recalled with a pang the promise he'd made out in the hallway. There was Howard Quincy Mason, who noticed him at the same time and waved hello. Boyd Carraway and June Emons were engaged in a conversation.

"Jeffrey, my boy," he said aloud, "you need another drink."

He made his way back to the bar and got his other drink. Then, feeling as though he could conquer the world, he inched his way out of the room as unobtrusively as he could. Once back out in the hallway, with the door closed behind him, he took another deep breath. Hell, he said to himself as he rounded the corner again, whatever Bill Hoehner can do I can do.

The patrolman and the sergeant were still in the hallway. Jeff greeted them both and had no difficulty getting back into Suite 412. The orange decor of the sitting room looked even more ghastly the second time around, especially since it clashed with the color of M. Morturier's blood. He had no idea what the color scheme in the other room, presumably the bedroom, was. Inspector Janssen didn't seem surprised to see him back.

"I would have invited you to join me for a drink, Inspector," Jeff said, "but I realize you're on duty."

Janssen nodded. Was that a twinkle in his eye?

"The victim ordered up a trolley with several different kinds of liquor—anyway, two kinds—and four glasses. That suggests a meeting of some kind."

As he said the words, Jeff realized the trolley was no longer in the room, nor had it been there when he was here before.

"We sent the glasses to the lab to be checked for prints," Janssen said. "Although that wouldn't do us any good unless one of the people here had an arrest record. As a matter of fact, we know who Morturier's guests were."

Jeff's mouth must have fallen open. Even Bill Hoehner didn't get that far that fast. But then, he worked alone, without any assistants, without a lab. Yet he was always a step ahead of his friend, Lieutenant Bailey.

"Morturier left word at the desk that as soon as any of the following people asked for him, the clerk was to send him right up: Don Boris. I wonder whether that's the same Don Boris who played left end for Washington? Jack Milner. Ravi Singh."

"Is there an APB out for them?" Jeff asked.

"Not yet. We know where they live. Morturier had an address book in his suitcase, and all three names were in there. I've sent my men out after them. How soon we get hold of them depends on whether they went straight to their homes or whether we have to hunt them down."

"So the desk clerk sent them up here," Jeff noted. "Did they come up separately?"

Janssen nodded.

"Did the clerk by any chance see them leave the hotel?"

"As a matter of fact, he did. The three of them—Boris, Milner, and Singh—left together at about a quarter past five."

"So unless Morturier had another visitor after they left, there are only two possibilities. Either the three of them murdered him—or, more likely, one of them did it while the other two watched—or else one of them returned here almost immediately after the three parted company."

"That seems likely enough," Janssen agreed.

"Did the clerk see anyone return here?"

"No. First of all, the lobby was getting busy by then. People were going to the coffee shop, and then there was your Christmas party. And if the killer came back, he might have returned and left via the service entrance."

It was Jeff's turn to nod. That part of it would have to wait till the police had a chance to question the three suspects.

"The message—" he began.

"The next letter, the one he started to write, could be the beginning of an *n*. Does that make sense?"

"Yes, it does," Jeff said. "And that is the way the French say *Indian*. Even without that last letter, the word couldn't be anything else."

"You're sure of that."

"Let's say I'm ninety-nine percent certain. You could consult an expert or an unabridged dictionary, and you'll probably do both of those anyway." He realized Janssen wanted a piece of evidence that could stand up in court. He had it. "Are your men going to bring the suspects back here?"

"If they can get hold of them in time, yes."

Splendid, Jeff thought. Then he had time to go and get another drink. He had purposely been standing with his back to the window, and the corpse—a fact that wasn't lost on the inspector. This time, though, he made a more dignified exit.

"I have to see a friend of mine next door, Inspector. But I'll be back in a few minutes."

Yes, Jeffrey my lad, he thought as he rounded the corner again, it's time for some liquid refreshment. The inspector may be on duty, but you're not. Besides, your brain needs the stimulation of Scotland's magic elixir. Bill Hoehner functioned on a diet of Scotch, scrambled eggs, and broads. The eggs could wait till later, and there was no time for a broad this evening. But the Scotch, thank God, was available, so why not take advantage of it?

"Jeffrey!" Geraldine Armour grabbed his arm as he reentered the suite. "I thought I saw you here before. Where did you disappear to?"

"I had to make a phone call downstairs," he lied. "Good party, Geraldine. And Merry Christmas." He gave her a kiss.

The party hadn't thinned out at all. Over at the bar somebody he didn't know was telling someone else he didn't know about his old college professor, who wanted to show his students at Christmastime what he thought of them, so he pinned a sprig of mistletoe to his coattails.

No he didn't, Jeff thought. I told that joke when I was in college. Still, it wasn't a bad story, and he wondered why he'd never used it. Chuck Steinway, one of the volunteer bartenders, didn't need to be told what Jeff's drink was. He immediately poured him a large Scotch.

"Thanks, Chuck. Merry Christmas."

"Merry Christmas to you, Jeff. Did you bring a present to put under the tree? We're going to be drawing them soon."

It had become traditional to put a package under the tree upon arrival and later draw one. Pot luck. As was to be expected, the gifts were mostly books.

"No, I didn't. I didn't know whether I'd be coming here at all tonight. This was sort of a last-minute decision. How about another drink, before the revolution?"

He finished his drink and once again worked his way toward the door and quietly slid out. He felt as if he were floating back to Suite 412. He wasn't drunk, by any means, but four large whiskeys on an empty stomach were beginning to tell on him.

The patrolman, smiling, opened the door for him.

"Merry Christmas," Jeff said to him and the sergeant.

Oh, Christ, that color again!

"Ah, Inspector!" He greeted Janssen as though he were an old friend. "Have our suspects shown up yet?"

Janssen seemed amused. "They're not here yet, but they're on their way, all three of them. We've had extraordinarily good luck on this case—so far. It's usually not this easy, believe me."

"I knew there was something I wanted to ask you before I went to get anoth—before I went to see my friend. Was this a robbery? As far as you can tell, was anything taken?"

"As far as we can tell, robbery was not the motive. If anything was taken, it wasn't cash. His wallet is loaded, over six hundred dollars, and we found two thousand dollars' worth of traveler's checks in his suitcase. There are also several bankbooks showing deposits here in New York, as well as in banks in Switzerland and in the Caribbean."

"It's beginning to look as if our Monsieur Morturier was a crook."

"There was nothing against him in this country, so I've just been informed, but according to French law his activities may well have been illegal."

Once again Jeff was impressed with the speed and thoroughness of the police work. The police had gotten here, when? Perhaps an hour and a half ago. How far would Bill Hoehner have gotten in that time? Not very far, he had to admit to himself, but you can bet he would have met at least one fantastic broad by then. Ah, well. Bill Hoehner's fans wanted broads, action, and snappy dialogue. Inspector Janssen's superiors wanted efficiency and results. To each his own.

"I'm curious, though, why a man with Morturier's money would stay in a place like this," Janssen said.

Jeff shrugged. "Perhaps out of sentiment. Maybe he stayed here before the war or right after the war, when the hotel was still first-rate. Perhaps it was recommended by someone who knew it then and didn't realize it had gone to seed. Maybe he just wanted to be inconspicuous.

"I wonder," he added, "what Morturier's game was."

"Whatever it was, it backfired on him."

Jeff thought hard, or tried to think. The rush of events this evening had been so fast he felt as if he were caught up in a whirl. He would never admit that the whiskey had befuddled his little gray cells. The inspector evidently believed this was no casual killing, even if it was unpremeditated. It was directly tied in with whatever the Frenchman's racket was. But what was it? Could one tell, by looking at him—Ugh! Never mind that.

Let's see. He was alive at five-fifteen. And he was dead at six. And we certainly know how he died. There wasn't much the medical examiner's PM could tell us. All each of the suspects had to do was stick to his story: The victim was alive when they left, and he himself never came back here.

But the victim, the victim himself told us who the murderer was. It was important that Janssen should make that stick. Even more important was that he, Jeff Merritt, needed another drink.

"Inspector, have I got time to go next door and say goodnight to someone before the suspects get here?"

"Yes, if you make it fast."

Shuttling back to the other suite, Jeff felt like Goldoni's Servant of Two Masters. People were unwrapping their presents, and he hoped they were happy with the books they got. The bar was unattended, and he simply went behind it, poured himself a double Scotch, and plunked down a dollar and a half. He moved away quickly, before he got stuck having to pour for other people.

In Gaelic, he thought, raising his glass, *uisgebeatha* was the water of life. And so it is. He hoped they could wrap up this case tonight. The case! He downed the rest of his drink and made for the door.

"Once more, once more unto the breach, dear friends."

His step back around the corner was jaunty but, if truth be told, not too steady.

"Are they here yet?" he asked his friend, the cop.

"Who?"

"The shushpecs . . . suspects."

"Nope."

"Good. I did wish you a Merry Christmas?" He clapped him on the shoulder. "Have a Happy New Year, too. Happy New Year, Sergeant."

"Thanks, Mr. Merritt. Merry Christmas and Happy New Year to you."

Back inside, the first and most obvious thing that caught his attention was that that *thing* was still lying there in front of the writing desk.

"Is he going to be a permanent fixture here?" Jeff asked.

"I want him here when our suspects are brought up," Janssen said. "Speaking of suspects"—there was that look of amusement again—"don't you want to know what their occupations are?"

"You mean you know that, too?"

"Jack Milner is a captain of a cargo liner, the *Santa Rosa*. Ravi Singh owns an import-export business, and Don Boris is the ex-football player."

"What does he do these days?"

"No present occupation."

"Any idea yet what Morturier did?"

"He said he was in business. An entrepreneur."

"So was Al Capone," Jeff cracked. Where had he read that line? Oh, of course. He'd written it. *Yellow-Belly Death*.

Sergeant Henry came in from the bedroom. "They're all here, Inspector. They're being brought in through the service entrance."

"Oh, Sergeant." Jeff stopped him before he could return to the other room. "What's the color in there?"

"Puke green." Sergeant Henry returned to the bedroom and his phone.

"I've had our suspects picked up for questioning," Janssen explained, "but they don't know what it's about yet. Except for the killer, of course. The others only suspect the police are on to them because they're involved in something that's not kosher. They're probably wondering how much we know. I let them cool their heels in our cars outside until all three suspects got here. Now they're all being brought up."

"So two of them will be genuinely shocked, and the third will have to fake shock."

"That's about it. But don't expect too much. He's had time to prepare himself."

Jeff felt dizzy and light-headed. But he mustn't let on . . . mustn't let on. There was a murderer to trap. Concentrate now. Three guys, meeting with Morturier . . . came separately, left together . . . inspector seems to think one of them came back and killed him . . . killed the Frenchman . . . probably right, the inspector . . . man of experience, and a gentleman . . .

The door opened, and the three suspects were brought in, each accompanied by two detectives. Jeff noticed that Sergeant Henry came out of the bedroom and joined their group. It was easy to tell who was who. Don Boris was a bull of a man, not quite as tall as the inspector, but heavier. He'd obviously gained weight since his playing days. Jack Milner was a thin, wiry man with a lined, suntanned face. Ravi Singh, as his name implied, was an Indian. He wasn't wearing a Nehru jacket, though. In fact, he wore a well-tailored pinstriped suit.

"What's this all about?" Jack Milner asked.

Inspector Janssen introduced himself and simply indicated the body near the window.

"Oh, Christ!" Milner exclaimed.

Jeff kept his eyes on the suspects, all three of whom looked surprised, but he couldn't tell who was sincere and who was faking.

"Is that all you have to say?" Janssen asked. "Doesn't any of you have anything to tell me?"

"I have something to tell you, Inspector," Ravi Singh replied. He seemed to have recovered the fastest. "Unlike my colleagues here, I am not a United States citizen, and so I must cooperate with the police. I only hope I will not be deported."

You'll be lucky if that's all that happens to you, Jeff thought.

His two "colleagues" looked daggers at the Indian, but Captain Milner, too, seemed to have recovered his wits. "Sure, go ahead and tell him," he said. "We haven't committed any crime—except for whoever killed the Froggie."

"It's okay by me," Don Boris said. "I haven't done anything wrong."

"Very well, then, Inspector," Ravi Singh said. "I will begin. How Mr. Boris and I first became acquainted is of little importance now, as a much more serious crime has been committed than the one my colleagues and I contemplated."

"Oh, for God's sake," Milner exploded, "you're not in a bazaar in Calcutta telling a story for rupees. Skip the comments and get the hell on with it."

"Have you noticed, Inspector, that whenever Anglo-Saxons are faced with a crisis, they immediately revert to racial slurs?"

"Get on with it," Janssen said coldly.

Singh bowed in acquiescence. "I first made Louis Morturier's acquaintance in Marseilles in September of last year. He was what you would call a jack-of-all-trades. I think he had an office in Marseilles, although exactly what he dealt in I have no idea. As we became better acquainted, he said he had a business proposition that would interest me. He was right, it did. I told him I had an acquaintance in New York, Mr. Boris, who might very well be interested in coming in with us. This, too, proved to be correct.

"So, in effect, we three became partners. But we needed a sea captain, and Mr. Morturier found him. That, of course, is Captain Milner here."

"Look," Milner said, "the corpse will have rotted and all of us died of old age if we let this guy go on. You won't have to worry about catching a killer.

"I carry cargo out of Cape Town. Morturier told us he knew of a mine in the rand where the Bantu workmen and the Afrikaans overseer could be bribed. He'd also have to bribe a couple of officials, but there'd be plenty left for us. The idea was to smuggle the gold out of South Africa and sell it on the open market, then deposit the money in a Swiss bank. He said we wouldn't be breaking any Swiss laws."

"He said we wouldn't be taking any risks at all," Don Boris chimed in.

"But things went wrong," Ravi Singh said. "Oh, my goodness yes, they went wrong."

He sounds like Peter Sellers, Jeff thought, but despite his lightheadedness he had enough presence of mind to stifle a giggle. Not without some effort, though.

"Somebody blabbed, and word got out," Milner said. "The Bantus and the overseer were arrested, and the whole operation collapsed.

One of the Bantus spilled the beans. Maybe the police tortured him. Anyway, a high official got arrested. I was in Cape Town when I heard about it."

"You understand, Inspector, there never was any actual gold smuggling," Ravi Singh said. "We have therefore not committed any crime, although for reasons of health it would behoove the three of us to stay out of South Africa."

"Damn right," Milner agreed vehemently. "I got out of there by the skin of my teeth. I didn't relish the idea of being questioned by their police, or getting thrown into one of their jails."

"Okay," Inspector Janssen said, "so your dishonest dream of easy wealth went up in smoke. What of it? What did you actually lose? And don't tell me it was your self-respect."

"No, Inspector, it was money," Milner said.

"Every cent I had," Boris added.

"Mr. Morturier told us that palms would have to be greased," Singh explained. "After all, it was the people in South Africa who were taking the real risks. They couldn't or wouldn't wait until we'd sold the first gold shipment. How did he put it? Oh, yes. Give them an aperitif, a taste of wealth, to whet their appetites and make them greedy for more."

"Ten thousand dollars," Milner said, "from each of us."

"Why was Morturier here in New York?" Janssen asked.

"He said it was on a business matter that had nothing to do with the South African business," Milner answered. "He didn't contact any of us, believe me. I found out he was in town and got hold of Boris and Singh. We forced him into this meeting. I wish to hell now we hadn't."

"What happened up here this afternoon?"

"We talked, we argued."

"We threatened, we pleaded," Singh added. "All to no avail, of course. Mr. Morturier kept insisting on the same thing he told me over the phone after the fiasco, when I telephoned long-distance to Marseilles. He said he lost more money than any of us, and that he owed us nothing. We were partners, and we took our chances."

"And how did you gentlemen feel about that?"

"How do you think we felt?" Don Boris replied.

"We were angry, goodness yes." (Jeff stuck his fist into his mouth.) "At one point Mr. Boris threatened to—how did he put it?—knock Mr. Morturier through the wall. But I managed to dissuade him."

Boris had given Singh a murderous look. "Okay, so I was mad," he said. "We were all mad and we said things. That was the least of them."

"In the end, as I said, it was all to no avail," Singh went on. "We three left the hotel together, in a most disconsolate mood."

"But Morturier was alive when we left here," Milner put in. "None of us touched him."

"Then what did you do?" Janssen asked.

"I returned to my place of business," Singh said, "where your inspectors picked me up."

"Detectives," Janssen corrected him. "I'm an inspector. Did you take a cab to your business?"

"Oh, no, Inspector. It's only a few blocks away, on Lexington Avenue. I walked there. I needed time for my anger to cool."

"Captain Milner?"

"We parted company right here at the corner," the captain said. "If it hadn't been for this goddamn murder, we'd probably never have seen each other again. I went back to my hotel and had a couple of drinks in the bar."

"Mr. Boris?"

"I went back to my place. What else was there to do? I was thinking of going out for a drink and a bite to eat when you guys picked me up."

"And of course not one of you came back here and killed Louis Morturier," Janssen said. "As soon as you left, he was so stricken with remorse he stabbed himself with the first weapon that came to hand."

Here it comes, Jeff told himself. He's given them the bait, and now he's about to spring the trap. The whole scene had an air of unreality, as though he were seeing it in a dream. The room wasn't actually spinning around him, but it seemed about to spin.

"But one of you did return," Janssen was saying, "as soon as the others were out of sight. He came back up here, and Morturier made the mistake, fatal it turned out, of letting him in. Or maybe the door was unlocked, and he came in without an invitation.

"Let's give the killer every benefit of the doubt. Let's say he didn't come up with the intention of committing murder. He came back to plead, even beg. He needed money desperately, and he would have settled, by that time, for less than ten thousand. But Morturier was adamant. Maybe he even threatened to have him thrown out of the hotel.

"Then the killer lost control. He grabbed the ice pick and stabbed Morturier. And after that he panicked. He had just enough presence of mind left to wipe his prints off the ice pick, but his only thought was to run. He didn't even go through the man's wallet or search the rooms for any money.

"The killer is the one, among the three of you, who knew why you were being brought up here. He must have remembered, once his head cleared, that the desk clerk had his name. He just wasn't expecting it to happen that fast. He also knows that he stabbed Morturier just about where I'm standing. When he left here, he thought Morturier was dead. But he wasn't, not quite. He managed to crawl over to the desk and pull down the pad and pencil."

There was dead silence in the room as everyone, including the policemen, turned toward the window.

"With his last ounce of strength, with his dying breath, Louis Morturier told us who his killer was." The inspector paused for effect again, as he looked at the tense, strained faces of his three suspects. "Ravi Singh, I arrest you for the murder of Louis Morturier. Sergeant Henry, read him his rights."

The look of shock and surprise on the Indian's face seemed genuine enough. He started to sputter incoherently.

"He's not your man, Inspector," Jeff said. He had been quiet so long the others had forgotten about him. Inspector Janssen looked at him inquisitively.

"I had to look this up for a story once." Jeff's speech was slurred, and he was making a great effort to enunciate distinctly. " 'S true of every European language. Every one. When they say Indians, they always mean American Indians. Indians from India are called Hindus —even if they're not Hindu." He was weaving dangerously by now.

"That's fine," Janssen said, "but we don't have an American Indian among our suspects." The light of understanding was beginning to dawn in his eyes, while at the same time the murderer moved toward the door.

"No, we don't," Jeff agreed with him. "But we do have a Redskin."

"Grab him, Henry!"

Don Boris may have been out of shape, but his years of training showed as he charged through the policemen who tried to hold him. He actually had the door open when Inspector Janssen caught him with a tackle and he and three other policemen brought him down and cuffed him.

The light had gone out of Jeffrey Merritt's eyes. "A Washington Redskin," he said, standing straight as a tree, as he pitched forward and passed out cold on the floor.

VAUDEVILLE
WHITLEY STRIEBER

October was bright; November began as a cold, gray month in the wartime year of 1943. It was in the first week of November, on the kind of night that made people hurry in the streets, that Jane Drane of Drane and Alexander was suffocated. Of course her name wasn't really Jane Drane, but that was her importance, and so we all called her Jane.

She died in her two rooms on the second floor of the Brearly on Washington Square. At the age of sixty-five Jane was a gangling, hilarious lady, very poor, sometimes with a look of remembrance in her eyes that approached poetry. She was haunted by the memory of fine days, but so were all the old vaudes. Drane and Alexander had been a knockout on the Keith's Big-Time Circuit in the year 1915.

Not everybody at the Brearly lived modestly. Alexander Snyder had rooms up on the fourteenth floor. Monty Woolley graced us with his stentorian presence when he was in New York, over from Hollywood or over from London. He was here for the long run of *The Man Who Came to Dinner* at the Music Box a couple of years ago, singing "Georgia on My Mind" in the halls and doing his lines on the stairway.

But most of us were endowed only with hopes or memories. We had some vaudes: Jane Drane and Arthur Fink of the famous Fink's

Mules, which had been popular for twenty years on the Big Time. And we had Carlotta Fewe, who had played opposite William Warfield in *Macbeth*, and had adopted the role of Lady M. permanently. Not a lady with whom one cared to dine.

Among us hopefuls, I am afraid that only I achieved any degree of notoriety, and it was not upon the stage.

Now that I am old, living in digs far worse than the beloved Brearly, I have my own memories, not least among them that first case, if it could be called a case. At the time it seemed only an interlude in an actor's struggle, but it was really the beginning of my adulthood. What I want to do is get things straight. It isn't that I dislike mystery. All human beings have some sort of relationship with mystery—we must, we can't clearly and finally define evil.

Evil had visited itself upon Jane Drane, even by modern standards. In 1943 there were far worse things happening in the world, but they were still behind the curtain. What happened to Miss Drane was right in front of me, a living mystery.

At the Brearly, we youth kept an eye on the older folk. I shared a two-roomer with John U. Kephart—who was to become Mr. James on the Blue Network's *Whispering Trees*—and Arnold Bigbee, who died on the second to last day of the war, shot through the heart by an eleven-year-old German boy.

The morning I discovered Jane, we three young hopefuls had just taken coffee together—coffee and rolls—and I said that I thought I might go knock on Miss Drane's door, as there was no sound from the radio. She always listened to *Arthur Godfrey*, drank tea, and smoked cigarettes in the morning. She smoked Fatimas, in the dark red box, I remember that well. As I went down the hall, I had just the slightest premonition of misfortune, I think. There is something a little thick about certain silences. They are oppressive. The silence I encountered walking down that hall was such a one—dangerous, unpleasant. I suppose that my mind was turning on alarms. Not only was there no radio, there was no smell of cigarette smoke, despite the fact that the transom above the door was open.

Worse, the *Sun* was lying on the floor at the door. It was already eight in the morning. Jane usually went out for the *News* "Night Owl" at eleven and then took in the *Sun* at six.

I knocked, waited, staring down at the headlines: MODEL DIES IN HOTEL FIRE. There was no answer, and I felt the silence, and the whole nature of the morning finally changed.

After a few minutes I went back to my rooms. What else could I do?

"Maybe we ought to tell Mr. Belli," Kephart suggested.

"Go back, knock harder," Bigbee said. "She's old, maybe she didn't hear."

Neither of them offered to help me, I noticed. But I went back and knocked harder. It was then that I tried the door and found that I could go in. I wish I could say that "in those days nobody in New York thought to lock doors," but I would be lying. In some ways the city was a harder place then than it is now. Not as ugly, perhaps, but the hospitals were terrible, the police were terrible, and a lot of crimes simply didn't get reported.

I saw her lying in a naked, bony heap midway between the bedroom and the living room. I was so stunned that at first I did not see that her hands were tied behind her back. Her face looked hideous. It was dark in color, her eyes were wide open. I realized that there was a rubber gag over her mouth and nose.

I rushed over to her and pulled off the gag. She wasn't breathing; she wasn't going to breathe. I stepped back, horrified and more than a little revolted. I will never forget the ugliness of that woman's agony, the groping, almost sensual cast of her mouth, the sadness in her distorted eyes.

What had happened was unimaginable. It was a violent, terrible city, was the New York of 1943, but this was totally unparalleled. Who in the world would do something like this to a poor old lady, an old vaudevillian who'd been washed up for twenty years?

Nowadays we are more used to bizarre crimes. The Brearly is the Hotel Henry today, full of hippies and drug dealers. In 1943 it was my home. In 1973 I'm scared to go near it. There has been a murder with barbed wire there, and a roomful of drug dealers burned to death.

But then—well, I won't say that we were better. I will say, though, that a murder like the one I had discovered was going to make the day of every crime reporter in New York City.

I went staggering down the hall crying little, silent sobs, more as if I had just witnessed the quiet death of a parent than discovered the grotesque murder of a comparative stranger.

Drane and Alexander had been a "sight act," Jane a lean six-footer, Alexander under five feet, a genial redheaded balloon of a man. His death, in 1931, had finished Jane. Vaudeville audiences were familiar with all the acts, and when Jane appeared with an equally small and round man named Tim O'Hughes at the old Fulton, everybody, including Jane and her new swain, cried so much the act had to go off the circuit.

Alexander: "Seven years ago I was wrecked on a desert isle. My mates were all drowned, but I was washed ashore—"

Drane: "And you haven't been washed since—I see!"

Vaudeville was a big, friendly family. The audiences considered themselves the sisters, brothers, and cousins of the performers. Once when Parrott and Beake tried to change their act at the Iroquois in Chicago, the audience pleaded so sorrowfully that they went back to the old routine and never changed again. Parrott and Beake were a staple of the shows from 1892 until 1926, one of the longest running acts in the history of show business.

I saw Drane and Alexander as a boy, at the Keith's Hippodrome. I saw them at the Palace, at Proctor's Roof, at the Moss Broadway. Do I really remember them? Yes, pretty well, largely because of their unusually bright costumes and Jane Drane's loud voice, and how much she made my father laugh. By the forties the old vaude turns seemed pretty bad. But that was the sophisticated era, Cole Porter lyrics and the smooth sound of the Jimmie Lunceford band.

During the vaudeville era we were still on the sunny part of the lane into the future. It's hard to remember that. When the lane began to get dark, around 1930 or so, vaudeville began to die. People couldn't bear all that happiness. It made them feel alone. Going home from the theater in the dark, beneath the grandeur of a universe turned malevolent, was just too hard on us. The public turned its back on vaudeville because it was too much fun.

Bast and Royce, the two "Bull-Garians," rushed past me in a state of extreme upset. When they reached Jane's apartment, they began screaming, both of them. And their voices were desolate, not only with sorrow but, it seemed to me, with fear also.

They were an odd act. Onstage these two careful gentlemen had been vulgar, loud, and stupid, banned from Keith's Circuit by Mr. Albee himself. They were what we now call "gay" men, but in those days we knew only that they were tender friends, and we accepted them on that basis. Since their retirement they had run a little clothing shop called M'Lady Boteet on lower Fifth Avenue. The dream of the old vaudes was always to open some little shop. They saved for it. They always knew that vaudeville would end, knew it in their bones. A lot of them died during the Depression. Some people must still remember seeing old vaudes, around '33 or '34, doing their turns in front of the new movie palaces, to entertain those in line. Max Kruger did that, and he had been a headliner in his day.

What was happening was like a nightmare. People were coming

out of their rooms, Mrs. Cuddyshack's cat got out and ran into Jane's place. Berton Bertoni, the popular waiter at the Stork who had been written up in "Talk of the Town" and was the richest of us all, burst out half dressed, and I was stunned to see that he was really a woman. She rushed into Jane's room, and her screams pealed through the halls like the music of a bell.

"Call the police," Kephart said. "Was it her heart?"

"She's been murdered," I shouted. "She's been murdered!"

That brought total and sudden silence.

"With a rubber gag," I added. From inside the room Bertoni screamed again.

We all crowded into the room, all except the best and most effective of us, my roommate Bigbee. He dashed back into our living room. I heard him talking over the telephone in a deep, shaking voice. As I stood with the others, clustered just inside Jane's doorway, I heard the grinding of sirens. In those days the radio car was still a new thing, and we were all astonished at the speed with which the police had acted. We looked at one another, our faces suddenly haggard, the scream and the horror going out of us.

I wondered if I might be looking at Jane's murderer. We were an odd group, after all, and it was not only an ugly crime, it was also odd.

The pounding of heavy feet on the stairs transfixed us. The appearance of two blue uniforms spread with brass buttons fascinated us. The two shining young faces with those dead eyes made us uneasy.

"Right in here, officers."

"Oh! The poor lady," one of the boys said. More sirens were wailing now, echoing through the steel-cold morning, rising over the distant honking and hubbub of Sixth Avenue.

Soon a group of five men came up the stairs, homicide detectives with a cameraman and a "duster," who at once started working over the scene.

"This the gag? Who touch it? You? Only you?"

"I pulled it down her chin, I—"

"She ain't been alive anytime recent. Gimme prints." He grabbed my right hand and jammed my fingers against a stamp pad, then onto a cardboard. "Nobody else touch it?"

Nobody had.

Another man came up the stairs, long overcoat, beaten homburg, stench of coffee, eggs, and cigarettes: "What we got, Jack?"

"S'murder. Smother job."

"Where's the coroner?"

"Coming, Captain. Ridin' the wagon, be here directly."

The captain lit a cigarette. "You folks please stay in your rooms, do you mind? We'll want to talk to each one of you." He looked around, as if having a sudden idea. "Who made the discovery?"

"I did."

"He touched the gag," the duster muttered. "I woulda had a couple of good ones, too. Thick imprints. The murderer musta held it down on her to make sure no air got in around her nose."

"You pulled off the gag?"

"I hoped—"

He nodded, dragging on his cigarette. "You know her?"

There was something insinuating about the way this man asked his question, and it made me feel at once angry and vulnerable. I didn't like the way the fingerprint man kept pointing out that my prints were on the gag. "I knew her a little bit."

"Well?"

"What?"

"What am I supposed to do, put in a nickel? Who was she? What was her age? What did she do? All of that."

"Her name's Jane Drane. She's an old vaudevillian, and my guess is she's in her sixties."

"Drane? You're kidding."

"The same."

" 'The baby swallowed my collar button!' 'Did you call the doctor?' 'Certainly. It's the only collar button I've got!' "

It wasn't one of Drane and Alexander's turns, I was fairly sure. They never did a married-couple act.

The captain hunched his shoulders, turning toward the remains as if leaning into a wind. "Get out of here," he suddenly shouted to the assembled crowd, who had ignored his instruction to return to their rooms. "You stay," he said to me. "We're going to block out the scene. We need you."

The others were taken aback. People in those days weren't used to casual rudeness. We still had a few illusions left in 1943. Nobody knew about what was happening in the Axis countries. Nobody knew a lot of things. Like what had really happened there, and the reason.

"You found her? When?"

"Fifteen minutes ago."

He looked at me. "Why you? Why not a housemaid, the milkman?"

"We don't have any housemaids here. We do our own housekeeping. And the milkman—well, you're better off going over to Washington Market if you're taking in as little as she did. She only used it in her coffee."

"You knew her, then?"

"That's what I was trying to say. I knew her. Sometimes I had coffee with her. This morning her place was quiet, and the *Star* was still on the stoop—"

"And she's old, and you were concerned so you went in."

"And I saw that—"

"I know, son. She was like a grandmother to you, the grandmother you never had—"

"I had a grandmother."

"She took her place. And you saw that gag, and it was just a natural damn stupid unfortunate impulse that you handled the thing!" His voice had risen as he spoke, almost to a scream. "I'm sorry," he said into the silence. "We got a nice, quiet precinct here, the Sixth. This is two murders in a week, both of performers."

"I didn't read about any other murder in the Village."

"One of those fancy boys. Pretty ugly. The papers don't want that junk, it makes Sweeny throw up."

The captain turned away from me. The coroner had arrived, a solidly built young man whistling under his breath, carrying a black Gladstone. He wore a streaming rubber raincoat. When I saw his fedora dripping on Jane's worn-out old rug, I wanted to cry.

Jane: "I remember the first time we got a call from Keith's office. A runner in a maroon uniform came up to our building. We were then living at the Western on Fifty-fifth Street. We lived well. Small Time was not a bad life if you did not mind travel. Alexander and I would do six shows a day, and try to make seven days per week. We got three hundred dollars' salary, and were a second bill. 'Drane and Alexander, Comic Novelty.' We got a lot of laughs. Was it because I am tall, or because he was short? My, we did argue about that! How quickly it all went. He died. He was the first man I had ever seen die. It was sudden. I always wondered if it was something I did, and if there would be anything more about it."

Suddenly there came into the room two men in neat white uniforms, carrying a canvas stretcher and gunnysack. They could not straighten Jane out, she had been lying there in that doorway too long, so they put her in the bag as best they could and carried her out, a knobby shape in the center of the stretcher.

It was just about unbearable. I left the rooms and went to get my coat and hat. I wanted to be in the streets, and no matter the weather. I envied the coroner his rubber raincoat. Such things were unobtainable now, even with ration coupons.

My own aged mac did a poor job of keeping me dry, especially the right shoulder, which leaked through an old tear I'd never been able to get repaired. I bought some of that Seal-All stuff they used to sell at the Rexall store, but it didn't do the trick.

I had an idea that I would go over to Sixth Avenue and have some coffee at the Knickerbocker on Fourteenth Street. My problem was that I was full of grief, and I did not know how to deal with that.

In 1943 I was innocent; I was among the last of the innocent. The nature of crime had not yet become clear to me. I still had conventional words and conventional definitions. Robbery and burglary were unlawful taking, also called theft. There was kidnapping, something that happened to the Lindberghs; we also had bunco and grand larceny, and murder, which meant what was done to Jane, and the electric chair, where the balance was restored.

I cannot entirely blame the times. I have a recurring image of my brother's death in the Pacific, his actual death. The little plane fluttering in the bright noontime, red flickering along its silver flanks, and the wispy smoke left by its amazing passage, smoke that is my brother.

I was completely out of contact with my family. In fact, it had ceased to exist. Later I discovered that my mother had lived in a bungalow in Jersey City, a bungalow that was to be burned to the ground in 1967 by an outraged, helpless mob of the same blacks whose parents said, "Yassuh," behind the counter of the Knickerbocker when a young man with his eyes swimming in tears croaked, "Java."

The thing that was bothering me was that Jane had suffered. Why did she have to suffer?

I did not know anything about the blue cave in the soul that is mystery.

Jane and I had once gone out to Holy Cross Cemetery together on the subway and then the trolley and put flowers on Alexander's grave. I had carried the flowers for the old woman, and she had made me feel as if I were rendering assistance to a real star.

She was a brilliant actress, but she had shunned the journey down into acting, preferring vaudeville's reliable salaries.

I have met an old actress. A few years ago my friend Jerry Patterson and I booked steerage on the *Berengaria* and spent five weeks in Europe, starving in London, in Paris, in Lyons. He took me to meet his great-aunt in the south of France. We found her, the famous star Mrs. Patrick Campbell, hiding her poverty in a miserable little ruin of a villa. "It's cold even here," she said. "I try not to be bitter. At night I dream that the chauffeur is helping me into a hearse. Will have a hearse? Poor Shaw." She was his Eliza Doolittle, the first woman to utter a curse upon a stage of England, the most famous actress of her time, a lifetime skidding in the black water in the center of the soul, the place where art waits to destroy you, and it did destroy her, leaving an impoverished old relic who spat, suddenly while we were having tea.

Jane would sing in the morning, the same song she sang to Alexander's grave: "I'll take you home again, Kathleen, though the sea be wide and wild." They really loved each other, the dwarf and the giant lady, loved each other with a passion no less deep for its freakish taint. Their public lives were spent on sunny, easy stages, while they suffered together in private over their impossible relationship, the sad little man and his tall ladylove.

At the age of sixty-five Jane was still over six feet. She told me that she weighed a hundred and twenty pounds. Seeing her that morning looking like a great, crashed stork, I could believe a hundred and ten pounds. "I carried him," she said to me once. "I remember how good it felt. We danced. I carried him. It was entirely different from carrying a baby. Goodness, we were rich, he and I. Drane and Alexander Orpheum and Pantages fought over us. Shubert's offered us the moon, but we knew they would never beat old Albee and the Keith's Circuit. Thank God we stayed with Albee. When the Shubert Circuit folded, a lot of those rebel acts never worked again. I remember Gus Grahame of Grahame's Children begged on his knees. He had seven children to feed. The last I heard, the oldest boy was a journeyman mechanical, and the others were selling newspapers and such. Street Arabs. Gus died a long time ago."

She would get that distant look, and serve me some more coffee "The vaudes all went for their coffee and smokes. The ladies preferred cigars. They worked better. Among the vaudes cigarettes were for children, cigars for women, and the devil only knows what the men smoked. Big, black stogies that were capable of making a horse go permanently insane. We weren't as bad as the circus folk. At least the hotels would let us in. Good Lord."

I sat in that Knickerbocker staring at my reflection in the coffee, listening to the radio—Artie Shaw, "Indian Love Call."

The vaudeville murders . . . torture, corruption, horrible perversion. They characterized their era, not as it believed itself to be and is remembered, but as it was. To me they reflect the dark, corrupt practice of life itself, the fundamental structure of society, the truth at the bottom of the world.

I suddenly realized that the captain had said that another performer had been murdered in the past week. Or rather, I realized the possible significance of what he had said. I wondered who that performer was and how the murder had been accomplished. In 1943 we did not think of serial murder and mass murder. In those days murder was always an astonishment, especially when it was not connected to some sort of hoodlum war.

I don't have the statistics, but my sense of it is that murder became an ordinary crime somewhere in the mid-sixties. It took a generation raised on television to commonize the extraordinary fact of the willful taking of life.

I had to find out which performer had been victimized besides Jane.

On my way over to the Sixth Precinct I had the further thought that it was odd the murder had been kept out of the papers. We had the old *Journal* then, and the *Mirror,* a tabloid that thrived on the seamiest, most sordid of crimes. And the *Police Gazette,* which occupied a prominent place in barbershops from Boston to San Francisco.

The precinct house was a grim Victorian affair, with two round lights on poles out front and the word POLICE painted in black letters upon their surfaces. The Sixth Precinct was placed as close to the docks it was originally built to protect as it could be and still be within sight of the Sixth Avenue Fire Tower, which was in 1943 an abandoned hulk next to the new Women's House of Detention.

I went struggling through the miserable rain, the clouds so low you could touch them, passing only an occasional stranger, another wet slicker and dripping hat, sometimes a whiff of perfume beneath a spread umbrella. I turned off Seventh Avenue just above Sheridan Square. Club Gaucho was closed at this hour of the morning, a dismal shade of its late-night self standing at the head of stodgy Christopher Street.

Kephart and I took Jane to the Gaucho not a week ago, guiding her along Fourth Street and watching with delight when she clapped her hands during a particularly good number. We were very pleased with ourselves, two young bachelors on a mission of charity, giving her a little entertainment when nobody else cared what she got, she who had entertained so many.

Until that day I was like most of my fellow New Yorkers. I had never been inside a police precinct. My familiarity with them came from Raft and Cagney movies. Indeed there was a high desk dominated by a sergeant. Against one wall was a bench on which a child of perhaps fourteen was sitting, very prim and silent, costumed like a woman. Her fists twisted the strap of a bag. She wore a necklace of false diamonds and a floppy old hat, as if she had been dressing up.

Three black men huddled in a far corner in threadbare broadcloth suits, speaking quietly among themselves. The place was full of policemen, all brass and blue, sitting at desks, some of them pounding typewriters with enormous hands, others shuffling papers and talking. From time to time a radio spluttered. Once a siren ground down outside, and I could see fancy boys being brought down off a Black Maria. Fancy boys and what I think must have been dress-ups, men who go around as women, now called transvestites. In those days they seemed as fantastic and disturbing as alligators in frocks would have been, and much more illegal.

Robbers and murderers were not among the chief criminals of the Village. Our crimes have ever been those at the edge of free expression.

"I would like to talk to a detective on the Jane Drane case," I said to the sergeant.

He leaned forward across the desk. "You have some evidence to give?"

"I'm a witness."

"You witnessed the crime? Weren't you interviewed?"

"I found Jane. We were friends. There are a few things I'd like to talk to a detective about."

"Go upstairs, look for Doyle or Barker. They're up there somewhere. Barker's the loo on the case."

I went up a metal stairway at the back of the room, past dirty green walls. From the basement came long, echoing sobs. Upstairs men were speaking softly. When I opened the door into the squad room, their voices were louder. They worked in a haze of cigarette and cigar smoke, and their words were for the most part curses. There was a lot of laughter, most of it rich and boozy.

Just inside the door I found a lean, unfriendly-looking man lounging behind a desk. He was reading the *Daily Variety,* of all things.

"I'm looking for Doyle or Barker. I wonder if you could help me?"

"Why?"

It was a somewhat open-ended question. Why was I looking, or why should he help me. "I am a witness in the Drane case. I have some more information." These men did not give me the impression that they would be well disposed to questions from a member of the public, even if a witness.

The lean man bestirred himself, unfolding his legs and putting his cigarette in an ashtray. "I'm Barker," he said. "Shoot."

"The captain mentioned that another performer had been murdered. I wondered if there might be any connection between the two cases."

He leaned back, staring at the fly-specked ceiling. "Oh, Lord. Do we have an armchair detective in this?"

"It's just that it wasn't in the papers."

"Not every murder is in the papers."

"A theater person?"

"A has-been."

"Jane was retired. She could be thought of as a has-been."

"Look, son, I admire you for your concern. Just listen to me, though. There's no connection between these two cases. No connection at all. Why the papers didn't pick up the last case, I don't know."

"May I know who it was?"

He looked at me. "You don't really hear me, do you? You don't talk my language. Well, the records are closed."

"But you just said—"

"I said I didn't know why the case wasn't picked up. Maybe the captain knows, maybe the commissioner knows, maybe only LaGuardia knows. But I don't know. And anyway, it's none of your damn business. Lookey here, it's nearly ten. If you have a job, the boss is mad as hell."

"I'm an actor."

"Tomorrow and tomorrow and tomorrow—a man with a coat like yours ought to give up whatever he's doing and join the army."

"I'm waiting to be drafted," I said. With that I left the oppressive place. At the time I did not really know it, but I had begun to investigate Jane's murder. I had no real method and no considered motive beyond a vague desire to catch the monster who had tortured her to death.

It did not take me long to discover a way to find out the particulars about the other actor who had been murdered. I went to the library and there took down a stack of issues of *The New York Times* covering the past week. Sure enough, I soon found the only obituary of an elderly actor.

His name was Barton Cook. I felt a distinct thrill of unease when I saw that he had also been a vaude. "Barton Cook, tenor in vaudeville from 1892 until 1934, at home, suddenly." The familiar obit euphemism for murder: *suddenly.*

Now, I could not believe that these murders were random. In those days we might not have known much about serial murderers and mass murderers, but we also did not believe in accident and coincidence. Somebody had killed two old vaudes within a week of each other. Both murders had taken place at home. It seemed to me that they were connected.

Although I did not know it at the time, I was in the process of taking the steps that began my adulthood. I really very much wanted to get things straight. At the time that didn't even seem like a motive, it was so deep in my blood. Now I understand that I wasn't even much interested in vengeance. I wanted to know what happened and why it happened. Is that the light that shines away evil?

I went marching back to the precinct, armed with my little treasure. I thought that they would be astonished at how quickly I had learned the name of the other murdered actor.

"So you're a regular shamus," the captain said when I found myself confronting him. As soon as I mentioned the name, Barker had ushered me into the captain's spotless office. It was enclosed on two sides in glass, so that he could keep an eye on his detectives in the squad room beyond. The office reeked of Lysol and lemon oil. The desk, totally clear of papers, was polished to a high shine. On it stood a brand-new Dictaphone and a telephone, both instruments gleaming as if waxed. Probably they were waxed. The captain himself sat behind the desk, smoking a cigarette. His suit was neat, but his eyes were tired, terribly so.

"A shamus?"

"You know. It's storybook talk for a private eye. You read the pulps, I'm sure. *Black Mask*?"

"I don't read the pulps. I read *The New Yorker* and *Collier's.*"

"Well, now, a high-toned man. One with nothing to do but waste police time on crackbrained theories. Two old actors are murdered within a week of each other. So you think there's a Jack the Ripper running around. Okay, I can see that. As a nonprofessional, you might draw that conclusion. But as a policeman who saw both corpses, you would see how silly that conclusion was. Cook was hit with what we call a blunt instrument, in this case probably a chair leg. Miss Drane, well, you know."

"Why was the Cook murder kept out of the papers?"

"Kept? *Kept?* My God, you are a suspicious soul. Ask the papers, if you want to know. I have no idea."

I sat watching the captain, wishing I could hear his thoughts. I had the strong impression that he was being honest with me without being straight, which made me extremely uneasy.

I couldn't deal with this level of deception. There is something particularly ugly about the paradox of the true lie.

I got out of there.

Walking down the street with the wet wind at my back, I felt certain that I should drop this matter. I had a life to lead, after all. They were auditioning for *Crazy Lady,* and I was due for a tryout at three. After that I was supposed to meet Janet Jean at the Pennsy for the tea dance. The Glen Miller band was there, and Janet was paying, since she was currently flush. She had landed a fine place in the chorus line at the Copa, and was making a hundred and fifty a week salary.

Suddenly I wanted very badly to be with Janet. There was something cold and ugly going on, and she was so warm.

The audition was hell. I muttered, I danced badly, my singing voice seemed thin and unreal. I got no more than three minutes, then I was dead. Afterward I went miserably off to the Pennsy, which was bright and full of life, hurrying waiters, bellboys, and a glittering, elegant crowd of debs and their idle, rich boyfriends.

"Oh God, that lovely old lady?" Janet said when I told her my news about Jane. "She was so decent. Why can't the police protect people?" She was wearing a green dress, white kid gloves, and a matching white pillbox hat. Her baby face was lovely, soft but full of life. She gave off a scent of Shalimar. Janet represented to me the possibility of a stable life, the world of salaries and five-room flats on Fifty-seventh Street, all I could not gain. I did not mention my performance at the audition, and she was tactful enough not to ask.

In some ways, discussing the case was a relief. "There was another old vaude murdered a week before, just a few blocks away. Totally different method."

"So?"

The band struck up "Blue Moon," and we did a foxtrot. I'd had a highball and some finger sandwiches and I felt better. Janet was nice to hold, a supple dancer. She stirred me. We were comrades in the theater, but that did not foreclose love. I'd met her at an audition.

Kephart had once offered me five dollars for an introduction. I'd turned him down flat.

"The murders are connected," I said after the dance.

"The police told you?"

"The police told me the opposite. But I think they're connected."

"Jane Drane was a decent old woman. What good is it, working all your life if you end up murdered?"

"It beats TB as a way out."

"It isn't fair. People have the right to live. Do the police know who did it?"

In some ways Janet was very innocent. I shook my head. "There's also the fact that nothing appeared in the papers. I can't believe that the *Mirror* passed up an "Actor Murdered" headline, but there wasn't a whisper. Not even the *Herald* reported it, and they cover the city very thoroughly."

"Who cares about a couple of old vaudes? That's why there was nothing in the papers. And you don't know about Jane. There hasn't been time for an edition."

"The afternoon papers are out. The *Post* ought to have something." I signaled the cigarette girl and had her bring me a *Post* and a *Journal.* There was nothing in either paper about Jane's death. "Not even an obit."

"I don't like the look in your eye. You stay out of this."

"You sound scared."

"I do because you don't. You never know what might happen. If these people were both killed by the same person, that person is desperate, to resort to such a thing. You stay out of it, Art. It's the kind of thing you don't want."

"I have to go to the morgue and identify Jane. They expect me there tomorrow."

"That's awful." She looked away. I did not continue talking about it. There was no reason to torture Janet.

We ordered another round, then did a swing routine to "Pennsylvania 6-5000." The crowd was excited, and we were having a good time. After the dance we sat drinking our Manhattans. Janet smoked a cigarette, looking at me in a way that transported me with lust.

I wanted to fill the moment with words. But I remained silent.

She laughed a little. "You and the night and the music?"

"I'm sorry. You're very beautiful right now, Janet."

"Thanks. I just got this hat yesterday. It's a Millicent."

"It isn't the hat." I wish that I could have declared myself. What prevents me? I think I probably lost Janet forever that afternoon. I've lost too many women since. Far too many. I look back on two lives: One is ashes, the other is devoted to getting things straight. That's the one I have chosen to live.

Things are not straight, not at all. They are far from it, and getting more and more crooked as time goes on. Back in those days, for example, we didn't have drugs in any quantity. You heard of reefer in use among musicians, and maybe cocaine, but nothing else. Reefer and coke. Crimes of innocence: murder and Black Maria and the captain.

A telephone ringing in the middle of the night: "Young man, this is Detective Barker." Voice slurred, very sweet, very sad. "Don't do this. You're a fool. This ain't a *Spirit Section.* That bastard captain, he plays for keeps. You understand me. *Forever.*" Then the metallic click, the buzzing of the instrument.

I telephoned the precinct and asked for Barker. He wasn't there.

"Operator?"

"Yes sir?"

"I just received a call. Can you tell me where it was from?"

"We have no way of doing that, sir."

"Surely you must. It wasn't five minutes ago."

"If it was an annoyance, I can let you speak to my supervisor."

I put the instrument down. There had been kindness in Barker's voice, but underlying it was something else, the same thing I had seen in the captain's eyes. It wasn't that they were tired, these men, but that they were beaten, dragged down, compromised.

I was startled to realize that they were also afraid. Thinking about it now, in the dead of the night, I realized that it was true.

I lay back in my bed, smoking and thinking. I sat up and stared out the window. The streets were dark. Nineteen forty-three was a dim-out year, and at three o'clock in the morning when the air was clear, you could see the stars.

I looked up at the Milky Way, a drift of smoke high above the black shadows of the buildings. A darker shape moved there, and I heard the deep whine of a plane, very high, a bomber moving from somewhere to somewhere in the cloak of the night.

Had I been a different man I would have called Janet and asked her to let me come to her. She would have agreed, I feel sure, and I would then have known the mystery of her arms. I did not call her, though. Instead I stood there staring and smoking. At length I got out my pint of rye and made myself a drink.

When I slept, I dreamed of Jane, a tall figure in the theater of death, with popping red eyes.

Next morning Arthur Godfrey was on the radio, Kephart was making coffee and toasting toast, and I was boiling a merry egg. "Let's have another cup of coffee, let's have another piece of pie," Julius LaRosa sang.

A Rodger van passed in the street below, its rumbling drawing my eye to the bright window. By the light of morning the world really did seem a better place, safer and more normal. Kephart had a *Herald.* "Looks like we didn't make the papers," he said. "Il Duce's having a rotten time in North Africa, though."

"Your number's up. That's the only reason you'd be looking at anything about the war."

"Greetings," Kephart said, tossing a letter on the kitchen table.

"You've been drafted!"

"Be it far from me. I'm not the addressee." I read the name: Arthur Bigbee.

"You opened his mail?"

"I didn't notice the name. If you'd seen that thing under the door, you'd have opened it too."

"I'm not afraid to fight. Actually, I'm spoiling to. And as soon as it's my turn, I will. Bigbee'll be thrilled."

"I see him as a seabee, chomping one of those Haddon House cigars of his and wearing nothing but boxer shorts and a sweaty undershirt, driving an armored bulldozer against the Japs."

"Sounds good to me."

I was drinking coffee when the phone rang. It was the morgue, and could I come for a ten-fifteen identification. So much for my breakfast, my mood, and my day.

"Doesn't she have any relatives?" Bigbee asked.

"I guess not. Otherwise why would I have to go for the identification?"

Bigbee gave a whoop, seeing his draft notice. "I have ten days," he yelled excitedly. "Oh, thanks Uncle, I've been looking forward to this. Boy, I hope I get to put a bullet in some Kraut's fat fanny!" He grabbed the phone, then slapped it down. "You fellas have been swell roommates! This is just incredible! I've gotta have a party." He snapped his fingers. "A hell of a party!" He grabbed the phone again and called his girl friend. We could hear excited screaming and sobbing on the other end of the line. He put down the phone. "Look, meet me and Betty at Elk's Rendezvous at nine tonight. Art, you bring Janet. Kephart, you get a date, too."

"I dunno, you can drop a lotta cash up in those Harlem places—"

"Oh, be quiet, Kephart, it's my treat. I can do no less for a couple of great pals. I'm goin' to war, boys!"

For a little while that morning, hitting my dwindling supply of rye despite the hour, I was able to forget the silent apartment at the end of the hall.

At nine-thirty I walked across Eighth Street to the Lexington Avenue stop on Astor Place. Oranges were back down to a penny each, and I bought one to tide me over until lunch. I was just descending into the subway when I noticed a streetcar on its way up Fourth Avenue. It was a perfect autumn morning, and after all the weeks of gray I couldn't bear to go down into the Stygian depths, so I ran for it.

We rocked along, bell clanging, fellow passengers happy and expansive from the return of the sun. None of them were going to the morgue, though. Death is such a dirty little secret.

My world was changing fast again, and I didn't like that. I'd been brought up in the Depression, an experience that had left me with one objective: get out of Ohio and stay out of Ohio forever. I was sick of sitting in miserable, cold schoolrooms, sick of sharing the shoes with my brother, of it taking weeks to be able to get up a nickel for the movies, and most of all sick of watching the people I loved work themselves to death to the tune of "Happy Days Are Here Again."

The silver screen was my preferred reality, that and the radio. We would sit up nights listening to Fred Allen on *Town Hall Tonight* or *Drene Time* or one of those programs. We kids were not allowed to listen to *Hermit's Cave* or *Inner Sanctum,* or any police program except *Gangbusters.* My father was ruined in the wheat crash in 1930. He was a prosperous man one day, the next day he came home, his tie askew, his face grave, got out of his brand-new Auburn and stood in the middle of the front yard crying. The whole family gathered, mother and Hermione from the kitchen, me and Rufus and Claire from the backyard. We circled him, touched him, finally were taken into his receiving, desperate arms.

I will never forget the hollow depth from which he spoke, saying that he was ruined, that he had not a penny for us, not even enough for mother to go to the grocery in the morning.

We lost the Auburn and the Ford, we lost the house, Hermione abandoned us, we children left Holy Cross School and matriculated at P.S. 2, our clothes wore out, we went from rooming house to rooming house. My father pumped gasoline, he swept floors, he sorted in the button factory, he hauled fertilizer, and finally he ran away.

Mother raised us with strong arms and what love she had left, amid the stink of Rinso and other people's laundry.

I dreamed of dancing with Mary Astor, of drinking with William Powell. I declaimed Shakespeare in the basement until the landlady forbade it, saying it put her meal boarders up in the dining room off their food. I memorized every word of *Long Lost Father,* doing the Barrymore role in a tenor, varying my tone for Donald Cook, Claude King, and Alan Mowbray, and using a falsetto for Helen Chandler.

Why didn't I set out for Hollywood instead of the Great White Way? I don't really know. Maybe because the bus tickets to New York were cheaper than to California. Maybe because I thought there'd be more opportunity in the theater. Or perhaps it was just the big buildings and the city's air of promise.

Now here I was, a New Yorker sure enough, going through the red-brick portals of the city morgue on as fine a November morning as you could wish.

I viewed Jane. They raised her on a little elevator behind a glass window. There were other people in the waiting room, a silent man, a sobbing young girl as perfect as a flower, each there to confirm some other tragedy.

When I left, I didn't want to have coffee or eat any lunch. I simply walked, trudging west toward Fifth Avenue through the tired tenements of the East Thirties, not really knowing where I was going. I wanted the glitter, the shine, the excitement of midtown.

In the event, I was headed toward Times Square. Maybe I was going to take in a movie. Davis and Howard in *Of Human Bondage* at the Apollo, a Zane Grey picture at the Lyric. Both former vaudeville houses, and Jane had both of them in her collection of bills. Sometimes I think that the teens, before the Great War, were the perfect time. The last of the days when people could still believe in their own essential goodness.

I passed the B&O office at Forty-second and Lex and was tempted to cross the street and go into the Commodore and find a nice, stiff drink. But what was I going to use for money? I was flush, I had forty cents.

Ahead there was a banner across the street appealing for the Greater New York Fund. Wonderful. Why not include us actors among the indigent? A panhandler moved past whispering, trolleys rumbled and clanged on Forty-second, a Buick honked and honked at a double-parked Bernard Baron truck. I reached Times Square and looked up the Great White Way. I'd worked it once in a while, a bit part here, a dancing number there. I could go on the boards, I could act, I could dance. Laughton and Leigh in *Sidewalks of London,* the dark rumbling blitz, the rain, the war and an old dead lady behind a glass window. Tears were streaming from my eyes, and I wanted to go home.

I had no home, though. My family broke up, God only knows where they are, nobody answers letters, mother's gone west, that's all I know. I thrust my hands in my pockets and struggled up Broadway, walking and walking. The Planters Peanut sign stared at me, reminding me that after all, life continues. I nearly got hit by a Broadway "B" trolley as it came around the curve onto Forty-second, then practically reeled into a Skyview Cab. "Hey, buddy," the driver called, "save yourself for Tojo!"

I stopped in at the Riker's just past Ripley's Museum on Forty-seventh and got a hamburger and a Coke. The food made me feel a little better, as did the laughter around me, the easy coming and going of ordinary folk.

The food took fifteen cents. I couldn't afford to spend the afternoon at the Palace or even the Apollo, so I went down Forty-seventh to Eighth Avenue. There, sandwiched in among the twenty-five-cent burlesque establishments was the little Hollywood Theater, three features for a dime. Leading the bill was Hugh Herbert in *Slightly Tempted.* Not a wonderful film, but sitting in that theater with the other bums and sad men, I would have given my soul for just ten minutes of Hugh Herbert's shining life.

Watching through a silver window into Herbert's heaven drove me a little crazy. It was in the middle of the picture that I decided I would defy Detective Barker's warning. I would defy them all. Somehow, I was going to get things straight again. I was going to find Jane's murderer and the murderer of the other old vaude.

How do you find a murderer? Some anonymous person comes into a rooming house and enters a room. There he or she kills an old lady. There's nothing left behind except a piece of rubber. It has no fingerprints on it, none except mine.

I was not a suspect, I know now, because the police knew perfectly well what was going on. At the time, though, it never occurred to me that I would have been under the utmost suspicion, had this been an ordinary murder case.

In the middle of the film I jumped up and ran right out of the house. I invested another nickel and took the Ninth Avenue El down to Fourteenth Street. It was now two o'clock in the afternoon. On the El I pondered my decision. How do you become a detective? Get a book from the library, take a course from one of the ads in the back of the pulps?

The answer to the last two questions is no and no, at least for me. I became a detective by trying to crack a case. Since then I've read a lot, seen a lot, thought a lot about the nature of crime. It's a web of antisocial behavior. One crime leads to another, and it all starts down at the bottom, where the desperate people live. A guy with hungry kids robs a store, then he has a little money, so he does some reefer. The reefer was brought in by a man who bribed Customs at the pier, and a union boss got hold of some of that bribe money, and he calmed down a cop with it, and so it goes, right up to the top, which is inhabited by politicians.

Thirty years as a private detective, and I am absolutely convinced that the politicians, not the Mafia, are the true kings of crime.

But it's 1973 now, another year in hell, and I know too much almost to bear. I'm so damn old and I hurt and I'm about as poor as I was then. Only now I don't have the enthusiasm. I'm not mad anymore, I'm just very careful. I suppose that makes me a professional. I'm remembering the Drane case as if from a great distance. It's a long time, thirty years. I have seen the curious darkening of the world. The bright things like the British Empire with all its pomp and lazy, unfair wealth are dead, and in their places stand the monolithic empires of the damned, the Soviet Union and Richard Nixon's bitter, rundown United States.

I've spent most of my adult life trying to get things straight, and I still can't do it. I've learned to climb in the spider web, but there seems to be no way to clear it out of the grim little corner where most of life is lived. I've cracked maybe fifty cases in my life, made my bread and butter off divorce like all us gumshoes, and spent a lot of time doing Shakespeare and Ibsen and Chekov alone in my apartment. I do all the parts, men, women, children. I can do anything, and I can damn well still dance, too.

I was so goddamn mad by the time I got home that afternoon that I all but broke down the front door of the Brearly letting myself in. I went right up to Jane's place and started looking around. I didn't know what I was looking for—the past, the truth.

Nowadays a crime scene like that would have been locked and

sealed by the police. Not then: The door wasn't even locked. New York was a very different place in 1943. I'm not saying it was better. It was much poorer, and there was a lot of crime around and the police had few really effective methods of solving it except for the third degree, which they used virtually all the time. To be a cop in those days you had to know how to rough a man up or terrify a woman. They were hard cases, the police. Most of them had been attracted to the job because of their ideals. Sooner or later they discovered the reality of the precinct house basement. That was enough to break any man, no matter how strong. I know, I was down there a few times.

I went through Jane's room with amateur thoroughness. I didn't know anything about the patterns people use to hide valuables. Nothing. So I did stupid things like look under the bed. And under the bed I found something so horrible that the memory of it still burns my gut with acid, even after thirty years.

In those days there was plenty of pornography around, but it was a deep, dark secret. You went up to the girlie shows and asked the usher. He'd take you into a room backstage where they'd have the magazines and little black boxes with five- and ten-minute blue movies inside. There were also pictures, wallet-size stuff, that guys sold out of their coats on Eighth Avenue.

I had never seen anything like what was under Jane's bed. She and Alexander might have been funny on the stage, the tall woman and the short man, but naked in bed they were downright weird. And the looks on their faces, the suffering behind the smiles made me feel rotten inside, just to look.

Without their costumes they were nothing—two freaks, a skinny woman with no breasts and a bulging little ball of a man bouncing around on top of her, under her, sitting in her lap. Even though they were naked and degraded in some hotel room, there remained about them that ineffable something, the gentle sweetness that had made their act great.

They could have made money at Hubert's Museum. They could have gone on the carny circuit, the long thin lady and the fat little man, the giantess and her dwarf slave. The farther down in the stack the uglier the pictures got, the more viciously exploitative. Now she was holding him upside down, and her face was a bitter scar. He looked scared. Now she had him under her arm and she was slapping his behind. Her eyes were cast down, as the Madonna's eyes are cast down in the old paintings.

LAVA PHOTOGRAPHERS, JUNE, *1930.* Stamped on a corner of the paper. Lava. I didn't know the name. 1930: Vaudeville is dying, Drane and Alexander are desperate has-beens. Joe Kennedy has bought out Albee and turned the whole Keith's Circuit into film theaters. Show people are starving. A world has ended.

What did they get for this? Fifty dollars, a hundred and fifty, a thousand? A desperate time always seems worse when it's happening. That's why I tell these people who see us getting ourselves kicked out of Vietnam and the president halfway to jail and New York City on the bankruptcy highway, I tell them all not to worry. In 1930, there was reason to worry, or in 1943 when a young man could get sent to the Pacific.

Then I saw the other pictures, the worst ones, the real, serious porno. And in them I saw Cook, the man who had been murdered, and two other men I recognized. Joe Bast and Robb Royce, the "Bull-Garians." I recalled hearing the two of them and Jane and another man—who must have been Cook—screaming at one another in her apartment. That was about two weeks ago.

Had they been arguing about these pictures? Joe and Robb were readily available; I could find out. My mind was racing, numbed. I simply did not understand the significance of what I was viewing, except that it had violent and terrifying sexual content. There was a series of tableaux in which a man whose face was vaguely familiar was made to service Jane in a way that shocked me so deeply that I still cannot put it down on paper, not even in this era of moral degradation.

I sat there stunned on the floor of that apartment. It was some little time before I realized that the captain was standing over me, hovering like some great bat ready to drop out of the night.

"What the hell are you doin', you stupid fool?"

"These pictures—"

"I thought we had all that stuff. It's just like my dopes not to look under the bed. For Christ's sake, give me that before you burn your eyes out. That isn't fit for a boy to see." He gathered up the pictures, wheezing as he worked. "Look at all this nonsense. You'd think those old vaudes'd try to be respectable. You'd think so! And you, you damn kid, what the hell do you mean entering a crime scene? I thought you might come here, though. That's why I waited, why I left the door open. Make it easy for both of us."

The photographs stuffed into his black briefcase, the captain slowly stood up. I got to my feet, too. I could feel the violence in him, a fierce current that made his eyes hard and his lips tight and made his fists tremble.

I wondered what awful thing was bad enough to scare the police. Not these pictures. Ugliness does not frighten men like the captain and Barker. Only one thing frightens them: power greater than their own.

I was leaving the apartment when the captain made a sudden move in my direction. He was very quick, and I was light, more a pile of matchsticks than a solid man, a Frank Sinatra with a five-dollar voice. His hand jerked me, dragged me, and dropped me on the bed, which groaned old protest. I was speechless with surprise. The captain kicked the door closed. "You're a bad boy," he whispered. "You got a call last night. Instructions, do you understand? *Instructions.*"

"You can't issue instructions to me. You don't want this case investigated—"

"Not by a member of the public who doesn't know one thing about what he's doing! Certainly not."

"You've kept it out of the papers—both murders."

"Kid, you're a damned fool. I don't control the newspapers."

"I'm sure you don't, but I'll bet somebody above you does. Somebody powerful enough to scare you."

"Leave it alone, son. It's police business. Your lady friend is dead. God knows, maybe she was worth your concern, but let me make something very clear: If you don't give this thing up, I'm going to have to do something about it."

His voice sounded so mild that I was deceived into trying to leave again. But he slapped me across the face so hard I saw an angry flash and heard a sound as if of a bus backfiring directly into my left ear. "Don't you move until I tell you to move!" He shook his head, rolled his eyes. "I'll tell you this much: You have been the subject of some dangerous discussion. People have talked about you in a very unpleasant way. Am I getting through to you?"

"You won't scare me off."

"*What?* Why in the world not? What have you got to gain? You must be as stupid as those damned old vaudeville hacks. I hope you're not as stubborn. Just listen, and try to get this through your head. People are getting killed."

The words seemed to vibrate in the air. I had a sudden, intense desire to get to poor Bast and Royce. I wanted to get to them right that minute. "I'm leaving."

"Not until you promise me you'll stay out of this mess."

"Are you arresting me, Captain?"

"Oh, Lord, you poor kid. You damned fool! No, I'm not arresting you." He stood aside, then he made another sudden movement. There was a dollar in his hand. "Here, sticks, go up to the Astor and buy yourself a steak."

I had nothing to say to him. As I was going downstairs, I heard a terrific thud and knew that he had put his fist through a wall. He must be hell on his kids, that man. A big, protective, frustrated gorilla, as neat and clean as your little grandmother. Dangerous.

My ear burned and rang. My cheek felt like a hot skillet was lying against it. So much for our celebration tonight at the Elk's Rendezvous. I'd be too black and blue to show my face. I was dizzy, mostly with rage. I hammered on the Bull-Garians' door. There followed a long period of silence. After a time I became aware that there was an eye in the peephole.

"I'm Arthur Byron from upstairs. Jane's friend. We met at her apartment about two years ago."

The eye did not go away.

"I want to talk to you about Jane. I want to find her murderer. Maybe you can help."

There was a click, and the door opened onto a dark, chaotic mass of aged newspapers, vaude bills, programs, bits of costumes, all surrounded by the yellowing remains of a living-room set, complete with rotted chintz curtains and a photograph of a young woman glued to a contorted-perspective table. The place smelled like old men and Wildroot.

Bast was unkempt, a solemn gentleman in a black double-breasted suit with a long line of drool connecting his chin and the base of his collar. He was the one who smelled of age, and it was he who had answered the door. Royce was if anything even older, but he was better preserved. He had a high mane of neat, yellow-white hair and wore a checkered suit of relatively recent vintage. The hair-tonic aroma was coming from him.

"Good afternoon," he said in a sullen rumble. "Welcome to our remains." His eyes twinkled. "Just a minute." With the gentleness of a mother, he went to his old friend and cleaned him up. He made no excuses for their condition, and I respected him for that.

"I saw the pictures," I said. I couldn't think of any other way to approach it. I just came right out with it.

"You want a cup of coffee?" Bast asked.

"No, thanks."

"Doesn't want a cup of coffee."

"No, Bill, he doesn't."

"I think she was killed because of the pictures."

"Sure," Royce said. "I know it damn well. We weren't going to give them up. Not for any price. What fools we were." He nodded toward his doddering friend. "There's the brains. 'The guy's gonna be a governor candidate,' says that one. 'We owe him a break.' His dad was in vaudeville, you know. John Green. He had a dog act, damn good. Did the whole thing from offstage. You never saw anything out front but the dogs. Played right up until the end. They ate the dogs, the way I hear it."

I knew with the suddenness of total revelation who the young man in the photographs was: Connie Green, state senator from the Fifth Senatorial District, Borough of Manhattan. Connie Green as a young man. Connie Green long ago, in harder times.

If he was bad, Connie Green could be the kind of power that would scare cops. Right then and there, I jumped to the wrong conclusion—the youthful, innocent conclusion. The kid's conclusion.

I hated him with all the venom of wronged youth. "I ought to get me a gun and just kill him," I said, slapping my fist into my palm.

"You want a cup of coffee?"

"He's fine, Bill. He doesn't want coffee."

"You don't want coffee?"

"Sure," I snapped at last. "Give me a cup of coffee."

"It won't help," Royce said sadly. "I was being facetious when I said Bill was our brains. His brains died years ago. If you want to know the truth, Cook wanted to give them the pictures. Jane and I said no. Him over there, he just asked if anybody wanted coffee." He laughed, a sneering, wheezing cry echoing out of the cavern of memory. "Connie Green was a nice boy. Hungry, just like the rest of us. You know how much Lava gave us for those pictures? Two hundred dollars each. Per person. That is *per person.* In 1930 that could be six months' money, if you didn't go dancing."

"This guy want coffee?"

"Pitiful. But we've been together an awful long time. Nineteen fifteen we met. I was a handler with the Foys. He was a solo comic, Billie Bast. He was second stringer on a bill with the Foys in Hartford, at the old Palace. The one that burned down, you remember, a couple of nuns God killed. That's one of his jokes. *God* killed. You can see why he was such a failure. He specialized in humor that was annoying. He was so pitiful, I thought I'd try to work out some ideas with him. Help the man. We laughed so hard together that night we've been together ever since. Right, Bill?"

"You've never been right in your life."

"He has his flashes, even yet, poor man. Listen, young fella, do you think you can save our lives?"

They had refused to give up the pictures, so now Green was simply killing them off.

"Give him the pictures."

"It's a rotten thing to do. We're loyal to the profession."

"Give him the pictures if you want to live. I can't save you."

"He could just come in here and get them. We're two old men, we can't stop him."

"You can go to the D.A. You can make trouble. If you give them to him, you might be allowed to live."

"Might be?"

"I don't know what else to say."

Royce picked up the phone. "I can beg for our lives, I guess. I know how to beg."

I couldn't bear to be inside that choking, stuffy apartment for another minute. I went upstairs and called Janet. Tonight was doubly out; not only was I an unsightly mess, she was working both floor shows at the Copa. We made arrangements to meet at midnight at the Gaucho. In the streets I'd wear a hat down over my eyes. The club was as dark as the far side of the moon.

It surprises me, in retrospect, that I still wasn't afraid. I was furious at Connie Green, disgusted with the police, and feeling awfully sorry for the old fools. Afraid I was not.

I'd been warned off the case twice, the second time with physical violence. The way people like these worked, my third warning would be a fatal one. At the time I simply didn't know that, or I would have bought a bus ticket to the coast, or ridden the rails, or done anything to get away from the danger I was in.

I suppose that the magnitude of the corruption was too much for me. Here was a noted politician working hand-in-glove with the police to strong-arm a bunch of old folks. Maybe Barker and Doyle were enforcers too, just like the captain. Maybe they were investigating murders that they had themselves committed.

There is no escape from the spider web. It's a lot bigger than it seems, until you give it some real study. I didn't know that, then. Fool that I was, I telephoned Green & Co. and asked to speak to Mr. Green.

"Mr. Green is in Albany today. May I tell him what it's about?"

"Tell him it's about some photographs. Mr. Lava's pictures."

"Thank you." I left my name and telephone number. What did I propose to do to Connie Green, threaten him? By now he had most of his pictures. All he needed to do was get the remaining copies and negatives from Bast and Royce. Judging from their appearance, this would not be a difficult task.

It hit me hard, then: Green had actually had people killed—helpless old people—to save his reputation. He was that cruel a man, that vicious a man.

The telephone rang.

"Green."

"Yes, I was calling about—"

"Do you have them?" There were tears in the man's voice.

"The police have most of them."

"The *police*? Not Captain Blankenship."

"That's the man."

There was a sigh. "Why do you want to see me?"

"There's something to discuss. A matter of murder."

"Who in hell are you? Where did you come from?"

"I'm from Ohio," I said.

Again he sighed. "I'm flying down to see you. I'll take the five-o'clock plane. It gets in at nine. We can meet tonight."

I thought of my face, and for the first time, of my life.

"We can meet," Green said more frantically. "Nine-thirty at my place, 275 Park Avenue."

I knew the building. It stood where Lever House was built back in the fifties. In 1943 Park between Forty-seventh and Fifty-seventh was as fine a residential neighborhood as existed in this city.

I still hadn't replied, which must have unnerved Green. "You'll come there," he said. "You've got to come!"

My mouth was dry. I was shaking, and I couldn't possibly keep the shake out of my voice. "No," I managed to blurt.

"What the hell do you want?"

"Good government." My God, I sounded idiotic.

There was a long pause. He was trying to figure something out. When he spoke again, even the great and powerful Connie Green sounded scared. "Where do we meet?"

"The Knickerbocker at Fourteenth and Sixth Avenue."

"What's the Knickerbocker? A club?"

"A coffee shop."

"I could be recognized."

"Mr. Green, I don't care." I hung up the phone. The image of Jane's gray-blanketed corpse swam before my eyes, rising from the depths of the morgue, the face turned toward the window by virtue of a block of wood jammed in behind her head. Her lips were open, questing so delicately for air.

Hers had been what the criminal world calls an enforcement killing, designed to frighten her coconspirators into submission. When the first murder hadn't worked, a simple bludgeoning, the second had followed, uglier and more violent. What might be done to Bast and Royce, I wondered. I didn't want to think about it.

Kephart came home at six, humming cheerfully until he saw me. "What happened to the other guy?"

"The other guy was a three-ton truck."

"You're not serious? You were hit by a truck?"

"Let's just say I was hit and let it go at that. Obviously you'll have to give my apologies to the young warrior. Tell him to send me some kraut."

"Jehosophat, you got hit hard."

"At least my face still works."

"Has Janet seen this?"

The thought of her getting further involved chilled me to my depths. "Don't tell her." My disease was deadly, and highly contagious.

Without another word I left the apartment. Behind me I could hear Kephart's startled shout. I didn't stop; I was already halfway down the stairs, and I was already living in another world. The bleak, dangerous reality that I now inhabited happened within the safe, warm world of Kephart and Janet and the other strivers who were my friends. They had hard lives, but there were harder lives there for the asking.

I knew: I'd gotten one. It has remained my life for the past thirty years. I'm used to it now, but in those days it seemed as awful and exotic as the Cabinet of Doctor Caligari.

The streets I entered were not my streets, not anymore. What significance did that radio car have, for example, the one just rounding the corner onto Sixth Avenue? Or the man running for the bus—was he doing that because he was late, or to cover the fact that he'd been watching my windows?

The Knickerbocker seemed a haven in the gray, deadly world, its lights flooding the sidewalk. Inside, there was the tang of hamburger and the toasty aroma of coffee, the kind of little affirmations that stand more strongly than we realize against the darkness. I took a booth by the window and held it down with a burger basket and a Pepsi.

Nine-thirty dragged closer, but very slowly. A couple of radio cars passed. A meat wagon swayed by screaming death. People huddled along the sidewalk, furtive, frightened, lonely beings on their way home to nowhere. How had I gotten myself trapped like this, waiting for a meeting with a monster?

A Street Arab came down the aisle selling the *Mirror.* I bought a copy and stared at the front page, a lurid photo of an Olds being dragged up out of the East River. Inside you could see a long, tapering leg and the arm of a man, its hand in a fist.

Another Olds pulled up to the curb, and a man stepped out. He was the kind of man who didn't worry about parking zones. His topcoat was of the finest cashmere, his hat gleaming, fine felt lovingly brushed. So this was Senator Green. Would he ever become governor? If Dewey chose not to run next time, anything was possible.

His face, partially shadowed by his hat, was carefully controlled, but it was a soft face. He looked into the restaurant, his eyebrows raised. I signaled to him.

When he was sitting across from me, the restaurant's neon revealed more about his face. Here was another man like the captain and Barker, a frightened man. His fear was more raw, though.

"You kill people," I said.

Slowly, he shook his head. "No. No, sir, I do not."

"You were the monkey in the pictures."

"God help me. I wanted to be an actor. I thought I was getting into vaudeville. Following my dad."

"Vaudeville was dead by '31."

"Have you ever been hungry?" He threw the question out like it was some kind of defense.

"Of course. Last time was a week ago, when I did a gig at a club and didn't get paid."

"You're an actor?"

"Trying. Song and dance. Anything for five bucks."

"You see, you see! This was fifty dollars. Fifty! In 1931! I was starving to death. It happened back then, believe me. I saw 'em all the time, the young men dying in the streets. Believe me!"

"You want some coffee?"

He nodded, and I signaled the counterman. "Two, Charlie."

"You're known in here?"

"Sure. I wouldn't go where I'm not known, not with a man like you."

"I'm a good man. I haven't done anything wrong! This is what you've got to understand."

At first I did not understand. But I saw the utter sincerity in his eyes, and I glimpsed a little truth. It was ugly, mean truth. The meanest I'd ever seen. It was also testable. "Do you want the pictures?"

"Is that what this is? A shakedown?"

What could I say? The captain had most of the pictures. The ones Bast and Royce had weren't going to end this man's problem, even if I got them for him. "Anybody try to shake you down before about this?"

"Me? No. Mr. Lava told me the negatives were burned. I just let it go and hoped for the best. Mr. Lava is dead these ten years."

Was this an act? The man sounded more and more innocent. I was beginning to buy his story. And with it, to understand how ugly the truth really was.

"You've never been approached about the pictures?"

He shook his head. His hands were twisting together. Tears filled the edges of his eyes. Then he said the truth, spoke it in all innocence. "Whoever has those pictures owns me."

We sat staring at one another. In the window behind Green's head, I saw the reflection of another man, this one standing out in the night, hesitating on the edge of the light. He stood just close enough to let me see a big manila envelope in his hand.

I understood, with a clarity that stunned, that the captain's presence out there was an act of kindness. The man knew a lot about me. He knew that I needed an answer. His presence sent me a clear message: My mystery was solved. But it was also a warning. If I said too much to Connie Green, my lights would go out.

Then the captain turned around and walked off. Why not? He knew that I was no fool. I had what I wanted; I wasn't going to demand more. The little man was stuck in the web, and he wasn't getting out.

Ownership of him—which he had sold for fifty dollars—had been transferred from the old vaudevillians to a new kind of owner, one who would work Mr. Green a lot harder. I sipped my coffee. A trolley clanged past, and I longed to be aboard, going anywhere as long as it was away from here.

Who had gotten Green? Whoever owned the captain, I suppose. I doubted I'd ever find out. But that was all right. I could learn not to care, seeing as I had no choice. What did matter to me was the solution to the murders, and I more or less had that.

"Is that all? Is that why you called me all the way down from Albany, to stare at me and drink coffee?"

"That's it."

"I don't understand."

"No, you probably don't. But you will, Mr. Green. Believe me, you will."

ABOUT THE AUTHORS

BILL ADLER is a well-known author, literary agent, and book packager. He is the creator of the number one mystery bestseller *Who Killed the Robins Family?*

THOMAS CHASTAIN the author of the bestsellers *Who Killed the Robins Family?* and *The Revenge of the Robins Family,* as well as a series of mystery-suspense novels including *Pandora's Box* and *Nightscape.* He serves on the board of directors of the Mystery Writers of America.

MARY HIGGINS CLARK was born and raised in New York City. A member of the board of directors of the Mystery Writers of America, she has written *Where Are the Children* and *Stillwatch,* and is currently completing a new novel, *Weep No More, My Lady.*

DOROTHY SALISBURY DAVIS has published twenty mystery novels since 1949. A past president of the Mystery Writers of America, she has had seven Edgar nominations and in 1985 received the MWA's Grand Master Award for lifetime achievement.

LUCY FREEMAN, former *New York Times* reporter and past president of the Mystery Writers of America, writes both mystery novels and true crime books, including *Betrayal, Psychologist with Gun,* and *Fight Against Fears.*

JOYCE HARRINGTON'S first mystery story, "The Purple Shroud," published in *Ellery Queen's Mystery Magazine* in 1972, won an Edgar Award from the Mystery Writers of America. Since then, she has written both short stories and novels, and has served on the MWA's board of directors.

WARREN MURPHY has written more than eighty novels. He co-authors the tongue-in-cheek adventure series *The Destroyer,* which has sold twenty-five million copies worldwide. With his wife, novelist Molly Cochran, he has won a best-book Edgar for *The Grandmaster.* He also won a Shamus from the Private Eye Writers of America for *The Ceiling of Hell.*

BERNARD ST. JAMES was born in Berlin of Romanian parents, spent his early childhood in Paris, and was educated in the United States. He is the author of four novels, and was awarded a National Endowment for the Arts Writers Fellowship in 1983 for his novel *The Seven Dreamers.*

WHITLEY STRIEBER is the author of such thrillers as *Wolfen* and *The Hunger.* More recently, he has written *Warday* and the bestseller *Nature's End.* His book for young adults *Wolf of Shadows* was named an Outstanding Children's Book of the Year in 1985 by the American Library Association and won the Olive Branch Award.